"Let's open up o... a path, then run like hell."

Domi nodded, finger curling around the trigger of her Combat Master. The fire of combat still burned brightly in her eyes.

"So much for catching Pollard by surprise," Brigid said, breathing hard.

"If nothing else," Kane replied, "maybe we can make it back to the redoubt before Pollard and lay a trap for him there."

Grant nodded curtly. "Just give the word."

Kane's gloved finger hovered over the trigger stud of his Sin Eater. The savages began another slow advance, moving in a deliberate tread, spreading out around them in a wide circle. Their dark faces were locked in masks of implacable ferocity, their eyes glittering with homicidal rage.

Kane did not enjoy killing outlanders—he had done too much of it as a Magistrate—but now that blood was spilled, there was no hope of talking their way out of the situation.

Other titles in this series:

JAMES AXLER

OUTLANDERS®

DOOM DYNASTY

THE IMPERATOR WARS

BOOK 1

A GOLD EAGLE BOOK FROM

WORLDWIDE®

TORONTO • NEW YORK • LONDON
AMSTERDAM • PARIS • SYDNEY • HAMBURG
STOCKHOLM • ATHENS • TOKYO • MILAN
MADRID • WARSAW • BUDAPEST • AUCKLAND

First edition November 2000
ISBN 0-373-63828-0

DOOM DYNASTY

Special thanks to Mark Ellis for his contribution to the
Outlanders concept, developed for Gold Eagle Books.

Only thin smoke without flame
From the cairns of stone and grass,
Yet this doom will go onward the same
Though Dynasties pass.
—Justin Geoffrey

The Road to Outlands—
From Secret Government Files to the Future

Almost two hundred years after the global holocaust, Kane, a former Magistrate of Cobaltville, often thought the world had been lucky to survive at all after a nuclear device detonated in the Russian embassy in Washington, D.C. The aftermath—forever known as skydark—reshaped continents and turned civilization into ashes.

Nearly depopulated, America became the Deathlands—poisoned by radiation, home to chaos and mutated life forms. Feudal rule reappeared in the form of baronies, while remote outposts clung to a brutish existence.

What eventually helped shape this wasteland were the redoubts, the secret preholocaust military installations with stores of weapons, and the home of gateways, the locational matter-transfer facilities. Some of the redoubts hid clues that had once fed wild theories of government cover-ups and alien visitations.

Rearmed from redoubt stockpiles, the barons consolidated their power and reclaimed technology for the villes. Their power, supported by some invisible authority, extended beyond their fortified walls to what was now called the Outlands. It was here that the rootstock of humanity survived, living with hellzones and chemical storms, hounded by Magistrates.

In the villes, rigid laws were enforced—to atone for the sins of the past and prepare the way for a better future. That was the barons' public credo and their right-to-rule.

Kane, along with friend and fellow Magistrate Grant, had upheld that claim until a fateful Outlands expedition. A displaced piece of technology...a question to a keeper of the archives...a vague clue about alien masters—and their world shifted radically. Suddenly, Brigid Baptiste, the archivist, faced summary execution, and

Grant a quick termination. For Kane there was forgiveness if he pledged his unquestioning allegiance to Baron Cobalt and his unknown masters and abandoned his friends.

But that allegiance would make him support a mysterious and alien power and deny loyalty and friends. Then what else was there?

Kane had been brought up solely to serve the ville. Brigid's only link with her family was her mother's red-gold hair, green eyes and supple form. Grant's clues to his lineage were his ebony skin and powerful physique. But Domi, she of the white hair, was an Outlander pressed into sexual servitude in Cobaltville. She at least knew her roots and was a reminder to the exiles that the outcasts belonged in the human family.

Parents, friends, community—the very rootedness of humanity was denied. With no continuity, there was no forward momentum to the future. And that was the crux—when Kane began to wonder if there *was* a future.

For Kane, it wouldn't do. So the only way was out—way, way out.

After their escape, they found shelter at the forgotten Cerberus redoubt headed by Lakesh, a scientist, Cobaltville's head archivist, and secret opponent of the barons.

With their past turned into a lie, their future threatened, only one thing was left to give meaning to the outcasts. The hunger for freedom, the will to resist the hostile influences. And perhaps, by opposing, end them.

Chapter 1

Toward the middle of an overcast autumn afternoon, with the sun finally breaking free from the black mass of thunderheads, the settlement of Port Morninglight was overwhelmed.

Upright sharpened logs were meant to serve as a protective palisade for the small collection of reed and thatch-roofed huts, but the barrier looked better suited for keeping livestock in than enemies out. The area around the stockade fence was open except for clusters of scraggly sage and mesquite that offered little cover. The squad of Magistrates couldn't approach without being seen, so they didn't expend any time or effort trying.

Before the attack commenced, Pollard didn't demand surrender, nor did the citizens ask for terms. They simply began shooting from parapets built on the palisade walls, first with bows and arrows, then with home-forged flintlocks. The twenty Magistrates under Pollard's command quickly realized it was easier to keep out of range of the crude .75-caliber miniballs than it was the four-foot-long arrows. The riflemen weren't very accurate, but the archers were. If not for their body armor, the Mags would have been pincushioned a dozen times over.

Only a single mortar launcher was needed to breach Port Morninglight's fortifications. The stripped-down PRB 424, taken from the Cobaltville armory, was assembled in a matter of minutes. Launched from only a hundred yards beyond the village's stockade fence, each 60 mm, high-ex round pulverized the logs and threw up great clouds of dust and grit. The echoes of the cannonade rolled across the barren sand dunes like prolonged thunderclaps. Four shells reduced a thirty-foot span of the wall to a heap of splinters and broken timbers.

Pollard dutifully led his men through the breach, clambering over the smoldering wreckage of the fence. Streamers of acrid black smoke veiled the interior of the settlement. Arrows and muskets were fired from behind the crude huts. Only a handful of armed defenders remained and once they loosed their last shots, they died under the autoblasters wielded by the Magistrates.

The Mag force suffered only one casualty, a triple-careless stupe named Mitchell who allowed a child to stab him in the throat with a filleting knife. The blade punched through his neck and into his brain stem, and he died without a murmur of surprise or protest.

Defying the vengeful snarls of the men who witnessed Mitchell's swift death, Pollard ordered the child to be bound, not chilled. He commanded two of his Mags to strip Mitchell of his armor and Kevlar undersheathing. Concealing physical evidence of the incursion was the mission's secondary priority.

After that, Pollard put his men to work rounding up the survivors. It didn't take long. He stood in the humid air, redolent with the coppery tang of blood and brine, watching as scarlet runnels cut crusted channels through the ground. A thousand flies crawled and feasted on them. He could hear the boom of the surf over the rise at the rear of the settlement. He had never seen either the Lantic or Cific oceans, but he kept his curiosity in check. He had never been in California, either, until dawn the day before, but he wasn't too interested in looking around.

So far he had seen very little of Baron Snakefish's territory that seemed worth coveting. The terrain around the little seaside ville of Port Morninglight was slashed through with dry streambeds and narrow ravines. Clumps of sagebrush surrounded the area like tufts of hair atop a balding man's pate. In the distance, humping up from the horizon, the gray peaks of the Sierra Nevada range shouldered the sky.

Although not an educated man by even the most charitable definition of the term, Pollard knew that when the nukes flew and the mushroom clouds scorched their way into the heavens, the San Andreas Fault had given one great final heave and thousands of square miles of California coastline dropped into the sea. For the past two centuries, the Cific had lapped less than thirty miles from the foothills of the Sierras.

A woman ran out of a hut, screaming as she fled from the black-armored killers. A Mag tripped her, and another pulled the homespun shift off her body. Pollard was about to order them away from the outlander female since she looked young, healthy and uninjured. Then he saw she was at least six months' pregnant. He turned away, allowing his men to take their pleasure.

He strode up to where MacMurphy and Swayze were herding the prisoners together. As per baronial edict, the survivors weren't executed. They were examined. The Mags arranged them into two columns, separating the old, the infirm and the seriously wounded from those who were young and suffered only superficial injuries. None of the eighteen survivors had come through the assault completely unscathed. Even children manned the walls, using slingshots.

Pollard inspected the youngest and most lightly injured of the prisoners, marching from one end of each column to the other, repressing a curse at the low number. There appeared to be only nine that met Baron Cobalt's standards. He had no idea of why the baron had assigned him to lead a Mag squad into California and capture outlanders. All he really knew about his mission was he'd been ordered to get in and out with healthy prisoners before Baron Snakefish learned that Mags from Cobaltville were in his territory.

Planting his gauntleted fists on his hips, Pollard

gazed at the nine people. A mixture of women, men and two teenagers, they averted their eyes. Their clothing consisted of simple tunics and pants, both of brightly colored cloth embroidered with fancy curlicues along the seams and hems. The tunics of the women bore beautifully crafted images of swans, cranes and fish, all worked in multicolored thread. The quality of the needlework and the fabric itself seemed too rich for a community of fisherpeople.

Pollard deliberately struck a pose as if he were on display in a museum case. He knew the sunlight glinting off the black polycarbonate exoskeleton encasing his stocky body lent him a fearsome aspect.

Like all hard-contact Magistrates, Pollard's armor was close-fitting, molded to conform to the biceps, triceps, pectorals and abdomen. Even with its Kevlar undersheathing, the armor was lightweight and provided no loose folds to snag against projections. The only spot of color anywhere on it was the small disk-shaped badge of office emblazoned on the left pectoral. It depicted, in crimson, a stylized, balanced scales of justice, superimposed over a nine-spoked wheel. The badge symbolized the Magistrate's oath to keep the wheels of justice turning in the nine villes.

Pollard's regulation side arm, the Sin Eater, was holstered on his right forearm. A big-bored automatic handblaster, it was less than fourteen inches in length at full extension with a magazine that carried twenty rounds of 9 mm ammo. When not in use, the stock folded over the top of the blaster, lying along the frame, reducing its holstered length to ten inches.

When the Sin Eater was needed, Pollard would simply tense his wrist tendons and sensitive actuators activated a flexible cable in the holster to snap the weapon smoothly into his waiting hand, the stock unfolding in the same motion. Since the Sin Eater had no trigger guard or safety, the blaster fired immediately upon touching his crooked index finger.

The weapon was more than a murderous weapon; it was a badge of office almost as important as the one he wore upon his breastplate. All Mags were expected to know it more intimately than anything else in the world.

Attached to his belt by a magnetic clip was his close-assault weapon. The Copperhead was a chopped-down autoblaster, gas-operated, with a 700-round-per-minute rate of fire. The magazine held fifteen rounds of 4.85 mm steel-jacketed bullets. Two feet in length, the CAW featured a grip and trigger unit that were placed in front of the breech to allow for one-handed use. An optical image-intensifier scope was fitted on top, as well as a laser autotargeter. Because of its low recoil, the Copperhead could be fired in a long, devastating full-auto burst.

Like the armor encasing his body, Pollard's visored helmet was made of black polycarbonate. Fitting over the upper half and back of his head, it left only a portion of the mouth and chin exposed. The slightly concave, red-tinted visor served two functions—it protected the eyes from foreign particles, and the electrochemical polymer was connected to a passive night sight that intensified ambient light to permit one-color night vision.

The tiny image-enhancer sensor mounted on the forehead of the helmet did not emit detectable rays, though its range was only twenty-five feet, even on a fairly clear night with strong moonlight.

There was another reason behind the helmet and the exoskeleton, which were designed to inspire awe and fear. When a man put on the armor, he was symbolically surrendering his identity in order to serve a cause greater than a mere individual life.

Pollard's father had chosen to smother his identity, as had his father before him. For that matter, all current Magistrates, the third generation, had exchanged personal hopes, dreams and desires for a life of service to a baron.

To the prisoners, Pollard said dispassionately, "We'll be moving out shortly and taking you with us. If you cooperate, you won't be harmed. If you resist, you'll be chilled on the spot. Those are your only choices."

None of them said anything as MacMurphy and Swayze moved down the column, fastening heavy, yokelike collars of leather and wood around their necks. The pair of Mags threaded a slim length of chain through staples on the collars, fettering the people together.

Pollard would have preferred to bind their hands,

as well, but the prisoners would make better time with their limbs unencumbered, especially over some of the appallingly rugged terrain they had to cross. Also, the barony of Snakefish lay only forty-odd miles to the northwest, and as far as he knew a patrol or trading convoy was on its way. The reports provided by the Intel section described how the fishing village of Port Morninglight was tolerated by Baron Snakefish because it provided his ville with a source of food other than that grown in the fields. The standing policy shared by most of the baronial oligarchy was to raze Outland settlements to the ground in order to prevent noncitizens from becoming self-sufficient and therefore rebellious.

Peeling back the cuff of his gauntlet, Pollard studied the LED face of his wrist chron, then glanced at the position of the sun. He swore beneath his breath, then bellowed to the Mags spread out around the village, "Pick up the pace, you bastards! We've got only five hours of daylight left!"

The Magistrates policing the killzone sped up their movements, snatching up spent cartridge cases and jamming them into canvas bags. Pollard wasn't too worried about the treaded tracks made by their boots in the soft, sandy soil, since the steady sea breeze would obliterate them in a matter of minutes. Baron Cobalt's order was to leave no clue, no hint of what happened to the residents of Port Morninglight—or at least no clue that could be traced back to him.

MacMurphy tugged at the length of chain, pulling

out most of the slack. Swayze attached a metal cross-bar to the trailing end. ''We're ready to go, sir,'' he announced.

Pollard nodded brusquely, pretending to ignore the baleful glares directed at him from the prisoners. Most of their faces were smoke streaked and begrimed, but at least they appeared to be in fairly good health. A woman stared boldly at him from beneath her hayrick tangle of dark blond hair.

''Where are you taking us, sec man?'' she demanded.

An obsolete term, ''sec man'' was applied to men who served in baronial security forces. Nowadays it was used only in the hinterlands and over the past century had become something of an insult. Magistrates weren't the descendants of ragtag crews of thuggish blastermen who obeyed self-styled barons; rather they were enforcers of law, opponents of anarchy, spiritually sanctioned to act as judge, jury and executioner.

That was the bare-bones history Pollard had been taught at the academy, but rather than correct the outlander woman, he cuffed her openhanded across the face. He didn't put much of his strength into the blow, since he mainly wanted to remind her of what she was. Still, she reeled backward, causing the entire line of prisoners to stumble and stagger.

As they regained their balance, cursing both him and the woman, Pollard opened the comm-link channel and spoke into the transceiver built into the jaw guard of his helmet. "Quantrell, Rance, Turner. Front and center."

Three armored men jogged toward him from all points of the perimeter. When they stood at attention in a semicircle around him, Pollard gestured diffidently to the column of survivors who were too wounded, too old or otherwise unfit to make the journey to the Sierras.

"Those are the culls," he said matter-of-factly. "Flash-blast them."

As one, in almost mechanical unison, the three Magistrates turned toward the men and women, the barrels of their Copperheads snapping up. The people bleated wordlessly in terror, broke formation and scattered.

The chattering, ripping rasps of three subguns on full-auto overwhelmed their screams. The rounds smashed into the running people, slapping them down amid scarlet sprays, their arms and legs flailing. Even after all of them had been hammered to the ground, the Copperheads continued to stutter, spent shell casings spewing from ejector ports like glittering rain.

The Mags didn't stop shooting until bolts snapped open loudly on empty chambers. The bodies lay where the steel-jacketed fusillade had battered them, crumpled in bullet-slashed heaps. The sandy soil soaked up their blood like a sponge, turning the ground around them into crimson-stained sludge.

Turner, Rance and Quantrell looked expectantly toward Pollard, awaiting further orders. Pollard impassively surveyed the three men, then jabbed a finger toward Rance. "You. You're the chosen man."

"Yes, sir." Rance's Sin Eater sprang from the forearm holster into his hand. He stepped forward, moving among the bodies, pointing the handblaster down and squeezing off a single round into every head.

The Magistrate selected to fire final head shots was always known as "the chosen man." Pollard had always considered the practice a waste of ammo, but it was part of some old, murky military tradition.

He strode away through the settlement. He saw a few goats in a wood-railed pen but no beasts of burden. There were freestanding racks with smoked fish and strips of seaweed stretched over the crossbars and a few heaps of clam shells, but little else in the way of foodstuffs. It was apparent Port Morninglight lived almost entirely on the bounty provided by the ocean.

Pollard paused to inspect a longbow lying on the ground. It was beautifully crafted, made of smooth, red-lacquered wood. Like their clothing, the weapon appeared too beautifully made to have been fashioned by the people of Port Morninglight. There was an elegance, an artistry to it, and he had seen none of that among the possessions of the residents. Nor did the wood look like any he had seen on the day-long march from Redoubt Charlie to the settlement.

Pollard had led his men down tree-dotted hillsides, then across a wind-scoured wilderness of ridges, spines of stone, dry riverbeds, fields of tumbled rock and acres of scrub brush. To refer to the confusing route as merely rugged was being more than imprecise; it was an outright lie. Several times he became disoriented, but he didn't allow his Mags to see him surreptitiously checking the map.

The men were already disoriented from arriving in Redoubt Charlie in groups of five. Except for Pollard, none of them had ever heard of a mat-trans unit before, much less stepped into one. The mat-trans gateways—jump chambers—were in hidden redoubts, underground fortresses scattered across the nuke-ravaged face of North America.

Pollard knew very little about the gateways, only what he had learned from his former superior officer, Salvo. He understood they could transport a man in a flicker of microseconds from place to place, but how this miracle was accomplished was beyond him, even if he stretched his imagination to its limits.

Over a year ago, such a mind-breaking concept was the last thing he had ever expected to encounter when he pursued a group of insurrectionists into Mesa Verde Canyon. Later, Salvo had tersely explained that the matter-transfer units transported both organic and inorganic material from point A to a point Z without the traveler stirring so much as a toe. As a menacing codicil to the explanation, Salvo added that the devices were the deepest, most ruthlessly safeguarded secrets of the unified baronies. If Pollard so much as hinted to anyone he knew they even existed, much less the fundamentals of their operation, his life span could be measured in minutes.

However, Pollard never bought into Salvo's version of how the insurrectionists knew of the device. He didn't ask questions, certainly not the wrong ones. He was content to be an active player in what was privately referred to as "Salvo's Vendetta."

He knew full well that had he stumbled upon a gateway without the knowledge of anyone other than Salvo, a swift execution was all he could look forward to in the way of career advancement.

Instead, he had been promoted—strictly through attrition, true enough—but he was now division commander and therefore privy to certain secrets. When briefed on the assignment by Griffin, the new Mag Division administrator, he was apprised of more than mission parameters. Those were fairly straightforward.

Since Griffin knew that the long-vanished Salvo had provided Pollard with a thumbnail history of the mat-trans units, he dispensed with supplying him with more information. Pollard easily recalled what Salvo had told him over a year ago—how the gateways were part of Project Cerberus, which was one of many research projects connected to the Totality Concept.

Over two centuries ago, before the sky darkened with massive quantities of pulverized rubble propelled into the atmosphere by hundreds of simultaneous atomic explosions, the Totality Concept was an ultra-top-secret scientific undertaking whose different research branches were housed in hidden redoubts. The official designations of the redoubts had been based on the old international radio code, as in "Charlie" representing the letter *C*.

During the mission briefing, Griffin supplied him with a string of numbers, confusing jumbles of digits he was to enter into the jump chamber's keypad controls. Destination-lock coordinates, Griffin called them. After handing Pollard a strip of paper bearing the numeric codes, he commanded him to memorize them, then destroy the paper.

For the two days preceding the jump from the mattrans unit hidden on A Level of Cobaltville's Administrative Monolith, Pollard had tried his best to commit the digits to memory, but ultimately he failed. He had already participated in several failed missions, so he was too afraid to inform Griffin he was unable to accomplish such a simple task.

The three digits and procedures to open and close the sec door in Redoubt Charlie were easy to remember, but the coordinates of where the prisoners were to be sent refused to be impressed into his mind. Therefore, he impressed them into his flesh. Using indelible ink, Pollard wrote them on the inside of his left wrist.

An alarmed shout dragged Pollard's attention back to the present. He whirled, visored eyes tracking across the village, squinting to see through the drifting veils of smoke. He heard the characteristic stutter of a Sin Eater set on triburst, the reports sounding like staccato whipcracks.

He spotted a man standing on the crest of a dune

on the far side of the village, waving his arms in a strange rhythmic manner. He held a pair of long-handled, flat, paddlelike objects in his hands. Pollard barely glimpsed the complex symbols inscribed on the surfaces before a storm of 9 mm rounds stitched a series of dark holes across his back.

The man's arm movements became spasmodic, and his entire body convulsed under the multiple impacts. He fell heavily, toppling face first to the sand.

Pollard watched as a Mag struggled up the slope of the dune. He wasn't sure which man it was until his helmet comm-link hissed with static and Franco's breathless voice said, "Chilled him, sir."

"So I see," Pollard growled. "What are those things he was waving around?"

Pollard saw Franco pluck one of the objects from the dead man's hand. His voice, sounding slightly troubled, said, "They're like fans, sir."

"Fans?" Pollard echoed derisively. "He wasn't waving them because he got overheated."

"No, sir." Franco turned, looking out toward the sea. His ebony-encased body suddenly stiffened. "I think you should take a look at this."

"What is it?" Pollard demanded, not wanting to scale the sand dune.

"I'm really not sure, sir," Franco admitted.

Uttering a grunt of disgust, Pollard stamped across the village, breathing shallowly through his splayed nostrils so as not to inhale too much of the astringent smoke. He lumbered up the dune, his boots slogging through the loose sand. Twice he nearly fell. By the time he reached the crest, he was panting, sweat sliding down his bulldog-jowled face.

The man Franco had backshot lay spread-eagled, his face buried in the sand. Blood streamed from his bullet-holed torso, puddling darkly around him. Pollard paid him no attention. Instead, he followed Franco's gaze, toward the open ocean.

A collection of small one-masted sailboats was beached upon the shore, among nets and fishing tackle. The heaving waves swept over jagged rock formations. The limitless blue expanse of the Cific evoked a spark of awe within him. The largest body of water he had ever seen was a lake, and its opposite shore was easily visible.

The ocean looked as vast as the sky, with foaming whitecaps instead of clouds. For an instant he couldn't help but wonder what lay on the other side of it. Pollard knew the tiny black specks barely visible on the horizon were barren islets known as the Western Isles, pieces of California that had not completely submerged.

Franco pointed in a southwesterly direction. "See it, sir?"

Pollard narrowed his eyes. "See what?"

"That fog bank."

Pollard stared hard, and finally spied a yellowish vaporous smudge far down the shoreline, about three-quarters of a mile away. He started to demand profanely why Franco had summoned him to look at a fog bank, when he realized the weather wasn't right for fog to form. Nor did the mist really look or behave like fog. It billowed against the wind, some scraps twisting away, but appearing very thick at the water-line—or just above it.

In a tense voice, Franco said, "For a second, I thought I saw something inside of it."

Shading his eyes with his hands, Pollard glimpsed a dark, indistinct shape within the heart of the cloud. For a microsecond, the sun glinted brightly from a reflective metallic surface. Then it was gone, obscured by the vapor.

Hefting the paddle-shaped object he had taken from the dead man, Franco declared anxiously, "Sir, I think this slagger was using these to signal…like the old semaphore code."

Lowering his hands, Pollard quickly studied the paddle in Franco's hand, noting how it did indeed resemble an oversize hand fan. The symbol inscribed on it was utterly unfamiliar, like a sunburst containing three geometric shapes. Although he had no way of knowing, it seemed Oriental in design. He didn't like the cold chill that suddenly crept up the base of his spine.

Franco tapped the sigil on the paddle. "I think this mark is called an ideograph. It means something."

Pollard did not respond, waiting for the younger man to say why it was significant.

"The fog may be a smoke screen generated by a

ship,'' Franco continued. ''He was either warning them off or calling for help with these.''

Neither possibility made Pollard's chill go away. Although the Intel section hadn't indicated that the ville of Snakefish possessed anything like a navy, there was no reason why its own Magistrates couldn't use boats to patrol the coast. Cobaltville and its surrounding territories were landlocked, and so the notion that another barony might employ seagoing craft had never occurred to him. Still, for a reason he could not name or understand, he knew if a boat lurked within the smear of fog, it had not been dispatched by Baron Snakefish.

He felt a jolt of near panic, a sudden mad desire to put as much distance between the sea and his prisoners as possible. At the same time, he fancied he could feel the numbers he had written on his wrist burning his skin.

Swiftly, Pollard opened the all-channel frequency on the helmet comm-link, barking, ''Every one of you bastards prepare to move out. We're triple-timing it. Standard deployment of personnel and firepower.''

He snapped the orders as he clumsily climbed down the dune. None of the men protested that they hadn't finished policing the area, and Pollard wouldn't have listened to them if they had. The artistry of the bows, the hand fans and the fog bank all slid together in his mind to create a mystery that, if not frightening, posed a threat to the success of his mission. He feared failing Baron Cobalt far more than whatever menace might be rising from the sea.

Pollard raised his voice in a roar, knowing it was unnecessary and knowing he concussed the eardrums of the entire Mag force. "You stupe bastards! I said, *Start moving!*"

Chapter 2

"Stop moving," Grant whispered, raising the knife to shoulder level.

Domi's eyes narrowed to slits, her snow-white lashes veiling the bloodred irises. "I'm not moving," she snapped fiercely, her shoulders trembling. "I'm shivering."

Grant grunted. "Stop it, or you're dead."

"It sees you," Kane said softly.

"With all those fucking eyes," retorted Grant, his characteristic lionlike roar of a voice muted to a rumble, "how could it not?"

Domi nipped at her full underlip. "I can feel it climbing," she murmured breathlessly.

The creature's six legs secured grips in the tough fabric of her khaki shirt and crept slowly up her back, its sickle-shaped pincers opening and closing reflexively.

Grant slid the titanium-jacketed point of his combat knife closer, but the mass of compound eyes constituting the bug's head rolled in his direction. He checked his movement, muttering, "Lakesh told us to expect mutie snakes, not mutie insects."

"It looks like a mutagenically altered relation to a

scorpion, and scorpions are arachnids, not insects,"
Brigid Baptiste noted.

Domi stopped short of snorting in exasperation, but
said lowly, "It's still a big fuckin' bug with a big
fuckin' stinger."

The black monster clinging to Domi's shirt did
hold the general contours of a scorpion, with a black,
shiny carapace, long foreclaws and stinger-tipped tail
that curled and quivered over its segmented back. But
the resemblance ended there. Nearly eight inches
long, with a cluster of eyes atop its streamlined body,
the scorpion-thing seemed to study the fourteen-inch
blade in Grant's hand, silently assessing its severity
as a threat. The manner in which it rolled its many
eyes in all directions was very disquieting.

"I don't think you can sneak up on it," Kane said
quietly.

The curved tail stretched out to half the length of
the creature's body and made a couple of forward
darts, as if in warning. A drop of amber venom
formed on the barbed point of the stinger. Grant carefully withdrew the knife from the bug's range of vision. After a watchful second, the scorpion began
climbing again.

The four people—and one mutie bug—crouched in
a clearing amid an expanse of shoulder-high scrub
brush. All around was a semiarid landscape, not quite
a desert but not a particularly hospitable place, either.
Here and there a solitary tree rose to break the mo-
notony of the tableland. Now and then a rare stream

cut a shallow dell across the terrain. The night before, they had made camp in such a dell. They could have pushed on, but all of them were tired after descending the rocky, arduous path from Redoubt Charlie.

Kane's eyes flicked toward the distant mountain slope, absently noting the miles-long scar of a two-century-old earth slip. He could see no trace of the entrance to the installation tucked beneath the lip of the peak above.

For a reason she had not explained, Domi had spread out her bedroll some distance from the rest of them. When she awakened, she found she was sharing her accommodations with an uninvited bunk mate.

Her urgent whisper drew Kane's attention back to her. "Do something before it lays eggs in my ear!"

Domi barely topped five feet in height, and she couldn't have weighed more than a hundred pounds. Her slender build was insolently curved, with generous hips, long slim legs and perky breasts.

A mop of ragged, close-cropped bone-white hair framed her pearly, hollow-cheeked face. Despite her albinism and burning red eyes, she was weirdly beautiful, particularly with her complexion, the color and texture of a polished pearl. Raised in the Outlands, she displayed the free style and outspoken rough manner acquired in the scramble for existence far from the relative luxury of the villes.

Grant backed away before straightening to his full height of six feet four inches. His face was locked in a stony mask as Domi scowled at him. The two people were a study in complete contrasts, not just physically but emotionally. Grant was broad shouldered and barrel-chested, and his high forehead was topped by short, gray-sprinkled hair. A down-sweeping mustache showed ebony against the dark brown of his face. He wore a black, high-collared coverall made of a Kevlar weave.

He hefted his knife uncertainly. "I'm open to suggestions."

To Domi, Brigid said soothingly, "Just sit tight. As long as it doesn't feel threatened, it won't sting you."

She tossed her loose tumbles of thick, wavy red-gold hair off her shoulders, affecting not to notice the dour, dubious glance Grant cast in her direction. Brigid's big, slightly slanted emerald eyes fixed on the scorpion-thing as it reached out tentatively with a foreclaw to touch the collar of Domi's shirt. Tall, long-legged with a willowy, athletic build, Brigid did not allow the apprehension mounting within her to show on her smoothly contoured face.

Kane eyed the position of the early-morning sun and said lowly, "We can't wait all day for the damn thing to make up its mind."

An inch over six feet, Kane was not as tall or as broad as Grant, but every line of his long-limbed body was hard and stripped of excess flesh. Most of his muscle mass was contained in his upper body, lending his physique a marked resemblance to a wolf. His longish dark hair held sun-touched highlights, and his high-planed face was deeply tanned. A thin, hairline scar showed white on his left cheek. His narrowed eyes were faded to a pale gray-blue, the color of the high sky at sunset. He wore a black coverall identical to Grant's.

Domi stiffened as she felt the pincer questing softly at her nape. She drew in a sharp breath between her teeth. The bug stopped as it tried to determine the nature of the new substance. Carefully, she reached down to pick up a fist-sized rock. In a steel-edged tone, Domi announced, "If nobody's going to do anything, I will."

"And if it stings you?" Grant challenged.

Domi hesitated, then gestured slightly toward the flat, metal-sheathed case lying at the edge of the campsite. "We got plenty medicine in that."

Under stress, her abbreviated mode of Outland speech became more pronounced.

"We don't know how virulent the venom is," Brigid pointed out. "Whether it's a blood or neurotoxin."

All anybody knew about the mutie scorpions was that their poison was hundreds of times more potent than that of their forebears, enabling them to kill almost anything that walked, crawled or swam. Domi let the rock drop from her hand, and she squeezed her eyes shut in fear. She did her best to minimize the shudder that racked her slight frame. The stinger at the end of the scorpion's tail rotated in a semicircle, as if it were connected to a ball-and-socket joint.

Touching the Sin Eater holstered at his forearm,

Kane said quietly, "Maybe one of us could pick it off."

"The Magistrates could be less than a mile away," Brigid objected. "They'd hear the shot."

Grant's lips peeled back from his teeth in a silent snarl of frustration. His "Fuck it!" was a harsh, angry rasp. He lunged forward, the blade of the combat knife flicking out in a lightning-fast thrust. Since the blade was blued, it didn't flash, but the double-edged point slashed through the scorpion's tail, right below its bulbous barbed tip.

With a crunch of cartilage, the stinger arced through the air, seemingly propelled by a geyser of greenish-yellow ichor. The twin pincers snapped open and shut, clicking in a castanet-like rhythm of silent agony.

Grant's equally swift backstroke inserted the point between the bug's underbelly and Domi's shirt. He jerked up and levered the mutie creature off her back, its clawed legs kicking convulsively. As it landed on its ridged back, he hurled the knife in a blur of motion. The blade pierced the creature's unarmored underside, cracked through its black shell and impaled it against the ground.

Domi came to her feet in a lunging rush, panting heavily. Whirling, she bent, grasped Grant's knife by its nylex handle, whipped it loose from the bug, then stomped down hard on the wriggling body. With a snarl of satisfaction, she twisted on the heel of her combat boot, grinding the bug deep into the sandy soil.

"*Hate* these nuke-shittin' things," she spit. "Always have!"

She calmly handed the knife back to Grant and started rolling up her sleeping bag as if nothing more interesting than swatting a sand flea had happened. Grant bent over and shoved the blade into the ground to clean it of the scorpion's blood. "Next time, I pick the campsite," he said to Kane.

Kane said nothing, returning his energies to the task that Domi's wake-up crisis had interrupted. He went back to donning the pieces of his armor, once again wishing it weren't so awkward to carry. The individual pieces couldn't fit in a backpack, so it was easier to wear regardless of the discomfort. Grant was in the same quandary—a bit worse, actually, since his own armor wasn't custom fitted like Kane's. It had belonged to a Mag named Anson, who had briefly joined Lakesh's group of exiles some years before. Anson ended the association by blowing out his brains with his own regulation Sin Eater. Learning the truth behind the nukecaust and the future of Earth had been too much for him to bear.

He had left behind his armor, and though a big man, he wasn't as big as Grant. Pieces of it pinched and chafed him in places where a man was not designed to be pinched and chafed. The helmet, unlike the rest of the armor, was a shade too large.

As Kane snapped the shin guards into place above

the top of his heavy-treaded, steel-toed boots, he glimpsed Brigid unfold a map and study it with slitted eyes. From a pocket of her khaki shirt she withdrew the symbol of her former office as a Cobaltville archivist. She slipped on the pair of rectangular-lensed, wire-framed spectacles and gazed first at the map, then behind them at the Sierra Nevada range. Although the eyeglasses were something of a reminder of her past life, they also served as a means to correct an astigmatism.

Still, she squinted at the map, first holding it close to her face then moving it back. Kane briefly wondered if her vision hadn't been further impaired by the head injury she suffered a little over a month before. Brigid seemed in good condition, and DeFore, the medic, had pronounced her fully recovered. The only visible sign of the wound that had laid her scalp open to the bone and put her in a coma for several days was a faintly red, horizontal line that crossed her right temple and disappeared into the roots of her hair. Her recovery time had been little short of uncanny. Kane was always impressed by the woman's tensile-spring resiliency.

However, he couldn't help but notice how she needed her glasses more and more in the weeks following her release from the infirmary in the Cerberus redoubt, which was built into the side of a Montana mountain peak. The redoubt could be reached from the outside only by a single treacherous road, so the mat-trans gateway usually ferried people and materials in and out.

"How far now?" Grant asked gruffly, struggling to seal his breast and back plate.

Brigid didn't answer for a long moment. When she did, her voice sounded uncertain. "Shouldn't be more than half a day's march."

"Shouldn't?" Kane repeated skeptically.

Irritably, Brigid shot back, "You know we didn't have any recent satellite pix of this region in the database—none more recent than fifty years, anyhow, long before Port Morninglight was settled."

The fact that the Cerberus redoubt could uplink with a Vela-class reconnaissance satellite and a Comsat had been a matter of astonishment to Brigid, Grant and Kane when they learned of it more than a year ago. Although all of them were aware that in predark years, the upper reaches of the planet's atmosphere had been clogged with orbiting satellites, many of them designed for spying and surveillance purposes, ville doctrines claimed that all satellites were now simply free-floating scrap metal.

Brigid tapped the map. "This is all Lakesh and Bry could improvise, and it's largely guesswork, based on maps before the nukecaust."

"Fuckin' Mags know their way around," Domi said bitterly, kicking dirt over the smoldering remains of their fire.

Kane bristled at the hint of challenge in the girl's voice. "They have access to an Intel section. The

Mag Divisions of the nine villes share information about Outland settlements. All we know about Port Morninglight is what Bry overheard when he hacked into their system and listened in on the comm channels."

Over the past few months, Bry, the resident tech-head of Cerberus, had established a communications link with the Comsat satellite both to personnel out in the field and to the Cobaltville computer systems. Since all the villes had a form of wireless communication, the primary obstacle was finding an undetected method of patching into the channels, and Bry had come up with a solution that involved using the redoubt's satellite uplinks. The overall objective was to find weak areas in Cobaltville defenses and baron-sanctioned operations in the Outlands. The technique was far from perfect; the electronic eavesdropping could be adversely affected by anything from weather fronts to sunspots.

However, the last thing any of them expected to overhear was a plan to covertly dispatch Mags from Cobaltville into the territory of Baron Snakefish. Such an act was not only unprecedented, but it was also strictly forbidden by the terms established in the Program of Unification more than ninety years before.

"We know the Mags arrived at Redoubt Charlie yesterday morning," Grant interjected. "And they're doing a good job of covering their tracks."

"Yeah," Kane agreed. "But why? Baron Snakefish's ville is at least sixty miles to the northwest. None of his Magistrates are likely to patrol out here.''

Brigid refolded the map and shoved it into a pocket of her whipcord trousers. Picking up her backpack, she shouldered into the straps. ''I'm more interested in why a contingent of Cobaltville Mags is making an incursion into another ville's territory, raiding a coastal Outland settlement. It's a treaty violation and could be construed as an act of war.''

No one argued with her. Instead, they picked up their packs and started walking through the scrub toward a distant green-brown tree line. As a concession to the warm temperature, Grant and Kane kept their helmets in their backpacks. They slung their Copperheads over their shoulders.

None of them knew much about the ville of Snakefish or the baron who had taken its unique and grotesque name as his own. All of the nine villes in the continent-spanning network were standardized, so there probably wasn't much that would be unfamiliar.

However, Snakefish possessed a certain historical significance inasmuch as it had been an important commerce center on the Cific coast in the century following skydark. Although roughly half the state of California lay beneath the sea, the region around the ville had received only a light once-over with neutron bombs. Much of the mammalian life was killed off, but many of the structures remained standing.

Several of the structures were part of a gasoline-processing complex, which in the decades following the holocaust made Snakefish one of the wealthiest villes in the country, at least by the standards of Deathlands. Other than having access to a resource more precious than the gold, the ville was the birthplace of a bizarre religious sect that worshiped the giant mutie rattlesnakes in the area. The religion and the source of the ville's wealth vanished at about the same time that sabotage caused the fuel refinery to explode. The ville itself burned to the ground, taking with it a goodly number of its two thousand inhabitants.

One of the few survivors was determined to rebuild the ville, to restore its former glory as the primary power on the far western coast. During the process, he took the name of Snakefish for himself. By the time of the Program of Unification, the new ville of Snakefish, although hardly as prosperous as its predecessor, was a power to be reckoned with and was absorbed into the ruling baronial oligarchy.

By the time the sun reached a midway point in the sky, both Kane and Grant were perspiring profusely. Neither man had worn the polycarbonate armor for any protracted length of time in a while, not since the op to the Western Isles. Even then they hadn't been on a forced march, so both men grew more uncomfortable and irritable with every mile.

Though the sandy soil was hard packed, they occasionally crossed areas where it was loose and their feet bogged down in it. When Domi stumbled, Grant reached out a hand to steady her. She jerked away from him, avoiding his touch.

Kane noted that Domi had yet to thank or even acknowledge Grant's actions in ending the threat of the scorpion. For that matter, she didn't even make eye contact with him. A palpable web of tension stretched between the two people, but Kane wasn't inclined to ask about it for a couple of reasons.

First and foremost, though his and Grant's partnership dated back over a dozen years to their joint careers as Cobaltville Mags, they rarely spoke of personal matters. Secondly, Kane knew as much as he cared to about Grant and Domi's relationship, and he guessed Domi's resentment derived from a sexual issue—or a lack of one.

Domi was certainly not a stranger to sex, since she'd more or less sold herself into service as a slave to Guana Teague in exchange for being smuggled into Cobaltville. She ended her term of service by the simple expedient of drawing a knife across his throat while he was distracted with strangling Grant.

Since that day, more than a year before, Domi had viewed Grant as a gallant black knight who rescued her from the shackles of Guana Teague's slavery. In reality, quite the reverse was true; Teague was crushing the life out of Grant beneath his three-hundred-plus pounds of flab when Domi expertly slit his throat.

Regardless of the facts, Domi had attached herself to Grant, and though her attempts at outright seduction were less frequent, she made it fiercely clear that Grant was hers and hers alone.

Despite that devotion, Domi possessed a hair-trigger temper in the most relaxed of circumstances. If questioned about her sullen attitude, she probably wouldn't stage a tantrum, but she was prone to extended sulks. She hadn't seemed very enthusiastic about joining them on the op in the first place, which was decidedly unusual. Normally, the albino refugee from the Outlands eagerly jumped at any opportunity to leave the vanadium walls of Cerberus.

Heaving a mental shrug, Kane placed the matter in his personal file drawer of unimportant matters. As long as Domi's efficiency with her .45-caliber Detonics Combat Master pistol was unimpaired, he wasn't going to concern himself with her emotional state.

As they pushed through the sagebrush, dotted with occasional saguaros, they saw very few signs of animal life. Domi pointed out some indistinguishable tracks that she tersely identified as a deer trail. A few minutes later, they came across odd, swirling, S-curve patterns in the sandy soil. They reminded Kane of large wag tires that been rolled around.

Domi nodded toward them. "Sidewinder. A *big* sidewinder."

Uneasily, Brigid asked. "Just how big?"

Domi's reply, if she had one, was drowned out by a rattling noise like a half ton of gravel being shaken inside of an empty oil drum.

Chapter 3

Grant and Kane skipped around, their Sin Eaters popping simultaneously into their hands, hearts thudding frantically within their polycarbonate-encased chests. Half-hidden by a tangled copse of mesquite and sage, a snake lay coiled tightly, its multibuttoned rattle vibrating furiously. The creature's striped and mottled hide helped it blend in with its sere surroundings. The serpent was about twenty yards away, so they were in no immediate danger.

"It's one of the mutie snakes that used to be worshiped around here," Brigid said, striving to sound calm. "I guess there are still a few alive."

"You think?" Kane asked with a cold sarcasm, trying to ignore the prickling at his nape.

Many species of animals that survived the nuclear exchange and the subsequent freezing temperatures of skydark had mutated into grotesque imitations of their progenitors. The first two or three generations of mutant animals had run toward polyploidism, a doubling or tripling of the chromosome complement. For a time, gargantuan buffalo and panthers and even wolves had roamed the Deathlands, but their increased size had greatly reduced their life spans. Only a few of the giant varieties existed any longer, or so all of them had been led to believe.

Still, it wasn't all that long ago since Kane, Grant and Domi had fought a gigantic constrictor in the jungles of Amazonia, one the local natives had decked out in a feathered headdress and christened Kukulkan, in homage to the ancient Mayan god.

This serpent was in no way as large as that one, perhaps only fifteen feet, but unlike Kukulkan it was a pit viper. As it lifted its wedge-shaped head, swaying on an arched neck, they saw a pair of six-inch-long teeth curving out from the maxillary bone of the upper jaw. Beads of colorless venom glistened on the needle points of the hollow fangs. Its forked tongue darted in and out between them, and the fetid odor of its breath clogged their nostrils.

Domi reached for her blaster snugged in a shoulder rig, but Kane said curtly, "A shot from that cannon will carry for miles around here. As long as it's not bothering us, we won't bother it."

"Rattler meat is good eating," she replied petulantly.

"We don't have the time to skin it and pack out the meat," Grant told her dourly. "You'll have to make do with our ration packs."

Domi acted as if she hadn't heard, turning away. Kane and Grant backed up carefully, keeping their eyes on the flattened skull of the snake, just visible over the top of the brush. Its cold, slit-pupiled eyes watched them as they retreated, and after a minute it stopped shaking its tail.

The four people trudged on and reached a grove of pines. Although it was cooler beneath the thickly needled boughs, there was more undergrowth. Kane walked point as he always did, chopping a path through the tangle of thorny mesquite with his combat knife. Despite the fact that Domi was wilderness born, Kane always assumed the position of point man. It was a habit he had acquired during his years as a Mag, and he saw no reason to abandon it. Grant had the utmost faith in Kane's instincts, what he referred to as his point man's sense. During their Mag days, because of his uncanny ability to sniff danger in the offing, he was always chosen to act as the advance scout. When he walked point, Kane felt electrically alive, sharply tuned to every nuance of his surroundings and what he was doing.

After an hour, Kane called a halt so they could rest and drink. They sat in a clearing and passed around a bottle of water, drinking sparingly. There was abundant insect life beneath the trees, butterflies, bees and wasps darting this way and that, but none of them seemed to be of the mutie variety.

Kane and Grant had seen a nest of mutie hornets, and both retained vividly unpleasant memories of their six-inch wingspans, bloated, striped bodies and barbed stingers dripping with poison.

Grant said in a grumbling tone, "I wish we would come across another redoubt with a cargo gateway, like the one at Redoubt Oscar. That way we could make the jump with a Sandcat and stop this forced-march shit.''

"Cerberus doesn't have a cargo unit," Kane pointed out. "So it doesn't really matter, unless we make the jump with the Cat in pieces and spend a couple of days trying to reassemble it.''

Grant grunted. "Rather a couple of days of that than walking in armor.''

As he handed the water bottle to Brigid, he added, "I still can't figure out why Baron Cobalt would send a force of his Mags into another baron's territory—to an Outland settlement, no less. Doesn't he have enough of his own?''

Brigid paused thoughtfully before taking a drink. "Maybe not. Or maybe he's saving them for something else. For whatever reason he dispatched the Magistrates, he's taking a big risk. If he's found out, he could alienate the rest of the oligarchy.''

"No pun intended," Kane interposed wryly.

Brigid threw him a fleeting smile. "That's right.''

All of them knew what every ville citizen knew about the formation of their society. In the century following skydark, self-proclaimed barons had warred against one another, each struggling for control and absolute power over territory. Then they realized that greater rewards were possible if unity in command, purpose and organization was achieved.

Territories were redefined, treaties struck among the barons, and the city-states became interconnected points in a continent-spanning network. More than ninety years ago, the Program of Unification was ratified during the Council of Front Royal, then ruthlessly employed. With Unity Through Action as the rallying cry, the reconstructed form of government was institutionalized and shared by all the formerly independent baronies.

The nine most powerful baronies that had survived the long wars over territorial expansion and resources divided control of the continent among themselves. A hierarchical ruling system was put into place, and the city-states adopted the name of the titular heads of state.

But few ville citizens knew the true nature of their rulers. The barons ruling the nine villes were more than the governing body of postnukecaust America— they were a living expression of the ancient god-king system. Their semidivine status derived from the means of their birth; they were hybrids of human and nonhuman, a blending of genetic material with the sole purpose of creating new humans to inherit the Earth. The barons served as a bridge between predark and postdark, the plenipotentiaries of the alien Archon Directorate itself.

According to what Kane, Brigid, Domi and Grant had been told by Lakesh upon their arrival at the Cerberus redoubt more than a year before, the entirety of human history was intertwined with the entities called Archons. Over the long track of time, the mysterious entities had been referred to by many names—demons, visitors, E.T.s and, finally and most simplistically, the Grays.

Archons traditionally allied themselves with conquerors and tyrants, conspiring with willing human pawns to control humankind through political chaos, staged wars, famines, plagues and natural disasters. Their goal was always the unification of the world under their control, with all nonessential and nonproductive humans eliminated.

As time progressed, the world and humankind changed too much for them to rule through fallible human intermediaries with any degree of effectiveness. The Archons had no choice but to reveal themselves openly to the men in power.

After World War II, a pact was formed between elements in the United States government and the Archons, essentially an exchange for high-tech knowledge. Part of the trade agreement allowed the Archons use of underground military bases. The agreement was known in ultra-top-secret documents as the Archon Directive. The power elite convinced themselves that the Archons were benevolent, with their primary interest in sharing technology that could make nuclear war obsolete. Much of this technology, based on Archon templates, was the foundation of the Totality Concept researches.

Following the nuclear holocaust of January 20, 2001, the Archon Directive became the Archon Directorate. During the first century after the holocaust, humanity was too scarce and widespread for effective control. The Archon's solution was a long-range hybridization program, combining the genetic material of humankind with their own race to construct a biological bridge.

Eventually, the Archon Directorate interceded directly in the development of the most powerful baronies, and instituted the Program of Unification to bring humanity back under its control. Through their intermediaries, the Archons prevented the rebuilding of a society analogous to the predark model. Aspects of the Program of Unification were designed to prevent a repetition of the inefficient preholocaust societal structure and also to hide the existence of the Archon Directorate and the Totality Concept from all but a minority of humanity.

But over the past few months, Brigid, Kane, Domi and Grant had learned that the elaborate backstory contained only bits of truth mixed in with outrageous fiction. The Archon Directorate did not exist except as a vast cover story, created in the twentieth century and grown larger with each succeeding generation. The only so-called Archon on Earth was Balam, the last of an extinct race that had once shared the planet with humankind. Even more shocking was Balam's assertion that he and his ancient folk were of human stock, not alien but alienated.

Balam claimed that the Archon Directorate was an appellation and a myth created by the predark government agencies as a control mechanism. Lakesh referred to it as the "Oz effect," wherein a single vulnerable entity created the illusion of being the representative of an all-powerful body.

Balam himself may have even coined the term Archon to describe his people. In ancient Gnostic texts, *archon* was applied to a parahuman world-governing force that imprisoned the divine spark in human souls. Kane had often wondered over the past few months if Balam had indeed created that appellation as a cryptic code to warn future generations.

The Cerberus exiles still didn't know how much to believe. But if nothing else, none of them subscribed any longer to the fatalistic belief that the human race had its day and only extinction lay ahead. Balam had indicated that was not true, only another control mechanism.

It was undeniable, however, that the barons, the half-human hybrids spawned from Balam's DNA, still ruled. Each of the fortress-cities with its individual, allegedly immortal god-king was supposed to be interdependent with the others, but the baronies operated on insular principles, and cooperation among them seemed to be grudging despite their shared goal of a unified world. They perceived humanity in general as either servants or as living storage vessels for transplant organs and fresh genetic material.

Although the nine barons were not immortal, they were as close as flesh-and-blood creatures could come to it. Due to their hybrid metabolisms, their longevities far exceeded those of humans. Barring accidents, illnesses—or assassinations—the barons' life spans could conceivably be measured by centuries.

But the price paid by the barons for their extended life spans was not cheap. They were physically fragile, prone to lethargy and their metabolisms easy prey for infections, which was one reason they tended to sequester themselves from the ville-bred humans they ruled. Once a year, all the barons traveled to the Dulce facility to have their blood filtered and their autoimmune systems boosted. In severe cases, even damaged organs were replaced from the storage banks of organic material stockpiled at the Dulce installation.

Built in the midtwentieth century to house several divisions of the Totality Concept, the vast genetic engineering facility beneath the Archuleta Mesa in Dulce was later turned over almost entirely to Overproject Excalibur, the governing body overseeing bioresearch programs.

Over the past thirty-odd years, the subterranean installation had become a combination of gestation facility, birthing ward and medical-treatment center. The hybrids, the self-proclaimed new humans, reproduced by a form of cloning and gene-splicing. Since the installation at Dulce had been rendered useless by the Cerberus personnel, extinction for the barons was less than a generation away if they did not have access to a secondary installation. Or so the Cerberus exiles fervently hoped.

As Kane led his companions on their journey, they

twice crossed shallow ribbons of water that Brigid identified as tributaries of the Stanislaus River.

"If we follow it," she said, "we'd probably come to the ruins of a predark town or two."

"So?" Domi asked darkly.

"So, we might find some items of historical interest."

Kane gave her bleak half grin. "This isn't a field trip, Baptiste. Besides, the trail moves away from the river, not along it."

When they emerged from the grove of trees, they found themselves on a two-lane blacktop road. The asphalt had a peculiar ripple pattern to it, and weeds sprouted from splits in the surface. Kane and Grant had seen the rippling effect before, out in the hell-zones. It was a characteristic result of earthquakes triggered by nuclear-bomb shock waves.

In a relieved voice, Brigid announced, "State Road 49. We're right on course."

During the prejump briefing, Brigid mentioned that the entire area around the Sierra Nevada foothills was the center of the California gold rush, three hundred or so years ago. Fueled by dreams of riches, prospectors crossed America's mountains, plains and deserts to pan for the precious nuggets. In response to the influx of fortune seekers, hundreds of mining towns sprang up around the mountain range. Within two decades, with the gold fields played out, most of the towns died.

None of her companions had any reason to doubt

Brigid's brief history of the region. Not only was she a former archivist, but she was also gifted with an eidetic, or "photographic," memory. She instantly recalled in detail everything she had ever seen or read. Due to her years as a historian, her mental stockpile of predark knowledge was profound.

They walked along the highway for only a mile before it was bisected by an earth slip, the rupture as clean as if made by an unimaginably huge knife blade. Beyond lay a great plain of parched desert terrain, dotted only with sagebrush, cacti and ocotilla shrubs.

All of them knew that the most far-ranging destruction during the holocaust took place on the West Coast. Soviet "earthshaker" bombs had been seeded by submarines along the unstable fault lines in the Pacific. When they were detonated, vast areas of land between the Cascades and the Sierra Nevadas bucked, heaved and burst apart as if the earth itself were giving birth.

The four people were able to climb down the face of the fall with little difficulty, reaching the bottom in a series of jumps. Stooping, Kane examined the ground, noting marks of booted feet that had been poorly swept over with sand.

On one knee, Grant poked at a half-obscured pattern. "Boot treads," he observed. "They look familiar to you?"

Kane lifted his right foot, tapping the sole. "Standard Mag-issue footwear. How old do you figure they are?''

Domi stepped forward, eyed the tracks and announced, ''Not more than six hours.'' She looked toward the sky. ''Be full dark afore we catch up with 'em.''

From her knapsack, Brigid took a compact set of microbinoculars. She peered through the eyepieces, adjusting the focus to accommodate her own slightly astigmatic vision. At first she saw nothing but a dry vista of sand, stone and clay. Then she distinguished a dark line, a deeper brown against the beige of the sand.

''The edge of the desert isn't far,'' she said.

''Define 'isn't far,''' Kane suggested.

''An hour. Two at the outside.''

Kane straightened. ''Let's double-time it, then.''

They strode swiftly across the arid ground, though clusters of cacti sprouting steely thorns made double-timing anything difficult and painful. The wind-drifted sand glimmered in long ripples, as if a sea had been suddenly frozen and turned to powder. It reflected the sunlight so brightly that all of them put on dark glasses. The ground was not smooth, although it looked deceptively so. All of them stumbled at least once on the sharp creases of rock hidden beneath siftings of sand.

Inside of a mile, the air was heavy with radiating waves of sheer, hellish heat. The desert hardpan seemed to soak it up and reflect it back. There was no shelter in sight from the rising inferno.

Domi, with her fair skin and sensitive eyes, suffered the worst, but she kept her complaints to herself. Kane and Grant quickly soaked their Kevlar undersheathings through with perspiration, making both feel as if they were wearing swamps. Despite Brigid's estimate of how far away the edge of the desert was, the afternoon drifted by in a haze of heat shimmers and sweat.

They slogged on through the sand. Cacti of twisted, distorted shapes grew nearby, but no trees, not even a decent sized bush. Kane was concerned that Brigid would tire quickly, but her swift, almost mannish stride never faltered.

With agonizing slowness, the sun dropped enough that its glare wasn't as intense. The terrain gradually became rockier, firmer underfoot, inclining downward into dusty arroyos, dry washes that petered out after short distances. The ground was still soft enough to show bootprints, and the four people followed them.

One shallow ravine led into a deep gorge, where sheer walls rose on every side, exposing layers of sediment stained with streaks of red and ocher. Rocks both large and small reared in their path, as well as scatterings of dense shrub brush. Gravel crunched beneath their tramping feet. An island of solid granite stood in front of them. It had once forced a river to divide itself into a pair of channels, one right and one left. Both of them meandered out of sight. During the nuke-triggered quakes, rivers and streams had been diverted, sometimes running together until they made a vast, raging torrent.

Kane came to a halt, carefully examining the stony ground. He saw no sign of bootprints, not even the faintest of scuff marks. He looked to the left and to the right, and said in a voice full of frustration, "We've lost the trail."

Grant looked at the ground with an offended expression on his face, almost as if he blamed it for not holding tracks. "Fucking fireblast. To have come this far—"

"We've still got two choices," Brigid said.

"Yeah," Kane agreed gloomily, "and one of them is wrong. It could take us miles away from the bastards."

They stood in silence for a long moment, all of them loath to choose a path and take the responsibility if it was the wrong one. Finally, with a sigh of resignation, Kane started walking toward the mouth of the right-hand channel.

Not surprisingly, Domi heard the distant sound first. All of her senses were honed to razor keenness due to her upbringing in the Outlands of Hells Canyon, Idaho. She hissed, gesturing sharply for everyone to halt. They obeyed her without question, standing stock-still, listening hard, nerves tingling. They heard nothing but the soughing of the wind.

"What?" Kane asked impatiently.

Domi opened her mouth to speak, closed it, then

shook her white-haired head, dark and damp now with sweat. "Thought I heard things. Voices, footsteps, stuff clanking."

Kane strained his hearing, still heard nothing and started to relax. Then he heard the faint noises—a distant murmur of voices at the far limit of audibility, coming from somewhere ahead of them. Within a moment, all of them heard faint, mixed sounds, cries of pain, curses of anger, metallic clinks and jingles. Kane quickly slipped out of his backpack and Grant did the same, dropping their Copperheads atop them.

Extending a hand toward Brigid, Kane demanded curtly, "The binoculars."

She gave them to him, and he slung them around his neck by the strap. He and Grant picked a path through a jumble of upthrust rocks and reached the deeply fissured gorge wall. They began scaling it quickly and easily. It wasn't long before the easy ascent gave way to a serious climb. Footholds were hard to come by, and some of the handholds were mere cracks in the smooth stone face, but they wedged their fingers in and pulled themselves along. Their fingers gripped cracks in the stone, and rivulets of gravel streamed beneath their boots, rattling and clicking.

Grant huffed and puffed and swore as he clambered up the gorge wall, wishing Domi had volunteered to take his place. Nimble and strong, she could climb like a scalded monkey.

Finally, they reached a shelf of rock jutting below the top of the gorge wall, and panting heavily, the two men pulled themselves on top of it. Moving on hands and knees, they crawled to a heap of loose stones on the far edge. Kane raised the microbinoculars, blew grit from the ruby-coated lenses and peered through the eyepieces. Except for the shimmering heat waves rising from the baked ground and an occasional birdcall, the air was still.

He caught a flicker of movement and swiftly he tightened the focus to bring distant details to crystal clarity. Two columns of obsidian-armored Magistrates approached the gorge from the far side. He estimated they were about six hundred yards away, ten Mags to a column. Two armored men bringing up the rear haphazardly used brooms improvised from intertwined mesquite and sage branches to sweep their trail.

Between the black, marching lines staggered six men and three women. Raggedly dressed, they were tethered to one another by yokes of thick leather and wood with a length chain. They cringed from a pair of Mags who urged them along with curses and strokes from the barrels of their Copperheads.

"I guess they got what they came for," Kane murmured.

Grant squinted, barely able to pick out the distant black figures. "Anybody we know?"

Kane swept the binoculars back and forth, then fixed on a burly, stocky man in the lead. As he watched, the man removed his helmet and palmed away a film of sweat from his pale moon face and bulldog jowls. His small eyes were nearly buried within fleshy, puffy bags.

"Well, well, well," Kane drawled, handing the binoculars to Grant. "Look who's walking point."

Grant peered through the eyepieces and grunted softly in mingled surprise and disgust. "Baron Cobalt must be slag-assed desperate to assign Pollard to lead this detail."

Kane smiled mirthlessly. "Good old Polly. Haven't seen him in a while."

"The last time I saw him," Grant intoned, "he was flat on his fat face with a broken nose, a mashed hand and mebbe a broken rib or two."

"Mebbe? You're not sure?"

The broad yoke of Grant's shoulders lifted in a negligent shrug. "It wasn't for lack of trying. If you're interested, you can always ask him."

Kane nodded. "I figure to do that very thing. Just as soon as they make camp."

Chapter 4

The channels the long-gone river had cut into the gorge formed a natural maze with ancillary branches and side passages that offered easy concealment. Grant, Kane, Domi and Brigid withdrew into a deep fissure in the canyon wall, on the opposite side of the rock island that the Magistrates approached. They crouched silently as, hidden by the formation, the columns passed them by.

As the sound of the grim procession faded, Brigid commented quietly, "They'll have to stop for the night soon."

Kane glanced at the sky, at the sun sliding down amid a flurry of feathery clouds tinted a light purple. "In an hour or so," he agreed. "We'll be able to find them with no problem."

He eased himself into a sitting position, his back against a rock wall. "We can wait here for a bit before moving out."

In relative silence, they ate from the MRE ration packs. The Cerberus redoubt had thousands of the concentrated foodstuffs in storage, enough to feed all of the installation's permanent residents for a life-time—if they ever got hungry enough.

The self-heat rations offered a wide variety of meals, but most of them tasted like damp cardboard. The few that didn't have the flavor of wet paper and glue tasted, according to Domi—who had the most indiscriminate of taste buds—like stickie shit. Still, the MREs contained all the vitamins and nutrients to keep people alive and healthy, just not happy.

"If I were Pollard—" Grant began.

"You'd chill yourself?" Kane broke in.

Grant regarded him with mild irritation. "Besides that. I'd wait until a few hours after dark before crossing the waste. When the moon is high."

Brigid nodded. "Makes sense. The air will be cooler. Less risk of any Mags suffering from heat prostration. No cover in the off chance any of the prisoners break away."

Domi spoke up, her high-pitched voice carrying a note of incredulity. "So we do what—the four of us go up against twenty 'forcers?"

"Nineteen if you don't count Pollard," Kane corrected.

"Just to free some rag-assed outlanders? Why?"

"There's more to it than that," Grant rumbled. "We need to find out why Baron Cobalt is invading a brother baron's territory."

Domi's lips twisted as if she tasted something sour. "Why do we need to? Why do we care? Let 'em fight it out themselves."

No one responded immediately to the girl's suggestion, although the notion wasn't a new one, at least not to Kane. During a recent op to the British Isles, after reacquainting himself with the Celtic warrior-priestess Fand, she had mentioned much the same tactic. He easily recalled her words: "Perhaps you could turn those ego-structures against one another, exploit that self-aggrandizement, destroy them from within, rather than without."

The concept appealed to him on a number of counts, primarily because the tyranny of the barons would be ended by none other than themselves.

Fixing his eyes on Domi, Grant said in a low, intense tone, "Mebbe going up against twenty Mags for nine outlanders isn't worth it. Mebbe it is stupe. But remember what happened to your own people in Hells Canyon. I imagine they would've been grateful if just one of us interfered."

Domi's face remained as expressionless as if it were chiseled out of porcelain, but Kane could guess the kind of thoughts wheeling through her head.

The memory of the Mag-orchestrated slaughter and mutilation of her people was still fresh. The girl did not have much of a past, but what little there was of it had been ruthlessly expunged by the forces of the villes.

Kane tested the sensitive spring-and-cable mechanism of his Sin Eater's holster, making sure it wasn't fouled by grit. Brigid looked over her own blaster, an Iver Johnson TP-9 autopistol, carefully cycling a round into the chamber. She frowned in dismay at the gritty, grating sound made by the slide mechanism.

Grant extended a hand toward her. "That needs to be stripped and cleaned before it's reliable again."

He turned toward Domi. "What about yours?"

Wordlessly, she drew her Combat Master and tested the action. It moved smoothly. Grant nodded in satisfaction and from his backpack removed a gun-cleaning kit. Spreading out a square of cloth, he field-stripped Brigid's autoblaster, meticulously oiling all of its moving parts.

Firearms had been a minor point of contention between Kane and Brigid for the past several months. For a while she had carried an H&K VP-70, then a Beretta, but she found the weight and recoil of both guns a little uncomfortable. She had opted for a .32-caliber Mauser at one point, but its range and accuracy depended on too many variables. She'd carried an Uzi for a bit, but never had to fire it. Kane had chosen the 9 mm Iver Johnson autoblaster for her, and he suspected she carried it just to keep him from carping about her lack of interest in guns.

As Grant cleaned her pistol, he said contemplatively, "Seems kind of strange that Pollard would be leading this mission—or involved in it at all. He's got a couple of major fuckups on his record, and without Salvo around to protect him, by all rights he should've been executed."

"By all rights," Kane said, "Salvo should've chilled him after he saw the gateway in Mesa Verde."

"With all of the baron's setbacks recently," Brigid

ventured, "it's possible he's been forced to make allowances, to relax the rules."

Grant grunted thoughtfully, snapping the pieces of her weapon back together. "Cobaltville took heavy losses in ordnance and manpower when they attacked Ambika's raiders. The baron probably hasn't replaced either. After that disaster, he probably doesn't trust too many of his advisers."

"We don't know what happened to Abrams," Kane replied.

A few months before Abrams, the Mag Division administrator had led a force of hard-contact Mags from Cobaltville into Montana to investigate the Cerberus redoubt and ascertain if it was playing host to three wanted seditionists—namely Kane, Grant and Brigid.

Lakesh had taken great pains over the years to establish the belief that that particular Totality Concept-related installation was hopelessly unsalvageable. However, when the search for them among all of the redoubts began in earnest, it was inevitable Cerberus would be investigated simply by a process of elimination.

The Magistrates were stopped and soundly defeated by Sky Dog's band of Amerindians in the flatlands bordering the foothills. Grant and Kane were instrumental in the victory, although they managed to keep their involvement concealed from the invading Mags. The survivors of the engagement were disarmed and allowed to go on their way, believing the Indians alone were responsible for their humiliation.

A mental image of a boxy jawline beneath a helmet's visor suddenly popped into the forefront of Kane's mind. He recalled how the general outline had struck him as familiar, but because of the fierce firefight raging around him, he hadn't devoted much thought to it.

Absently, with a harsh chuckle lurking in the back of his throat, he said, "I'll be dipped in swampie shit."

Brigid glanced at him in distaste, and Grant angled questioning eyebrows in his direction. "What?"

"Remember the assault force of Mags under Abrams's command? Pollard was the driver of his Sandcat."

Sandcats were armored, overland fast-attack vehicles used by the villes. One had been appropriated by Lakesh and stored in Cerberus.

"How do you know that?" Grant demanded.

"I saw the son of a bitch—only for a couple of seconds, but because I was so busy trying to keep that damn war wag under control I didn't make the connection until just now."

Grant made a "hmm" sound of contemplation as he fitted the grip back into the frame of the Iver Johnson. "At best, by all the old protocols, the choicest assignment Pollard could hope for would be walking pedestrian patrol in Tartarus, not leading a squad into another baron's sphere of influence."

Since ville society was strictly class-and caste-based, the residential towers reflected those divisions. At the bottom level of the villes was the servant class, who lived in abject squalor in consciously designed ghettos known as the Tartarus Pits, named after the abyss below Hell where Zeus confined the Titans. They swarmed with a heterogeneous population of serfs and cheap labor.

Sounding a little mystified, Brigid inquired, "What are the old protocols?"

The corners of Kane's mouth quirked in a mirthless smile. "If a Mag squad fucked up, even though the commander was held accountable, every man in it was disciplined to some extent or another."

"Yeah," Grant put in. "Depending on the decision of the disciplinary tribunal, sometimes you just lost your rank, sometimes you were assigned scut work for six months or so. Worst case, you were cashiered out, your citizenship stripped away. You'd be reclassified as an outlander and exiled from the ville. In really extreme instances, you were executed. Most of the time, execution is considered too merciful."

Brigid knew that a citizen's reclassification to that of an outlander was in some ways worse than death. It was a form of nonexistence. For people who had been born outside the direct influence of the villes, who worked the farms, toiled in the fields or simply roamed from place to place, being an outlander wasn't a punishment—it was simply the way things were. They knew they were reviled by the ville bred.

To be recognized as a person with a right to exist, one had to belong to ville society, even if only in the lowest caste.

Those who chose not to, or were not chosen to belong, were the outlanders. They were the expendables, the free labor force, the cannon fodder, the convenient enemies of order, the useless eaters. She, Grant, Kane and all of the exiles in Cerberus were outlanders. Only Domi was one by birth, so in the kingdom of the disenfranchised, she was the pretender to the throne.

"So," Brigid said, "regardless of the fact Abrams would shoulder the lion's share of the blame, you're saying Pollard shouldn't be in charge of a latrine-scrubbing detail, much less a force of hard-contact Magistrates. At least by the protocols in place when you two were Mags."

Kane nodded. "Exactly."

Brigid opened her mouth to say something else, but Domi suddenly half rose, tilting her head to one side, expression one of concentration. "Hush," she commanded.

Her companions fell silent, watching her expectantly. After a few seconds, she said tensely, "Heard something."

"Mebbe a couple of Mag stragglers," Grant opined quietly.

Domi shook her head. "No, this sound was different. Sort of like metal scraping against metal."

Kane and Grant exchanged weary glances. Neither

man cared to make the strenuous climb back up the gorge wall to the ledge a second time. Unslinging the binoculars, Kane handed them to the albino girl. "Why don't you take a look-see this time?"

Her pale lips pursed, then curved in an impudent smile. "Not up to it anymore? You're acting as old as Grant."

Gruffly, Grant shot back, "And you're young enough to pull your own weight on this op just like the rest of us."

Crimson anger glittered in Domi's eyes, but it faded as quickly as it flared. She took the binoculars and glided as gracefully as a wraith out of the fissure.

After a minute, when it seemed likely she was out of earshot, Brigid asked in a half whisper, "What's going on with her?"

Grant lifted a shoulder in a dismissive shrug. "You know how moody she is. Sometimes everything gets on her nerves."

"True," Brigid agreed. "But her problem doesn't seem to be with everybody, just you."

Grant, concentrating on reassembling her Iver Johnson, didn't respond.

"Did you have a fight with her?" Brigid pressed. "Over what?"

A distinctly uncomfortable expression crossed Grant's dark face, but he quickly molded it into a threatening scowl. Staring directly into her face, he growled, "Drop it."

"But if she's—"

"I said *drop it.*"

Brigid blinked at him in surprise. She had grown accustomed to Grant's grumbling manner, as if he were somebody's curmudgeonly but essentially good-hearted uncle. Now she detected a genuine edge of anger in the way he bit out the words, a warning she was overstepping her bounds.

She glanced toward Kane, hoping he would contribute something to her line of questioning. Instead, he gazed steadily out into the gorge, as if a nearby outcropping was a source of total fascination for him.

Brigid felt a surge of annoyance, but she tamped it down before it became anger. She knew full well how the two men observed an unspoken pact not to interfere in each other's private life. If and when they disagreed, they settled the issue between themselves, usually in private.

Domi returned in less than ten minutes, her white hair tinted beige with the fine powdery sand. Sounding only a little out of breath, she said, "Saw something at the far end of the ravine, 'bout a mile away."

"Saw what?" Kane demanded, straightening. "More Mags?"

"Don't think so. The light is bad, so all I saw was a little flash of metal."

"A wag?" Grant inquired.

Domi frowned. "Didn't hear anything. All I saw was a flash, only for a second."

"Could be people from the settlement," Brigid suggested. "Trailing the Magistrates."

"Could be," Kane conceded hesitantly.

"Or," Grant said, "it could be nothing at all, or at least nothing to do with this."

"Could be," Kane repeated. He stood, reaching for his helmet. "Let's leave most of our stuff here. Just bring the essentials. By the time we catch up to Pollard, he'll have called a halt. We'll come back and get it after."

"After what?" Domi asked, an undercurrent of challenge in her voice.

"After whatever happens," Kane replied coldly, sliding the helmet over his head.

Grant handed Brigid her blaster and rose, taking his own helmet from his backpack and putting it on. The snapping shut of the underjaw lock guards seemed preternaturally loud.

Looking at the two men with their features all but concealed behind the red-tinted visors, Brigid repressed a shiver of fear. The gaze she gave them was the same wary look she might cast toward a pair of tigers, if she came across them in her living room.

Although she owed Kane and Grant her life and had shared many dangers with them, when they were outfitted in full armor they ceased to be the men she knew. She could sense the change that came over them.

They weren't exiles now, nor were they soldiers or even her comrades. Grant and Kane had slipped back into their Magistrate personas as easily as other men slipped into dressing gowns. Once again Brigid had to forcibly remind herself that the two men had spent their entire adult lives as killers—superbly trained and conditioned enforcers, not only carrying the legal license to deal death but the spiritual sanction, as well.

"Everybody got their comm channels set?" Kane asked, shouldering the war bag and his Copperhead. Even his voice sounded frosty and remote.

Brigid and Domi flipped open the covers of their transcomm units, little palm-sized radiophones, and made sure the frequencies were in tune with the helmet comm-links.

"Set," Brigid declared crisply, shouldering the flat case containing basic survival stores.

"We'll move out slow and easy," Grant said. "There's no need to hurry. If you hurry, you're likely to get careless, and if you get careless you're likely to make noise."

"It's not probable," Kane stated, "but Pollard may've posted a couple of sentries to watch their backtrail if he thinks they're being followed."

Domi and Brigid nodded in understanding.

Kane turned toward the shadowed, stony maze, walking heel-to-toe as he always did in a potential killzone. "Let's get it done."

There was no need for him to say more. The four people walked in a single file, with about six feet separating each of them. No one spoke.

They had worked their way less than a hundred yards into the gathering gloom when faintly came the sputter of autofire. The reports were overlaid by a scream of pure terror. It was long, drawn out and undeniably masculine.

Chapter 5

Kane saw little reason to increase his pace. Whatever caused the commotion was far ahead of them. He doubted they would have heard it at all except the sound was carried by the wind and echoed off the labyrinthine rock walls.

"What the hell was that?" Grant demanded in a husky whisper.

Kane shook his head, indicating the matter was of little importance and continued to stride forward. Full darkness came swiftly to the canyon, seeming to flow like streams of ink down the walls and ooze out of the mouths of the side channels.

Stars began to gleam, cold and white against the vast indigo tapestry of the sky. Grant's and Kane's image enhancers brought into sharp relief everything around them. They saw small rocks that had been overturned by the passage of many feet and dim scuff marks in the dust. They were faint, but they were sufficient to mark a trail. Kane and Grant followed them, instinctively placing their feet so as to raise a minimum of dust and not dislodge loose stones.

The trail led across the rock-strewn gorge floor, winding and bending in a succession of narrow kinks.

Grant, for all of his size, moved through the darkened defile as surefooted as a cat. Surprisingly, it was the wilderness-born Domi who stumbled a couple of times. She swore under her breath each time until Brigid told her to shush.

At every bend Kane's sixth sense, his point man's sense, went on high alert for an ambush, but the path twisted on with no one and nothing to bar their way. Even though the Mags had a long start, their prisoners would slow them, and Kane saw no reason to take chances with hurrying.

Although he hadn't discounted Domi's report of seeing a flash of metal, he didn't devote much thought to it. His prey lay ahead, not behind. Still, the notion of being trapped in a squeeze play in the confines of the gorge didn't exactly help him enjoy the evening's walk. He told himself Pollard wasn't intelligent or foolhardy enough to divide his forces.

However, he felt a grudging admiration for Pollard's choice of routes. The average Magistrate, assuming any were dispatched by Baron Snakefish, would be completely bewildered by what little trail was left by Pollard and his men. If the Mags didn't know exactly who or what they were tracking, they would have given up the hunt at sunset.

The canyon pitched to the left and widened, then narrowed, descended and finally opened into a field of upthrust stones. Nerves tingling, eyes narrowed, he came to a complete stop. He gestured behind him, signaling his three companions to halt.

The dark boulders stood like lonely sentinels, guarding only desolation. The dozen rocks were all of similar sizes and shapes, approximately eight feet tall with the facing sides quarried flat. They were arranged in two rows with an aisle of about ten feet between them. Other than trying to scale the steep, downsloping walls of the gorge, a traveler would have no choice but to traverse the aisle, as if walking a mineral gauntlet.

Kane knew it wasn't a natural rock formation. Someone had gone to a lot of time and effort to place the megaliths in such a fashion. The setup was so obvious, he wondered why there wasn't a sign posted that read Watch Out for Trap.

As he scrutinized the stones, he saw the flat faces were covered by crude carvings, serpentine whorls and squiggles. In a whisper, he called Brigid up to stand beside him. "What do you make of those?"

As she squinted toward them, a cloud whipped past the moon, and its lambent glow shone on the standing stones and their inscriptions. "They're obviously artificially arranged."

"I figured that out for myself," he said dryly. "What I want to know is why they're there at all."

She shot him a sideways glare, an irritation born of exertion and tension glittering in her sea-green eyes. "All I can sell is speculation."

"I'll buy some if that's all you've got."

Running her fingers through her tousled red-gold mane, she said lowly, "We know a snake cult practiced in this region. This could be a holy place, where ceremonies or meetings were held.''

He nodded curtly. ''Pollard and his party came this way, so I guess we can too.''

Kane checked his wrist chron and saw with a twinge of surprise they had been walking for a little over forty-five minutes. He was on the verge of asking if anybody wanted to take a rest break when Domi's high, stressed-out voice squawked through his helmet comm-link and into his right ear. ''We're being followed!''

Grant and Kane pivoted almost simultaneously on their heels, peering into the murk behind them. They saw no sign of Domi. Grant growled into his transceiver, ''Where the hell are you?''

''Heard noises,'' her voice responded, the tone so sharp it made both Kane and Grant wince. ''I hung back for a recce.''

''Get your ass back up here,'' Kane commanded.

''But—''

''Now!''

He turned to Brigid. ''Did you hear anything behind you?''

She hadn't heard Domi's side of the brief conversion, but she easily guessed what it was about. ''Not a thing. I didn't even notice she'd dropped back.''

Within a couple of minutes, Domi emerged with a ghostly grace from the gloom. She stared defiantly at Kane and Grant, saying doggedly, ''Definitely somebody behind us. They know how to move fast and quiet, and they're wearing some kind of metal on their clothes."

"How do you know that?" Grant asked.

"Heard it scrape against rock a couple of times. I figure there's more than one tracking us."

Kane groped for a dismissive response but instantly recalled all the times in the past when the girl's sharp senses had alerted them to danger.

Planting her fists on her flaring hips, Domi demanded truculently, "You believe me, right?"

"Right," Kane replied brusquely. "How far behind are they?"

"Can't be sure. Like I said, they're moving fast."

"Take a guess," Grant suggested.

The girl's chalk-white brow furrowed in concentration. "Mebbe thirty minutes. Mebbe less."

Kane swung around toward the field of stones. He gestured. "Let's get across and find a place to lay up for a bit. Mebbe we can find out who it is."

"What about Pollard and his prisoners?" Brigid inquired, her tone slightly troubled. "Why did they come this way instead of retracing their steps?"

Grant replied, "To throw off tracers. The ground is harder here and won't hold prints."

"What I meant," Brigid said, "is if Pollard doesn't make camp and decides to cross the desert, we could lose him while we're laying low."

"Even if he crosses tonight," Kane stated, "we know where he's heading. Let's move out. Stay as quiet as you can. Don't even breathe hard."

Carefully, Kane stepped forward. The loud crunch of a shard of shale under his boot lifted the hair on his nape and sent a jolt of adrenaline surging through his body. He froze in midstep, angry and embarrassed. Behind him he heard Domi doing a poor job of muffling a cruel snicker, then Brigid hissing her to silence.

Taking a deep, calming breath, Kane began walking again, feeling the flush of shame heating his face and neck. The warmth quickly faded, replaced by the chill of mounting tension. His point man's sense insistently rang as he approached the double row of upright boulders. The ophidian coilings chipped into the rock faces were more visible the closer he came, and he repressed a shudder of loathing.

He had always prided himself on being free of phobias, but with a touch of chagrin he realized he had developed a fear of reptiles over the past year. It wasn't an irrational fear, but derived from unpleasant experience. First there was his encounter with Lord Strongbow and his mutagenically altered Imperial Dragoons, with their scale-ringed, snakish eyes. That was bad enough, but his fear reached its culmination during his nightmarish battle with Kukulkan atop a ziggurat in South America.

When Kane reached the first pair of standing stones, he tensed his wrist and the Sin Eater sprang into his hand. He glanced behind him and saw not only Grant with his weapon filling his hand but Brigid and Domi fisting their blasters, as well.

Kane continued striding forward, doing his best not to break into a sprint. He sensed other presences, felt malignant eyes watching him from the shadows where his night sight could not reach. The feeling ate at his nerve ends like acid.

Passing between the boulders, he saw that three of them bore bullet pocks, all near the base. He knew they were recent, probably less than an hour old.

Buzzing rattles, like a combination of a snarling chain saw and a stick being dragged over a picket fence, penetrated even the polystyrene lining of his helmet. He rocked to a sudden halt, his throat tightening in almost painful spasm.

Out of small burrows in the bases of the megalithic stones reared the wedge-shaped heads of diamondback rattlers. Hissing sibilantly, they slid out and looped themselves into sinuous, twisting coils, their tongues flickering out to taste the human scent.

In a panic-stricken fraction of a second, Kane realized that although the snakes were large with heads the size of his fist, they weren't monstrous in size like the mutie they'd seen earlier. Unless, he thought sourly, these were fresh hatchlings and the enormous mother slithered somewhere nearby.

Despite the fact his Sin Eater snapped up automatically in reaction to the threat, Kane didn't press the trigger stud. In an urgent whisper, he said over his shoulder, "Don't shoot unless you have to. Keep moving."

Gritting his teeth so tightly his jaw muscles ached,

Kane concentrated on putting one foot in front of the other, his eyes darting back and forth beneath his visor. He tried to keep to the exact center of the aisle between the standing stones so as to maintain a distance of at least four feet between him and the snakes. He was aware however, the distance wasn't a safe one since all the snakes looked to be a minimum of six feet long, and he knew they could strike more than half of their length.

One of the snakes struck at his left leg, its jaws closing with a snap barely six inches from his knee. It required all of his willpower not to jump aside. Such an action would bring him within reach of the snake on his right.

Cold sweat beaded on his forehead beneath the lining of his helmet. It was a frightful trap and he wondered briefly both about the diabolical brain that had concocted it, and how he could put a 9 mm hollow-point round through it.

Obviously, someone had to tend the diamondbacks, bring them food, pamper them in order to keep them in the vicinity. If he hadn't already witnessed how the Amazonian Indians deified their mutated anaconda, he wouldn't have believed humans would serve a serpent.

Kane continued walking and the rattlesnakes continued to hiss, shake their tails and strike. Their venom-dripping fangs came within fractional margins, but they missed. At the edges of his hearing, he heard Grant mumbling under his breath behind him.

"Oh, I love this, I really get a fucking big kick out of this...."

Kane closed his mind to Grant's profane mantra, focusing only on reaching the end of the ghastly gauntlet. He wasn't particularly worried about himself or Grant, since the fangs of even the biggest diamondback wouldn't penetrate their armor, but Domi and Brigid weren't so protected. Although they wore high-topped jump boots of thick leather and trousers of tough whipcord, he wasn't sure if the material of either article was dense enough to deflect penetration of needle-tipped teeth.

If the women were as uncertain of it as he was, they gave no sign. They didn't utter a sound, not so much as an outcry of disgust, so he ceased to worry about them. Even if one of them were bitten, Brigid's medical kit contained ampoules of antivenin.

By the time Kane passed between the final pair of megaliths, his heart trip-hammered as if he had just sprinted two miles flat out. Sweat flowed down his body beneath his Kevlar undersheathing. He kept walking, not turning his head to check the progress of his companions until he was well past the last of the standing stones.

Within seconds Grant joined him, then Brigid, her jade eyes startlingly bright in a face drained of all color. She was almost as pale as Domi. All three people trembled slightly from the adrenaline coursing through their bloodstreams. They waited for Domi to complete the gauntlet, watching as she cautiously strode along the aisle, expression composed and detached.

Her composure broke when a snake on her right, its temper evidently more aroused than its brethren, squirmed away from the base of the megalith to block her path. It reared up, jaws agape, rattle buzzing.

Grant lunged forward, the bore of his Sin Eater centering on the serpent, but Kane restrained him with an arm. "Wait!"

Silver suddenly gleamed in Domi's fist. All of them recognized the serrated, nine-inch-long knife. It was her only memento of her six months as Guana Teague's sex slave. It was the same knife with which she had cut the man's triple-chinned throat.

Domi took a tentative step forward. The diamondback's flat-snouted, wedge-shaped head struck at her leg. Not crying out, Domi's convulsive movement to evade it brought her within reach of a serpent on the other side, and she shifted like lightning to avoid the flash of its fangs.

Then all the snakes swayed and struck at her feet, ankles, calves and knees, whatever portion of her limbs chanced to be nearest to them. Domi couldn't leap over them or pass between the stones to safety. She could only whirl and wheel and twist her body to avoid the strokes, and each time she moved to dodge one diamondback, she put herself in range of another.

She shifted position constantly, even though she could move only a short space in any direction, and

the venom-filled fangs menaced her with every motion. Only someone with the reflexes of the wilderness
born could have lived more than ten seconds in the
aisle.

Domi became a blur of bewildering motion. The
heads missed her by hairsbreadths, and she matched
her coordination and eye against the speed of the
coiled, darting demons. The long blade in her hand
flickered almost as swiftly as the forked tongues of
the rattlers. It sliced the air in flat, circular arcs, then
cleanly sheared through scales, muscles and bone. A
fanged head leaped from a mottled, scaled body amid
a spouting of blood, black in the dim light.

It seemed to Grant, Brigid and Kane the snakes
struck with a rhythm, as if they worked in tandem. If
so, Domi and her slashing knife attuned themselves
to the rhythm. Even in the uncertain light, they saw
the hard, stitched-on smile creasing Domi's lips as if
she enjoyed herself immensely.

As she skipped lightly among hissing, rattling serpents, her long knife flashed in quick strokes. With
each motion a headless, blood-spurting trunk thrashed
in postmortem spasms.

Amazingly, the diamondbacks began to retreat toward their nests at the bases of the megalithic stones.
They still struck at her, but now it was in self-defense,
and their button-tipped tails buzzed in fear, not with
menace.

Domi slid gracefully between two of the diamondbacks and at the precise instant they struck at her, she

performed a pivoting pirouette, and the pair of blunt heads collided with a sound like two blocks of wood knocking together. The snakes, driven to a hissing, rattling frenzy of terror, attacked each other, their bodies intertwining and knotting, fangs sinking repeatedly into scaled coils.

Domi's spin brought her to the end of the aisle, and she half fell into Grant's arms. Her fierce eyes glittered like polished rubies—or drops of fresh blood. She panted hard, but not from exertion. The expression on her scarlet-spattered face was beatific, satiated, as if she had just undergone a sexual experience.

"Are you all right?" Grant demanded, his anxiety turning his tone into a husky half snarl. "Did any of them bite you?"

Pushing herself away from his armored chest, Domi swayed dizzily for a few seconds. She turned her head and spit contemptuously toward the field of stones. "Not fast enough to bite me." She brandished her knife, the blade carmined and sticky. "Bit them instead. Taught them big-time lesson."

"Yeah," Kane said, not bothering to disguise his sarcasm. "Once word gets out, all the snakes in the world will think twice about provoking you again."

Domi stared levelly into his face. Confidently, she declared, "They will."

Kane opened his mouth to respond, decided not to waste his breath and contented himself with shaking his head in exasperated disbelief.

Dabbing at the sheen of tension-induced perspiration at her hairline, Brigid commented darkly, "Let's be on our way."

They did so, Domi affecting a jaunty, hip-swinging swagger. Whatever had wrought the change in the girl's personality over the past few weeks, it had turned her from a spirited but reliable ally into a wild card, and Kane wasn't comfortable with the transformation. Judging by the frown tugging at the corners of Brigid's lips, neither was she.

They strode into a narrow pass framed by perpendicular ramparts of stone. They weren't very high, less than twenty feet. The cleft ran fairly straight and at the far end, moonlight shimmered on the desert sand. The sky was clear and speckled with stars. Before they were halfway through, they came across the body of a man lying facedown in the pebble-strewed dirt.

When Kane rolled the body over, the cause of death was immediately evident. The man's face and limbs were swollen to half again their normal size and tinged a purplish-blue from the venom injected into him through the six puncture marks on his legs.

Kneeling beside the corpse, Kane eyed his coarse, homespun clothing. "An outlander, one of Pollard's prisoners. When they came through the snakes, he was one of the unlucky ones."

Grant nodded. "That's the reason for the shots we heard. The Mags panicked."

"Can't blame them much," Brigid said wryly.

Straightening, Kane looked around. "Whoever is

the warder of the snakes can't be too far away, since he or she or they have to feed and water them. They probably heard the shots.''

''Mebbe,'' Grant conceded. ''But if they saw the Mags, they probably dug a hole and pulled the dirt in after them.''

''I hope you're right,'' Kane replied. ''This is about the best place for an ambush I ever did see.''

From ahead and above them came the scuff and scutter of feet. Rocks suddenly fell into the pass, tumbling from both sides of the narrow pass. It wasn't an avalanche; it was a barrage.

Brigid uttered a wordless cry of surprise, and Grant half roared a curse. Kane dodged a square block of stone that thudded to the ground less than an inch from his right boot. Swinging his head up, he caught only a glimpse of wild, scabby creatures with hair hanging in knotted masses to their waists.

Then a rock twice the size of his head smashed into the crown of his helmet and sent him plunging into darkness.

Chapter 6

The evening prayer service of the Ophidian Way was interrupted halfway through. Father Jaramillo chanted, "And blessed are the rattle and the skin of the great worms."

Before the congregation could shout back the traditional response, "The Lord loves the worms of the earth, all that crawls and stings," the breeze carried the unmistakable crackle of blasterfire.

Father Jaramillo's flock of thirty twisted on the benches made of flat stones, mouths agape in fearful wonder. Blasterfire was rarely heard over the past couple of decades. Some of the younger members had never even seen a blaster, much less heard one fire, so there was much whispering among themselves in their own dialect.

Jaramillo cut off their apprehensive murmurings with savage gestures of his bare, scab-encrusted arms. "Unbelievers cross the Sepulcher of Sacred Snakes!" he shouted, champing teeth that had been worn almost to the gums from a lifetime of eating roots with a high silicon content. "Infidels!"

His congregation gaped at him incredulously. Nico, his nephew, gasped, "No way!"

"Way!" Jaramillo snapped. "Very much way! Infidels with blasters, draggin' their shit 'crost our holy ground! They violate a sacred place, erected by Brother Mote himself!"

His voice hit a high, trembling pitch of scandalized outrage, and his congregation picked up on it. Spittle flying from their lips, they howled in unison, "They violate a sacred place!"

The men of Jaramillo's clan were short and stocky, with spindly limbs. Thick hair grew low over their broad brows and hung in matted braids about their shoulders and backs. For the most part, they wore breechclouts and moccasins. The women were very slight of build, almost fragile, except their bare arms and legs rippled with wire-taut muscles. Their pinched faces held the furtive, cunning expressions of she-foxes.

Physically, Jaramillo was no different than the other men in the gathering. However, he wore the minister's mantle, a long apronlike garment decorated with swirling designs worked in red thread to represent the movements of sidewinders. Because he wore the mantle, Jaramillo knew the spirit of the scale and rattle would demand blood and souls in retribution, so he began a passionate, shrieking tirade, turning the evening service into a hate rally, pumping up his followers with the heat of religious zeal. Since all of his male forebears had ministered the tenets of the Ophidian Way, he knew exactly how to do it, what trigger words to use.

Jaramillo reminded the clan of its duty, telling his followers how it was laid out in the texts of Brother Mote, the basis of most of the congregation's lifestyle and belief system.

Generations ago, according to legend, the Ophidian Way had been founded when Snakefish was a thriving, populous ville. Every home in the township displayed the holy snake emblem. Brother Mote, the founder of the order, had reputedly carved the symbols in the rock, the same symbols, ever after called the Sepulcher of the Sacred Snakes. Like Mote, Jaramillo was its guardian, the caretaker of the serpents.

As a rite of passage, before they could father children, all male congregation members were required to walk the sepulcher. If they were bitten and recovered, then it was believed they had been cleansed of their sins. If they died, they were viewed as righteous sacrifices to the sacred snakes.

True, there weren't as many sacred snakes as there had been during Brother Mote's day, certainly very few of the gigantic ones, but there were still enough for the congregation to maintain its fundamentalist faith.

The diamondbacks living in the sepulcher ate better, frequently more often than Jaramillo's clan. Field mice, rats and vermin of all sorts were trapped and fed to the snakes, not just to keep them in the area but in the hopes they would grow as large as their huge antecedents. That hope was pretty much a vain one. Only in the past ten years had a rattler been hatched that actually attained a size comparable to the holy worms of yesteryear.

Jaramillo named it Gideon and conditioned his people to pay it homage, to love it unquestioningly, even when it killed three of them in a four-year period. It was a damnable choice for Jaramillo to make, since for the holy serpents to be served properly, they required people to attend to their needs.

Sometimes if the hunting was poor, Gideon would slither into their village. The clansmen and the women dropped to their knees and passively awaited their fate as the great snake selected a meal, as if his family of worshippers were nothing but a pack of rats. But by strict interpretation of the Ophidian Way canon, Gideon's venom slew only the ungodly, even though one of his victims had been a two-year-old child.

Jaramillo convinced himself and his followers the sacrifices were part of a very old tradition. He knew the history of the Ophidian Way, as set down in Brother Mote's texts, did not derive so much from the Christian fundamentalist snake-handling sects of rural predark America as from ancient times—from the days of Montezuma the sorcerer king and his sacred serpent, a *biboron*, a monster rattlesnake.

The great divine serpent was worshipped in the black shadows of Aztec pyramids long before America was discovered. The priests raised huge snakes, believing them all to be messengers of the gods. According to the folklore of his people, the Indians of the Taos Pueblo in New Mexico sheltered one of Montezuma's divine serpents. The tale also maintained that on special feast days infants were fed to the gigantic rattlesnake. Whether or not such a story was true, Brother Mote had promoted the same belief in sacred snakes when he created the Ophidian Way more than a century before. It was only a continuation of native American religion, and he borrowed heavily from the mythography.

However, not only had the Ophidian Way lost many of its holy serpents since Mote's time, but the faith had lost almost all of its popularity, as well. Acolytes of the Ophidian Way were considered criminals, so the congregation didn't dare venture too near Port Morninglight and certainly not even within sight of the ville of Snakefish itself.

Jaramillo was deeply offended that the ville bore the name of the birthplace of his religion, but its baron saw no hypocrisy in dispatching black-armored heretics to hunt down adherents to the very order that the original ville had venerated. Some of the younger people occasionally wondered what it was like in the big-walled ville, but Jaramillo insisted the world beyond their canyons and desert was filled with soul-shredding dangers. Their land was the only true land, and now blasphemers invaded it. Even the nearby ruins of the old predark town were forbidden to the clan. Seeing the houses, as overgrown and dilapidated as they were, could give them ideas of another way of life.

Jaramillo continued to exhort his congregation, but he knew that mere words, no matter how passionately they were spoken, weren't sufficient to motivate the people to attack armed men—especially if they were the armored 'forcers in service to Baron Snakefish.

Although it was not a holy day, Jaramillo took the medicine brazier from beneath the makeshift altar and prepared it for the ceremony of commitment. The brazier was a the huge, bleached-out skull of Azarel, one of the sacred snakes deified by Brother Mote during his ministry and elevated to the status of a holy relic.

Despite its age, the skull still retained the pair of long hollow fangs curving down from the upper jaw. From a wooden box beneath the altar, Jaramillo took fistfuls of a dried, brownish green herb and crammed them into the empty sockets that once held Azarel's venom sacs. He touched a torch to the herbs until they began to smolder, then he blew gently to fan the sparks. A pungent, sickeningly sweet odor arose.

Grayish white smoke boiled from the tips of the hollow fangs. As the vapors thickened, the women shook diamondback rattles and chanted, "Blessed be the fang and the hollow needle. Blessed is the crushing and the coil."

Jamarillo called the men of the congregation forward and directed them to place their lips on the fangs and inhale the smoke. In pairs they did so, bending and sucking deeply, more than one succumbing to a severe coughing fit. The vapors produced by the burning herbs were astringent and powerful.

The herbal concoction had many names, but it was best known as *Cannabis lupus,* the werewolf weed. It was a rare narcotic, hard to find even in the hindmost regions of the Outlands. Composed of a mutated form of marijuana and mixed with peyote and telache, the weed stimulated the hindbrain, sometimes known as the reptile brain. It triggered an atavistic regression, allowing those who inhaled the fumes to wallow in ruthless bestiality. Its influence made men fearless and bloodthirsty, but while in its brutal grip, they could just as easily turn on their comrades as on an enemy.

When it was his turn, Jamarillo deeply inhaled the hot, acrid smoke and felt the first deadly thrill of its effects touch him. He felt the hunger in him, the blood lust, the stirring of the beast that lay so close beneath his skin.

The torchlight danced on the upturned faces of his followers, their eyes glowing with the beautiful madness. They laughed slobberingly, sounding more like yipping coyotes than riotous humans.

At Jamarillo's command, they shambled to their wickiups and returned with their weapons, a collection of stone-headed axes, clubs, chert knives and spears fashioned from lightweight wood. The women would not accompany them, since the order could not afford to lose any of them. They were needed for breeding. Besides, in a struggle against infidels, they had no sense of proportion or restraint, even though a number of them could throw rocks with deadly accuracy.

Mind clouded, madness singing in his blood, Jaramillo screeched, "If they have defiled the sepulcher, you know what we must do!"

His clan howled back, shaking their weapons toward the sky. "Righteous sacrifice!"

Chapter 7

Kane didn't completely lose consciousness, nor did he fall, but only because of the stone-knobbed wall at his back. Still, he wondered absently for a few seconds why the constellations wheeled so wildly in the heavens.

It required another few seconds for the whirling, vertiginous feeling to settle down into an insistent throbbing, reminding him of a hangover he had suffered a year or so ago, just prior to his escape from Cobaltville.

Blinking hard to dispel the amoeba-shaped floaters swimming across his vision, Kane's night sight showed him monochromatic shaggy figures bounding from the top of one wall to the other, snarling with discolored, gapped teeth. They heaved rocks over their heads and hurled them down with fierce cries. They were all fairly small in stature, with slitted coal-chip eyes and leathery sun-browned skin that gave them the look of Amerindians.

He heard Grant roar angrily, "No blasters! No blasters!"

Struggling back erect, putting his feet beneath him, Kane began a shambling run toward the far end of the pass. The rocky ramparts were like the jaws of a trap, inexorably closing on the four people. He warded off stones falling from above, but a couple of heavy rocks struck him on his polycarbonate-encased shoulders and made him stagger drunkenly.

He heard Domi yip in pain and anger, followed by a breathless cry from Brigid. He worried about her taking a blow to the skull, and he momentarily considered dropping back to protect her with his armored body. But to do so would jam up Grant and Domi.

Kane reached the mouth of the cleft and sprinted into open, sand-covered terrain. His surge of relief was instantly replaced by a jolt of fear. Digging in his heels, he rocked to such a sudden stop that Grant nearly slammed into him.

Spread out in a semicircle, a horde of small, shaggy figures shrieked hysterically, throwing fist-sized rocks at the four outlanders. Kane caught only a few of the words, garbled as they were, but the crazed accusations had something to do with slaying the sacred snakes and dragging shit over holy ground.

More of the figures moved in, emerging from the shadows wielding stone-and-wood clubs. Their motions were animalistic, partially bent over, eyes jerking back and forth furtively. Though small in stature, their limbs rippled with twisted, knotted sinew and stringy muscle tissue.

One of them thrust at Kane with a crude spear, the sharpened flint shard fitted into a notch at the end of the wooden shaft jabbing toward his face. Slapping it aside with his Copperhead, Kane delivered a snap kick to the man's groin, driving his testicles almost up to his navel.

Another savage who came too close suffered a milder fate with the heel of Brigid's jump boot to the jaw, which splintered a few of his already rotted teeth.

As the two shaggy men staggered away, one bent double and the other spitting blood and bone, stones began whizzing again. Grant and Kane put Domi and Brigid between them, forming a protective bulwark. Rocks bounced from their black exoskeletons without doing serious harm. Kane could not help but allot the half-naked wild men a certain amount of credit for their cunning—by dumping stones on them in the narrow pass, he and his companions were forced out into the open, literally into the arms of the larger body.

The barrage of stones ceased, and the small people glided around them, hefting spears and bludgeons in rope-muscled arms. A quick head count showed Kane at least twenty of them, perhaps more skulking out in the shadows. Even though the primitive weapons couldn't penetrate his and Grant's armor, they would be overwhelmed by sheer force of numbers, and the stone knives would seek weak points in their polycarbonate sheathings.

A man wearing a short, ragged mantle over his gaunt frame shrieked a torrent of gibberish at the four outlanders, his eyes blazing from beneath a wild tangle of hair. He bounded, leaped and gesticulated as if he were suffering a spastic fit. The wild-eyed and -haired savages slowly advanced, blood-chilling hissing noises issuing from their lips. Although they sounded more like imitations of faulty steam valves, Kane guessed they were sibilant vocalizations intended to emulate the hissing of serpents.

"Blades," Grant snapped, drawing his combat knife from his boot sheath.

Kane did likewise. Domi hadn't resheathed hers, and Brigid unsheathed her own knife, a Fairbairn-Sykes commando dagger. As the hissing hit a high, whistling note like a score of teakettles on full boil, a knot of savages suddenly made a concerted rush, trying to bowl them over through numbers and momentum.

Grant lashed out with the barrel of his Sin Eater, the heavy frame crashing against a skull and shattering it. The savage yelped, hands clasped to the bleeding split in his scalp and bone. Screaming, he fell to the ground in the path of two of his comrades. All three toppled in a tangle of thrashing limbs.

Domi wielded her knife like a butcher's cleaver, chopping a thrusting spear haft in two, then driving the pommel into the wielder's face, breaking his nose. Her lips creased in a smile, and her eyes blazing, she moved like a wraith, constantly shifting position and stabbing and slashing as she did so. Two men went down, a belly and a throat spurting blood, with Domi's mocking laughter in their ears.

A crude stone ax swung out of the mass of men toward Brigid's lower belly. She dodged it and kicked the savage's kneecap loose with the metal-reinforced toe of her boot. He hopped away, plucking at his maimed leg and howling in agony.

Kane swung his razor-edge blade in a flat, fast arc. He felt the point drag through flesh, and a savage reeled away, his hands at his deeply gashed throat, blood bubbles bursting on his lips and squirting from between his fingers. Crimson droplets splashed over Kane's visor.

The savages engaged in a reluctant, stubborn retreat, snarling and hissing in rage. The wounded backed away, whining. Five near-naked bodies lay on the sand in widening pools of blood. The survivors didn't retreat far, just out of reach of the deadly knives in the fists of the four people. They glared through matted screens of hair, and the hissing sounds began anew.

"We've got no choice now," Grant side-mouthed in a panting whisper. "We were lucky that time, but now they know what to expect. We'll have to use our blasters, or they'll chill us all."

"I know," Kane agreed gloomily, gulping air. "Let's open up on full auto, cut a path, then run like hell. Brigid, Domi, you cover our backs."

Domi nodded, finger curling around the trigger of her Combat Master. The fire of combat still burned brightly in her eyes.

"So much for catching Pollard by surprise," Brigid said, breathing hard.

"If nothing else," Kane replied, "maybe we can

make it back to the redoubt before Pollard, and lay a trap for him there. But we have to stay alive long enough to do that."

Grant nodded curtly. "Just give the word."

Kane's gloved finger hovered over the trigger stud of his Sin Eater. The savages began another slow advance, moving in a measured tread, spreading out around them in a wide circle. Their swart, dark faces were masks of implacable ferocity, their eyes glittering with homicidal rage.

Kane did not enjoy killing outlanders—he had done too much of it as a Magistrate—but now that blood was spilled, there was no hope of talking their way out of the situation. For whatever reason, these people had devoted their lives to this hard land. All they knew was that it belonged to them, and they'd keep it at the price of their own blood.

Shooting to wound was not an option. The Sin Eater's rounds impacted against flesh at 335 pounds of pressure per square inch. Even a bullet striking a limb resulted in heart-stopping hydrostatic shock, so in order to escape the savages they would probably have to slaughter the majority of them.

Brigid murmured musingly, "Most of those people look like they're related to an Indian tribe…interbred with indigenous Hispanics."

"I don't give a shit if they've interbred with Mormons," Grant rasped. "Look at their eyes. They're fused out, flying high on something."

"On three," Kane announced impatiently.

Grant nodded shortly, raising his blaster. "Set."

Kane eyed the distance between his Sin Eater and the nearest group of savages, took a deep breath and said, "One—"

Even over the hissing emanating from more than a dozen mouths, a vibrating thrum was clearly audible. Kane caught only a brief, almost subliminal streak of movement flashing overhead. With a resonant, meaty thud, an arrow nearly four feet in length drove into the chest of a spear-wielding savage. It almost went completely through his torso.

The impact smashed him backward, bowling three of his people off their feet. Another shaft was speeding through the air before the first target's body had settled to the ground.

It struck a man in the clavicle with a grisly cracking of bone, penetrating into the lungs. He screamed like a wounded animal and went over on his back, blood fountaining from his open mouth.

The savages uttered cries of confusion, which swiftly turned to fear when a third arrow struck a man in the upper thigh. The barbed point protruded from the other side of his leg, a squirt of bright, arterial-red blood accompanying it. The little man writhed, clutching convulsively at the shaft. Kane knew if he removed the arrow, the femoral artery would open up like a faucet and he would bleed to death in a matter of minutes.

The shaggy-haired horde began a disorganized, clumsy retreat, hooting in terror at the murderous projectiles that had felled three of their own in almost as many seconds. Kane did not dare turn his head to locate the source of the deadly arrows, but he could tell by the quality of workmanship, from the steel tips to the fletching, they weren't of Native American origin. The wood of the shafts caught highlights from the moon and stars, giving them the impression of being lacquered.

The man wearing the ragged mantle screeched at his people, shaking his fists, obviously exhorting them to do their duty. The savages hesitated in their retreat, heeding his words if not anxious to immediately obey them.

Another arrow flashed overhead, then punched through the right eye socket of the man in the mantle. The back of his head broke open, the point driving a wad of brain matter ahead of it. The greasy mass spilled onto the sand, followed an instant later by his spasming body.

A wail of horror exploded from the throats of the small, dark men. Almost as if they had rehearsed the action, the entire horde turned and raced away across the hard-packed sand. Kane figured the skull-impaled man had been a chief or someone of importance, and his sudden death broke the nerve of his followers.

Swiftly, he and his companions turned, their eyes seeking and then fastening on the ornately armored figure poised atop the rocky ramparts. It stood in a bizarre, almost hallucinatory contrast to the barren surroundings.

Each segment of the armor was made from wafers of metal held together by small, delicate chains and overlaid with a dark brown lacquer. The overlapping plates were trimmed in scarlet and gold. Between flaring shoulder epaulets, a war helmet fanned out with twin sweeps of curving metal like dark wings seen edge-on in flight. The helmet bore a sickle moon on top, positioned between a slender pair of foot-long antlers of softly gleaming alloy.

The face guard, wrought of a semitransparent material, presented an inhuman visage of a snarling animal, either a lion or a tiger. Obsidian eyes glittered through the slitted eyeholes.

A quiver of the long arrows dangled from the figure's shoulder. Two slightly curved long swords in black scabbards swung back from each hip, thrust through a broad blue sash.

Even as the four people gazed in astonishment, the masked figure raised a very long laminated bow, holding the string by an ivory thumbgrip. Surprisingly delicate hands and slim arms extended the bow forward, bringing it down from above the sickle moon mounted on the foreport of the helmet and to eye level in one smooth motion. The arrow was released, leaving the string of the bow humming musically.

All of them heard the smack of impact and a gargling cry, but they did not take their eyes off the figure above them. Grant was the first to speak, in a hushed, hoarse whisper. "What the fuck is that?"

Brigid supplied the answer in an equally muted tone. "Samurai."

Chapter 8

"Don't know what samurai is," Domi bit out, centering the sights of her Combat Master on the figure, "but I don't like the sound of it."

Instantly, with almost supernatural swiftness, an arrow was plucked from the quiver, knocked into the bowstring and drawn. The barbed steel point was pointing directly at the outlander girl. No one spoke. The four outlanders and the samurai stared at one another in a frozen tableau.

Brigid's lips moved slightly, and her brow creased in concentration as she dredged deep into her eidetic memory. Then she took a tentative half step forward, making a very deliberate show of snugging her Iver Johnson pistol back into its waistband slide holster. In a very courteous tone she called up, *"Anato yuku ne mutta ka?"*

Whatever reaction Brigid's question was intended to elicit, the last thing any of them expected to hear was a laugh. Although it was muffled because of the visor, it was still an unmistakable laugh of genuine amusement.

A hollow voice floated down to them, a voice neither high nor low. It stayed in the middle range but was pleasingly melodic. "No, as a point of fact, I didn't sleep well at all, but thank you for asking."

The language was flawless, unaccented English. A jittery, abashed smile played over Brigid's lips. She nodded contritely and said, "I apologize. I've never had the opportunity to speak your tongue. I thought I was asking if you would put down your weapon."

The antlers mounted on the helmet inclined toward her a fraction of an inch. "Your pronunciation was very good, nevertheless. As for your question, *hai*. Yes. I will if the rest of you will."

Dropping her voice to a whisper, Brigid addressed her three companions. "Let's do it. We owe him our lives."

Kane hesitated, glanced toward Grant, who after a frowning second of thought, nodded in agreement. Both men carefully pushed their Sin Eaters back into their forearm holsters, the spring lock catching with a meaningful click. They resheathed their combat knives, as well. Only Domi kept her blaster trained on the armored, horned figure above them.

"Leather it, Domi," Grant told her gruffly.

The girl shook her head. "Don't trust anybody whose face I can't see."

"We don't expect you to trust him," Brigid whispered urgently. "But you can show some basic respect. He saved us, after all."

The girl's lips curled in a sneer. "Didn't need saving."

"Leather it," Grant repeated, a hard, uncompromising edge to his voice.

With a wordless utterance of disgust, Domi shoved the Combat Master into her shoulder rig, but she kept her knife unsheathed, dangling at the end of her right arm.

The samurai swiftly and expertly relaxed the tension on the bowstring, replaced the long arrow in the quiver and with a surprising grace descended the rocky slope in a series of running leaps.

"What language was that you used, Baptiste?" Kane asked in a low tone.

"Japanese. I'm not very conversant with it. I've only read it in the database, not spoken it."

Kane was surprised she knew even imperfect Japanese, although he shouldn't have been. Brigid spoke Russian, a smattering of Chinese, German and even Lakota, the tongue of the Sioux Indians.

"What's a samurai anyway?" Domi demanded in a fierce whisper.

Tersely, Brigid answered, "They were the knights of medieval Japan. They began as the military elite, then became the political elite. The samurai were warriors of legendary skill."

Domi eyed the ornamented armor of the samurai and muttered disdainfully, "He looks more like a legendary gaudy lad."

If the samurai overheard the remark, he apparently didn't understand the Outlands euphemism for male prostitute—or if he did, he chose to ignore it. The helmeted figure approached them, his right hand resting on the cylindrical hilt of a sword. Not only were his hands slender, smooth and sinewy, but they also seemed very small. In fact, the closer the armored figure drew to them, the smaller he seemed. Even with the antlers topping the helmet, Kane doubted he was much taller than Domi.

Brigid bowed and said, "*Ah domo arigato*. We thank you for what you did for us."

"I merely extended you a warrior's courtesy," responded the hollow voice. "I could see you didn't wish to do battle with the primitives and were reluctant to employ your firearms."

"You've been following us," Domi challenged.

The helmet wagged from side to side. "No. I was following a much larger group, one that murdered the people of Port Morninglight and took others prisoner. At first I thought you were part of them, stragglers mayhaps. Then I realized you were also tracking them, and wishing to be quiet about it."

"What's Port Morninglight to you?" Grant demanded.

The armored figure did not reply for a long moment. It seemed the gaze behind the molded, snarling visor studied Grant's face intently. "Perhaps," the soft voice said, "we should take off our helmets and face each other like honest warriors. I do not confide in anyone until I have looked into their eyes."

Grant's lips twitched in a fleeting scowl, which meant he appreciated the samurai's sentiments. He unsnapped the underjaw locking guard of his helmet. After a brief contemplative moment, Kane did likewise, sliding his helmet up and over his head. The samurai followed suit, thumbing open two toggles on the bottom rim of the helmet and tugging it off.

Then Kane saw why the samurai's figure was so slight, the hands so small. Glossy black hair tumbled down over the flaring shoulder epaulets. A small, beautifully shaped mouth stretched in a wan smile, above which was a smoothly curving bone structure under sculptured flesh. The woman's complexion was a very pale gold with roses and milk for an accent. The almond-shaped eyes shone as fierce and proud as those of a young eagle.

Grant felt a sudden, disconcerting clenching in his chest. He didn't know why except he was looking at one of the most beautiful and exotic women he had ever seen in his life.

Her dark eyes swept over them in an appraising stare, and her lips curved in a smile. "You can meet the most interesting people in the desert."

"May I ask the name of our rescuer?" Brigid inquired.

The woman inclined her head on a neck that to Grant seemed to be as long and as graceful as a swan's. "I am Shizuka, first lieutenant to Captain Kiyomasa. We are Tigers of Heaven, in service to our high daimyo, Lord Takaun."

Scraps of memory, more like impressions, ghosted through the minds of Brigid, Grant and Kane. The

Tigers of Heaven touched faint chords of recognition, of an armored security force of samurai who traveled the spaceways—

The recollection slipped through the fingers of their minds like smoke. All of them knew the impressions weren't memories of events that had actually happened, at least not in their reality. They were the traces of their experiences on parallel worlds, when their minds possessed the bodies of their alternate universe selves, their doppelgängers.

The three of them had no clear recollections of those mirror realities any longer. Even Brigid with her eidetic memory could only consciously recall disconnected fragments.

Shizuka's dark eyes flitted from Grant to Kane to Brigid. "Is there something wrong?"

Before any of them could reply, Domi said loudly, aggressively, "You bet your ass something's wrong! Who sent you to follow us?"

Very humbly, the woman answered, "My captain. When stealth and tracking skills are required, I am always chosen."

Domi brayed a derisive laugh. "You need to practice your skills. I heard you from a mile away."

Kane tried to shush Domi into silence, but she ignored him. Rudely she snapped, "Where did you come from? Are you working for a baron?"

Shizuka regarded her calmly. Although her eyes went cold, her voice was silky soft. "I regret your confusion, but I have questions of my own. It is one reason I went to the effort of saving you from the *eta,* the handlers of offal.''

Red rage flared in Domi's eyes. ''We coulda taken 'em! Needed no help from you!''

''Domi—'' Brigid began admonishingly.

''*Hai, so desu.* Yes, I understand.'' Shizuka bowed slightly, only a half bow, and she did it in such a way that even Domi knew it was a deliberate insult. ''I should not have interfered. You alone could have saved your companions with the ferocity of your words.''

Domi's lips writhed over her teeth in a silent snarl and she lunged forward, her knife whipping up. Steel met steel with a ringing clangor. Shizuka's sword had slid from its scabbard with lightning speed. The flat blade blocked Domi's knife, then returned to the scabbard. Shizuka had not moved from her bowing posture. Although her face remained expressionless, she winked conspiratorially at Domi.

Kane stared, replaying the blurred movements in his mind. Domi gaped, as well, then with a strangulated screech of humiliated fury starting up her throat, she thrust for Shizuka's lower belly.

The sword rasped from the scabbard again, Shizuka stepped sideways in a sliding dance motion and Domi's knife missed its target. Instantly, she heeled around, leading with the blade. Holding her sword in a two-handed grip, Shizuka parried the knife slash almost negligently.

Kane and Grant started to rush forward to intervene, but Domi's maddened voice rose in a shout. "Stay out of this! I won't chill her, but I'll put my mark on her!"

Shizuka said calmly, serenely, "I promise not to harm the child. She is brave, but she needs a lesson in manners."

"Look who's talking, bitch!" Domi growled angrily. She sprang to the attack, her knife weaving a web of steel in the air between her and the Japanese woman. Shizuka caught all her blows on her sword, and ringing chimes rose toward the sky.

Domi held her blade point upward as did all experienced knife fighters, but she might as well not have had it at all for the good it did penetrating Shizuka's guard. She tried a reverse slash, the flat of the blade lying along her forearm, but the samurai beat it effortlessly aside.

Brigid, Kane and Grant knew Shizuka was treating Domi to an object lesson in the art of the sword. Kane had to admit it was beautiful. Never had he seen such a style, certainly not in the kind of swordplay Quayle had demonstrated against him a month or so ago. Shizuka could have carved up the one-eyed cutlass master like a turkey.

It quickly became evident that Domi's words to the contrary, she intended to kill her opponent. Sucking in a lungful of air with a growl of frustration, she rushed at Shizuka, striking wildly. She came on in a relentless surge, ever the aggressor in any combat.

The clang and clash of steel was an almost continuous cacophony.

Domi stabbed and thrust for the woman's armpit and her upper thighs, seeking to sever the major arteries there. The samurai did not back away and she stood untouched, parrying and blocking without much strain or even thought.

Eyes glittering like blood-drenched rubies, Domi uttered a shrill cry and plunged forward, knife darting low for a hamstringing cut. Shizuka's sword deflected Domi's blade, held it and wrenched it away in a blindingly fast corkscrew motion. Domi's cry died on her lips as her knife flew from her hand and landed yards away in the sand.

For an instant, she stared at Shizuka, then cut her eyes to her knife. Her expression twisted in disbelief, in furious astonishment. With a spitting snarl of rage, she clawed for the butt of her holstered blaster. Shizuka backstepped swiftly, raising her blade in a double-fisted grip.

A single long-legged bound put Grant between the samurai and the albino. His big gloved hand closed completely around Domi's right wrist. She strained against him, sweat glistening on her forehead, veins swelling in her temples. Her breath hissed sharply between clenched teeth.

"Stand down," he rumbled threateningly. "Stand down, or I swear to God I'll take your blaster away and hog-tie you with the holster."

Her crimson eyes burned into his with a defiant

glare. He met it unflinchingly, unblinkingly. Then, by degrees, the fierce heat of fury guttered out, and some of the tension went out of her posture. She released the butt of her pistol. Dropping her gaze to the ground, she muttered, "Let me go."

Grant released her, towering over her for a moment to make sure she wouldn't try to unleather her blaster again. All she did was grimace and massage her wrist.

He turned to Shizuka, making a resigned gesture. "I'm sorry. It's been a long day."

The woman nodded graciously, reversed her grip on her sword and slid it back into the scabbard with two swift, economical moves. "And full of hardship. She is young and undisciplined, but I admire her courage."

Domi did not react to the compliment.

Kane cleared his throat. "And I admire your restraint. But the fact is, she did make a couple of interesting points, regardless of her poor manners. Where did you come from? Surely not Japan."

Stolidly, Shizuka said, "It is unlikely you have heard of my home. And if you have, then my daimyo's advisers should be severely punished."

She swept a strand of raven hair back from her high forehead. "Permit me to communicate with my captain. If he wishes for you to know more, then I must receive the permission from him."

Reaching into her sash, she produced a black square of pressed plastic, not much larger than the palm of her hand. It was a smaller version of the trans-comms used by the Cerberus personnel.

Grant eyed it with interest. "What's the range on that thing?"

She used a thumb to flip open the cover. "Depending on the weather and the terrain, about three miles."

"That's quite the distance for a comm that small," Kane said dubiously.

With a touch of wry amusement in her voice, Shizuka replied, "Among the many traditions of my people is a devotion to miniaturization."

She walked away a few paces, lifted the comm to her ear and spoke softly into it. While she was so occupied, Grant plucked Domi's knife from the desert floor and presented it to her, pommel first. Without a word, the girl took it and thrust it firmly into the leather sheath at the small of her back.

"You were way out of line," he told her quietly. "She's an expert with her sword. You're damn lucky all she did was disarm you, not decapitate you."

Domi acted as if she hadn't heard. Wheeling, she stalked away to lean against an outcrop of flint, arms folded over her chest. Grant gusted out a weary sigh and turned his back to her.

Kane moved beside him, saying lowly, "I don't know what's going on with her, but she's making trouble we don't need. Straighten her out."

Grant's brows knit together, casting his eyes into shadow. "How do you expect me to do that?"

"Somebody better," Brigid put in. "Obviously, Shizuka isn't the only samurai in the vicinity. Until we know how many Tigers of Heaven are around and why, we have to be at our diplomatic best. And that includes Domi."

Grant's face locked in an impassive mask, as if it were carved from teak. "Then you tell her about diplomacy. I'm not her damn daddy or her husband. You two were the ones who insisted she come on this op, not me."

Kane and Brigid arched their eyebrows at him at the same time. Before either one could speak, Shizuka strode back, returning the comm to her sash. "Captain Kiyomasa will arrive shortly with the rest of the force. He wishes to meet you before any information about us is given out."

"Understandable," Brigid replied. "But it appears we have the same goal—catching up to those who attacked Port Morninglight. Our reasons may differ, though."

"Do you know who the attackers are?" the woman asked.

Brigid opened her mouth to answer, but Kane interjected dryly, "We wish to meet with Captain Kiyomasa before any more information about us is given out."

Shizuka's eyes flashed first in irritation, then in appreciation. "You have a sharp wit and I like that. Since I've provided you with my name—and a lesson in swordsmanship—the least you can do is tell me who you are.''

Introductions were made all around, and Shizuka bowed to each one of them in turn, including Domi, who made a studied show of ignoring her.

Tapping her chin musingly, Brigid said, ''Your name is an honorable one with historical significance. As I recall, Shizuka Gozen was a heroine of feudal Japan.''

Shizuka's eyes widened in surprise, and she flashed Brigid a gratified smile. ''I had not expected to meet any Westerner so educated about my people, especially out here. *Hai,* I was named in honor of Shizuka Gozen, a member of a great samurai family during the reign of Yoritomo, the first shogun. During the eleventh century, she was in love with Yoritomo's brother and rival for the throne, Yoshitsure. He became a fugitive, and Shizuka was forced into Yoritomo's harem.

''One evening, when she was ordered to entertain him, she defiantly sang a song in praise of his brother. The shogun was so enraged that when Shizuka gave birth to a male child, he had the baby murdered before her eyes.''

Brigid winced. ''And she became something of a martyr to women's rights in male-dominated Japan.''

Shizuka nodded proudly. ''Indeed. That I carry her name is a matter of pride.''

She turned toward Grant, examining the red Magistrate's badge affixed to the molded left pectoral of his breastplate. "Speaking of pride, what significance does that peculiar emblem hold?"

Grant's answer was stiffly formal. "None now. It used to have a bit."

Kane repressed a smile. Between the two of them, Grant still had the most difficulty accepting his criminal status.

"Was it the symbol of some lord you served?"

"In a way," Kane replied cautiously, hiding his astonishment that Shizuka apparently knew nothing of the Magistrate Divisions or the baronial oligarchy. She obviously did not come from America, but he seriously doubted she hailed directly from Japan.

"Why do you continue to wear it?" the woman pressed. She kept her eyes on Grant's face even though Kane had spoken last. "Is it to spite your former master?"

"It's more in the way of protective coloration," Grant answered.

Gravely, Shizuka said, "So you are like *ronin*, masterless samurai. Wanderers. Mercenaries."

Grant thrust out his lantern jaw pugnaciously. "We're not mercies. We have no master or lord to serve, but that doesn't make us hired killers."

Shizuka quickly ducked her head in embarrassment. "I have offended you. Please forgive me. It is apparent you follow the code of Bushido. I am not the only one here with poor manners."

Suddenly, there was a faint scuff of feet on sand, a clink of stone against stone. All of them turned toward the pass, and an apparition stepped from its mouth. His elaborate armor featured overlapping plates of silver and black, and his breastplate was engraved with the sign of the mantis. Over this was a long surcoat of blue silk accented by white-and-red embroidery. His broad helmet bore long outcurving horns, and combined with the lowered face guard, which held the aspect of a demon. A flat, mirror-bright blade glinted in his right hand. The four samurai who followed him out of the cleft did not bear naked swords, but all of them cradled longblasters in their arms.

Grant murmured uncertainly, "Arisaka Type 38 carbines. World War II vintage. I wonder where they found them?"

Kane wasn't surprised by Grant's immediate identification of the rifles. Not only was the man a superb marksman, but he was also something of a weapons historian. However, Kane was more concerned with the way the short barrels of the rifle swung toward him and his companions.

The Tigers of Heaven not only looked as if they knew how to use the three-century-old blasters, but also like they wanted to use them—very badly.

Chapter 9

With a click of releasing solenoids and the faint whir of tiny electric motors, the Sin Eaters sprang into Grant's and Kane's hands. Although they didn't aim their blasters, the Tigers of Heaven swiftly spread out so as not to present easy targets.

Shizuka strode to the man with the demonic face guard and spoke quietly to him, a deferential note in her tone. The man listened for a moment, then motioned peremptorily to the samurai behind him. Without hesitation, they lowered the Arisaka carbines.

Backstepping carefully, Shizuka reached a point equidistant between the Tigers and the four outlanders. She bowed toward the demon-faced samurai. "May I introduce Captain Kiyomasa."

The man scabbarded his sword with the same sharp, quick movement they had seen Shizuka display. He lifted his visor on tiny hinges and stared at them impassively. His features were full fleshed, with a sharp hooked nose set below heavy eyebrows. His eyes were very thin slits with no emotion in them. Only a penetrating intelligence gave them any spark. A thin mustache drooped at the corners of his unsmiling slash of a mouth. There were faint scars on his face, and Kane was sure there were more under his armor.

As Shizuka introduced the four of them, Kiyomasa surveyed them one by one, as if silently gauging their capacity and skills for violence. Kane did his best to meet that judgmental stare without blinking. The armored man did not speak, yet he felt the impact of his presence.

Finally, when Kane's eyes were on the verge of watering, Kiyomasa stopped the visual examination and uttered a grunt, as if satisfied. He bowed his head toward them, the Tigers behind him almost immediately assumed parade-rest positions, resting the stocks of their rifles on the ground, holding them by the barrels.

Brigid returned the man's bow, and after a moment's hesitation, Grant and Kane followed suit, holstering their blasters. Domi only stared with thinly veiled suspicion.

In a flat, uninflected tone Kiyomasa declared, "My lieutenant has informed me we apparently share the same goal, to avenge the slaughter of Port Morninglight. That is good. There is nothing like spilling the blood of a mutual enemy to make new friends."

Judging by the man's voice, he had few feelings but a lot of authority. Choosing her words with care, her tone courteous without being unctuous, Brigid said, "We are not so much interested in avenging the murders as discovering the reason behind them and why prisoners were taken."

Kiyomasa grunted again, as if to indicate puzzlement. "Such actions are not common here?"

"Not exactly," Kane put in. "There are gangs of marauders and bands of savages, but it's unusual for the type of men whom we follow to do something like this."

The samurai nodded curtly. "Ah. Then you know who they are."

"Yes." Kane said nothing more, meeting Kiyomasa's expectant stare expressionlessly.

Shizuka spoke quietly. "Perhaps we should agree to an exchange of information. A question for a question, an answer for an answer."

Kiyomasa reexamined the four people standing before him. He spoke briefly to Shizuka in a whisper, then said, "Inasmuch as my lieutenant saved you from the savages, you may discharge the debt by telling me the identities of the raiders."

Kane glanced questioningly at Brigid, then toward Grant. He was reticent by nature and had become more so since his exile. A casual word spoken to the wrong person in the wrong place could spell death for everyone in Cerberus and perhaps even the destruction of the installation itself.

Brigid surprised him slightly by saying, "There doesn't seem to be any reason to hold out on them. We're just as curious about them as they are about us. It's the diplomatic thing to do."

Kiyomasa suddenly dropped to his knees and swiftly arranged his legs in a lotus position. Shizuka did so, as well. The samurai motioned with his hand. "Speak, Kane-san."

Brigid, Kane and Grant lowered themselves to the ground. The two men failed miserably when they tried to smoothly cross legs as Kiyomasa and Shizuka had done. After a moment of grunting effort, they managed. Domi did not sit down. She remained leaning against the rock formation.

Kane began speaking quickly, doing far more than simply identifying the raiders of Port Morninglight as Magistrates. Such a simple answer would not satisfy Kiyomasa and would only lead to a protracted question-and-answer session. The man obviously was not a fool, and Kane could not treat him like one.

To save time he decided to provide an overview of the baronies. He described how the Magistrates were the organizational descendants of a proposed global police force of the late twentieth century, one that had judicial, as well as law-enforcement powers. He supplied only a few specifics, soft-pedaling the patrilineal traditions of the Mags.

There seemed little reason to conceal his and Grant's own long associations with the Magistrates. He stressed the kind of firepower used by the armored enforcers, so Kiyomasa would not become overconfident in the swords, bows and ancient carbines carried by his Tigers. Although he mentioned Cerberus, he did so only in passing and glossed over its actual location.

As he spoke, Kane surreptitiously watched Kiyomasa's reaction to what he was told. His face remained as immobile as his helmet's face guard, although he nodded at times, as if he understood a fine point. When he was done, Kiyomasa lowered his eyelids and said nothing for a brief span of time.

Then, inhaling sharply through his splayed nostrils, he said, "Our friends at Port Morninglight told us a few things about the barons and the Magistrates. Your knowledge is far more detailed than theirs, yet nothing you said is at variance with what we were already told."

Irritated, Kane demanded, "Why didn't you tell me what you already knew to save us all some time?"

"Forgive me, Kane-san," the Tiger captain replied politely. "Although I need information, I needed to know if you spoke falsehoods before I confided in you. I hope you understand."

Kane nodded. "I suppose I do."

Kiyomasa bowed formally. "*Hai.* Now it is my turn."

The man began his tale in a precise monotone that was an unsettling counterpoint to the fanciful language he employed to relate a strange yet lyrical story. He took the four outlanders back through the long centuries past.

Long, long before the skies darkened on the island empire that the West called Japan and the East called Nippon, millennia passed during which the common folk honored their emperor as the living descendant of the gods. And though the emperor was adored as divine, he had no true power. To deal in earthly, mortal matters was to degrade his lofty position.

The society was strictly caste based, and everyone a grade higher had the power of death over those below him. One merely had to say the word and the person was immediately executed. If he was samurai or of a noble family, he was allowed to commit a ritual suicide, called seppuku.

Noblemen called daimyos took over the common chores of administering the empire. They held great prestige and when combined with the practice of the samurai code called Bushido, the way of the warrior, they were the powers to be reckoned with, not the emperor.

Kane couldn't help but wonder if the daimyos held the same reverence for their god-king as the commoner did. To them, he was only an instrument by which power could be obtained, the population controlled—much like the way the baronies operated.

By the mid-twentieth century, Japan's martial philosophy had earned it the questionable distinction of being the first country to suffer from the effects of nuclear weapons. The nation put aside its blades, called *katanas,* its deification of samurai as folk heroes and its exaltation of a noble death. Instead it focused on technology and ironically enough, harnessing atomic power to make a safe and nearly eternal energy source. By the end of the twentieth century, the land of the rising sun was the premier economic power in the Cific Basin.

On January 20, 2001, the day of the dark sky, a chain reaction triggered not only meltdowns but explosions in Japan's nuclear reactors. Those in turn sparked volcanic eruptions and earthquakes of such magnitude all of the smaller islands around Nippon sank without a trace. Northern Honshu, the largest province, was inundated by tsunamis, tidal waves a thousand feet high, according to legend.

All that remained of the land of the rising sun was a mountainous island, barely 150 miles long, and no more than seventy miles wide at its broadest point. By the time survivors crept out of shelters and climbed down from mountain peaks, almost none of the technology that had made the country a world economic power remained intact.

But since the Japanese were an extraordinarily industrious race, they rebuilt their nation with the little they could salvage from the ruins. The first post-skydark generation wrung its living from the sea, as had their ancestors centuries before.

The old feudal system was revived as an extreme reaction to how westernized Nippon had become before the holocaust. The new society was a return to the old ways of shoguns, samurai and peasants.

The peasants were put to work, utilizing what little resources remained on the island. Many of the old skills had been lost, and so the industries that sprang up on the coastal areas pumped pollutants and toxins into both the sea and the air.

When a shogun by the name of Mashashige attempted to reverse this poisoning of Nippon, and end growing civil unrest by peaceful means, he was violently opposed by his own brother. Open warfare broke out, and the slaughter decimated both factions. Although Lord Mashashige was gone, his memory and name lived on in his clan, in the House of Mashashige.

In the century following this disastrous coup, a new house came to prominence. The House of Ashikaga had once been the power in the land until overthrown by Mashashige. This was a house comprised of heretic lords who came to prominence during the anarchy following the war between brothers.

They were an uncultured clan whose family before skydark were merchants, not nobles or warriors. By good fortune, cunning and brutality incredible even in a land of cruelty, they rose to wield unparalleled power. They swore to restore order and prosperity to Nippon as a basis to rally forces to them. Only the House of Mashashige refused their support.

It did not take long before the Ashikaga clan proved it was less devoted to restoring order to Nippon than to destroying the House of Mashashige, wiping its seed from the face of the earth. To achieve such an end, the Ashikaga clan employed assassins, religious cults and even private armies ruled by self-appointed warlords who served equally self-appointed god-kings. These factions often fought among themselves, and so the edge of the sword ruled the country, not the scepter. Death had no meaning, no honor.

Due to these internecine conflicts, the country was in a state of civil war with the lords and landowners choosing sides or straddling the fence, while paying lip service until they saw which way the stick would float. Many of them were disillusioned by the rule of the House of Ashikaga.

The daimyo of the House of Mashashige, Lord Takaun, made one last attempt to not only reclaim his clan's power but also to restore some semblance of order and dignity to his country. He failed and the House of Ashikaga would not give him a second chance. They vowed to exterminate the Mashashige clan to the last of the line.

Lord Takaun had no choice but to flee, to go into exile. Taking with him as many family members, retainers, advisers and samurai as a small fleet of ships could hold, they set sail into the Cific. Their destination was the island chain once known as the Hawaiians.

But the heavens broke open with the unchained fury of the *tai-fun*, the typhoon. The storm drove the little fleet far off course. The ships had no choice but to make landfall on the first halfway habitable piece of dry ground they came across.

This turned out to be a richly forested isle, the tip of a larger land mass that had been submerged during the nukecaust. Evidently, it had slowly risen from the waters over the past two centuries, and supported a wide variety of animal and vegetable life. Lord Takaun decreed it would support theirs, as well. The exiles from Nippon claimed it as their own and named it New Edo, after the imperial city of feudal Japan.

Of course there were many problems to overcome during the first few years of colonization. Demons and monsters haunted the craggy coves and inland forests. They had a malevolent intelligence and would creep into the camp at night to urinate in the well water or defecate in the gardens. More than one samurai was slain during that time, their heads taken.

But the House of Mashashige not only persevered, it thrived, hacking out first a settlement, then an entire city from the wilderness. And now a new empire was rising, free of the corruption and cruelty of Nippon.

Kiyomasa finished his story and stared dispassionately at Kane. Dead silence reigned for what felt like an awkwardly long time. Then, apropos of nothing, Grant shifted position and muttered, "Well."

"Well what?" Shizuka challenged, although a hint of laughter lurked at the back of her throat.

"Well," Grant repeated tonelessly, trying to smile. "That's the damnedest story I've heard in a long time."

Kiyomasa's eyes narrowed to barely perceptible slits. "No more than your own tale of god-king barons and Magistrates who serve them like samurai. Your view of our history is colored by your gaijin perceptions."

"What's *gaijin* mean?" Kane inquired, stumbling slightly over the pronunciation.

"A foreigner," Shizuka replied.

Grant clenched his jaw muscles tightly, his face returning to its semipermanent scowl. "I believe your captain has it backward. It's my country we're in."

Sensing a brewing verbal battle that might become physical, Brigid asked hastily, "Captain, how long ago was this?"

"Eight years," Kiyomasa answered promptly. "Last month."

"And in those eight years you made exploratory voyages to other islands and to the mainland?"

"*Hai.* Scouting and spying expeditions to what you call the Western Islands." The man's grim mouth twitched in distaste. "They were overrun by mongrel pirates and Chinese. We did not care to treat with them. But at Port Morninglight we were welcomed. New Edo has traded regularly with them for the past three years. They always treated us fairly and respectfully. They kept their word not to talk about us, to speak the location of New Edo. They were our friends."

"So," Kane ventured, "you were making one of your trading visits to Port Morninglight when you found it razed and you decided to track the perps."

"Perps?" Shizuka echoed quizzically.

"Perpetrators."

"*Ah so deska.* English is almost a second tongue among my people, the old language of business and politics. Still, there are some nuances of it which we have yet to master."

"You could've fooled me," Grant commented.

Shizuka threw a smile his way, and even Kane noticed how it was too wide to be simply an acknowledgment of Grant's compliment. He hoped Domi didn't notice it.

"As we approached the port," Kiyomasa continued, "we saw one of our friends warning us away."

"Warning you how?" Brigid asked.

"With signal fans we supplied them with. We taught them basic code maneuvers, as well. I ordered our ship's smoke screen generator activated. It concealed us from the murderers but it concealed them from our eyes, as well."

Kane frowned. "When you came ashore, you decided to avenge the deaths of the people?"

"*Hai.* And to recover the prisoners and take them back to New Edo if they wish it."

"Why?"

Kiyomasa eyed him speculatively. "I thought you would understand, Kane-san. Port Morninglight and its citizens are under the protection of Lord Takaun. It is a matter of honor."

"I do understand," Kane stated. "I hope you understand that while we don't want the Mags to escape unpunished, we need at least one of them alive as a source of information."

Shizuka leaned toward Kiyomasa and whispered softly to him. The tone and timbre of her voice sounded very gentle. The man drew in a long breath through his nostrils as if steeling himself to perform an unpleasant task. "I shall reveal another reason why the murderers cannot be allowed to escape. I had a woman in Port Morninglight.''

Kane blinked in surprise. ''A woman? Your wife?''

''My woman,'' Kiyomasa replied flatly. ''She carried my child. I found her violated and shot through the belly and the head.''

Brigid murmured in horror, in sympathy. Kane felt a jolt of compassion and realized the samurai's unemotional demeanor was a pose, a facade. And with a sinking sensation in the pit of his stomach, he also realized he couldn't hope to dissuade Kiyomasa from walking the vengeance trail.

''I'm very sorry to hear this,'' said Kane in a subdued voice. ''But it doesn't change things for me or my friends. The stakes are very high, and we need information from the men you stalk.''

Kiyomasa nodded. ''*So desu.* I understand your wishes. Let us tarry no longer.''

He and Shizuka rose together, uncrossing their ankles, rocking forward on their knees, then on their heels. They came to their feet in one smooth motion, apparently without effort regardless of their armor. Kane managed to do so, but Grant had to push himself up with his hands. He seemed embarrassed, averting his face from Shizuka.

Kiyomasa called the other Tigers of Heaven forward and introduced them so swiftly Kane had only the vaguest idea of which name belonged to who—Jozure, Ibichi, Kuroda, Odo. As Kiyomasa spoke each name, the man lifted his faceplate long enough to nod, then snapped it back into the down position again.

The imprints of the passage of many feet were easily visible in the sandy soil, but it required a few minutes to distinguish the tracks of the savages from the Mags. The group of ten started off, leaving the corpses of the savages to lie unattended on the sand. Shizuka, Grant and Kane replaced their helmets. The other Tigers moved with a surprising degree of stealth, despite the amount of metal they wore and carried.

It appeared Pollard's Magistrates no longer cared about covering up their trail. The gauntlet of snakes had either spooked them so much they forgot to sweep their tracks, or they hoped any pursuers would fall prey to the bites of the diamondbacks.

Grant, who at first seemed inclined to walk beside Shizuka, dropped back to speak quietly to Brigid. "How much of Kiyomasa's story should we believe?"

"Without any evidence to contrary," she answered, "we might as well accept all of it as gospel. Besides, the bare bones match up with an account in the *Wyeth Codex*."

Grant nodded, seeming to be both relieved and comforted.

The *Codex* was a journal of sorts by Mildred Winona Wyeth, one of the enduring legends of the Deathlands. Born in the twentieth century, Wyeth had slept through the nukecaust and skydark in cryonic suspension. She was revived after nearly a hundred years by another semimythical figure of the Deathlands, Ryan Cawdor. Wyeth joined Cawdor's band of survivalists who journeyed the length and breadth of postholocaust America. At some point in her journeys, she found a working computer and recorded many of their experiences and adventures.

"She even went to Japan?" Kane asked skeptically.

"And a lot of other places. She was one well-traveled lady."

As they walked, Brigid saw how Domi seemed content to lag behind, which both annoyed and disturbed her. She gestured for the girl to come forward, but she only shook her head. Brigid fervently hoped after her humiliation at the hands of Shizuka, Domi wasn't scheming some form of payback.

A two-mile hike brought them to the crest of a low range, more of a sprawling foothill to the Sierra Nevadas. They stood at the brow of the hill and stared at the collection of ruins below them.

The buildings of the town were gutted shells, its streets choked with rubble and debris. It was a settlement long dead, at least since the nukecaust. Mesquite bushes grew in open courtyards bounded by the remnants of once tall walls and cluttered with the wreckage of long collapsed roofs. Scrubby grass grew in the pockets of windblown dust and weathered detritus.

"Looks like you'll get in a little archaeology practice after all, Baptiste," Kane said quietly to Brigid.

They looked down at the still-visible pattern of streets and lanes, laid out in a grid. A nearby river sparkled clearly in the moonlight, running slow and quiet. Not far downstream it was joined by another flow of water.

"They're down there," Shizuka announced, her voice muffled by her full-face visor. "They could have gone around the place, but the fact they did not shows they intend to spend the night."

Kane and Grant silently agreed with her assessment. Pollard wouldn't want to trudge across the wasteland at night, regardless of the cooler temperatures. The town offered more shelter than sand dunes, and they could rest with a degree of comfort.

Kiyomasa grunted as if satisfied. "We shall find them easily."

Quietly, Kane said, "Once we do, remember how revenge is not our mission priority."

"Point out a murderer you wish spared," Kiyomasa retorted with a touch of impatience in his tone. "If at all possible, he will be. However, sparing child-killing cowards is not part of the *otoko no michi*."

"The what?"

"The manly and honorable samurai tradition." Over his shoulder, Kiyomasa spoke to the Tigers in his own tongue. They began to fan out, slinging their carbines over their shoulders and drawing their swords.

"Unclean weapons like guns have their uses," the captain continued, "but only the *katana*—the sword—can quench the samurai's thirst for vengeance."

Kane contemplated the meaning of Kiyomasa's remark for a couple of seconds, then swiftly stepped to the lip of the ridge. With a geniality he didn't feel, he said, "I'll take point. It's part of *my* tradition."

Kiyomasa stared at him with an indefinable expression on his face then lowered his visor with a short, slapping motion. "*Ah so deska,* Kane-san."

Kane wasn't sure what he said, but he assumed— and hoped—Kiyomasa wasn't warning him to keep out of his way.

Chapter 10

Kane picked his way slowly down the steep decline, his companions and the Tigers of Heaven following at a discreet distance. When he reached the outskirts of the ruins, he waited and watched and listened for a minute. There was something both fascinating and repellent about the houses, roofless and silent in the night. Many of the fallen walls showed black glassy surfaces, as if they had been exposed to intense heat and the stones vitrified. Peeping through tangled vines here and there, he saw the rust-red streaks of what had once been vehicles, which gave him some idea of the many years the city had lain unattended. By the standards of the Outlands, scavengers should have put the wags to other uses long ago.

He tried to find some hint for the cause of the city's collapse, but there was no sign of a single catastrophe, no bomb craters, no evidence of shelling. Despite the fact some of the ruins showed signs of fire-blackening, others did not. Some buildings still stood among others that were no more than ragged foundations. Wide dark bands of dried mud discolored many of the walls, from the ground to half their heights. Evidently, the two rivers tended to flood intermittently.

Kane gestured and his party joined him, the Tigers again impressing him with how quickly and relatively silently they moved in their armor. He stalked down a broad avenue. Farthest from the edge of the river, the city was better preserved than elsewhere. Here most of the buildings still stood. They were low, long structures set upon terraces and facing curving streets. The streets were narrow, and they had to keep to the center for the bushes and creepers had narrowed it still further.

Many of the plants bore flowers, and Brigid wondered aloud if they had once been part of gardens that overgrew and overflowed to make a continuous thicket. The area had all the appearances of a residential section of the city, what she knew were once called suburbs.

Brigid said, "I think this place was what the pre-darkers called a commuter community, a specially built or expanded township for people who worked in large metropolitan areas but didn't want to live or raise their children there."

A few minutes later, Brigid pointed out a big square of plastic rearing from the ground, almost covered by bramble bushes. It depicted a cartoony Sun wearing a big smile, a sombrero and dark glasses. The bright read copy read Welcome to Vista del Sol—Our Future's So Bright We Need Shades!

Kane didn't know whether to laugh or scoff.

On impulse, as they passed one of the rambling houses, Kane strode up a walk to peer inside. Grant, Domi and Brigid followed him, the Tigers waiting out on the street. The doorway was wide and tall. The wooden frame disintegrated into fine powder when he brushed against it with a shoulder. Inside all was a shambles. Dead leaves filled the hallways, and the rooms showed evidence of being long-unused nests for vermin.

The interior smelled musty, which was not surprising, but it also held another odor, faint but detectable. Domi sniffed and said quietly, "Smoke."

It was the first word she had spoken in more than an hour. Kane and Brigid experimentally sniffed the air and detected the faint odor of wood smoke. Grant did not bother, inasmuch as his nose had been broken three times in the past and always poorly reset. A running joke during his Mag days was that Grant could eat a hearty dinner with a dead skunk lying right next to his plate.

They followed the scent of smoke out of the residential section and down a side lane. The street ahead of them looked as if it had been a mix of storefronts and apartment buildings. Many of the structures lacked roofs, and there wasn't a single pane of glass visible in any of the windows.

Kane once again took the point, leading them quickly along the narrow, overgrown alleys and through deep shadow between roofless walls. They passed doorways leading into nothing but darkness.

Up ahead he caught the murmur of voices, the muffled clink of steel. The odor of smoke thickened. The alley took a sharp turn and butted up against the base of a high wall, about eight feet tall. It extended from the side of a multistoried apartment complex, forming a wide square enclosure on its rear side. The designers of the building had gone in for a Spanish Mission style architecture, meant to evoke the days of hidalgos and caballeros. Fake adobe covered over bricks, and a square, bell-tower-like cupola rose from the top of the structure. Most of the adobe stucco had peeled away from the walls decades before, revealing the mortared brick beneath.

Thick, flowering vines sprouted from the brickwork. Using hand signals, Kane informed his party of his intentions. Kiyomasa nodded brusquely, and he and Grant made a stirrup out of their hands. They heaved Kane high enough so he could see what lay on the other side of the wall.

In a spacious but litter-strewn courtyard, a few Magistrates were pacing restlessly, but most of them sat around a small fire, eating their rations from the self-heat packages. They stared at the flames and smothered yawns. Several of the Mags lounged on the flagstones with their helmets off, Pollard included. Kane recognized several—Franklin, Hotchkiss, Brady. A few others he knew by sight but not by name.

An empty swimming pool, half-filled with scraggly tumbleweeds and debris, served as the prisoners' holding cell. They huddled together against a curving wall. All of them looked exhausted, their faces haggard and begrimed. They were fed scantily by a Mag and given enough water to keep life in them, but not much more. Their fetters were not loosened, but they were allowed to sprawl around as they might.

Pollard stood some distance from the fire, a cup of coffee sub in his ungloved right hand. He gazed vacantly at the pool, not really seeing it, as if he were lost in thought. Kane saw the faint scar bisecting his right eyebrow, the memento of the day Grant rescued Lakesh from the Cobaltville cell blocks.

He wished Grant hadn't left the bastard alive, or at the very least had crippled him. Kane and Grant had known Pollard for years, and they had never liked him. He was a simple, brutal, uncompromising man, always toeing the mark and obeying his superiors' orders without question. He made the perfect blunt instrument, and in Pollard's mind, that quality made him the ideal Magistrate. More than once he had evinced jealousy of Kane's and Grant's reputations.

Kane saw equipment packs piled in a corner, on the opposite side of the compound from the prisoners. Other than the Sin Eaters, the only blasters in sight were the standard-issue Copperheads. He figured grens were stowed somewhere, since they were part of the normal hard-contact complement of ordnance.

Kane made a swift head count and noticed four of the twenty Magistrates were nowhere in sight. He assumed they were on sentry duty somewhere outside the walled compound, patrolling the perimeter. A wide, dark doorway gaped in the side of the building, but he doubted any of the Mags were inside. It was very defensible ground Pollard had chosen. The only opening in the wall was a narrow arched entranceway.

He gestured to Kiyomasa and Grant. They eased him down to the ground, and he strode back into the alley, indicating the others should follow him.

"We've got four Mags unaccounted for," he reported in a grim whisper. "They're on guard somewhere, so we've got to be on triple red. If we're spotted and they raise an alarm, Pollard and his men could hold us off for a long time."

"What do you suggest?" Kiyomasa inquired.

"We'll split up. I'll get inside the building and come up on them from the inside. The rest of you circle the zone, find the guards and take them out. Secure the way into and out of the compound."

Kiyomasa nodded. "*Hai*. A sound strategy."

"One more thing," Kane added. "I've spotted the man we need alive. His name is Pollard." He supplied Kiyomasa with his physical description. "Disable him if you have to, but don't kill him."

Turning to the four Tigers, Kiyomasa repeated Kane's words. They all responded with head nods.

Kane opened the war bag and removed three grens, a CS gas canister and a pair of Alsatex concussion flash-bangs.

"I'll go with you," Brigid volunteered, reaching for a concussion gren.

Domi gave Grant and Shizuka a narrow-eyed glance and extended her hand to Kane. "Me, too."

Kane handed her a flash-bang. "Be careful with it."

Domi regarded him with an up-from-under glare. "I'm not a child."

Grant stepped beside Shizuka and, facing Kane, he lifted his right index finger to his nose and snapped it away in the wry "one percent" salute. It was a gesture he and Kane had developed during their Mag days and reserved for undertakings with small ratios of success.

Kane returned it gravely. "Let's get it done."

GRANT, SHIZUKA, ODO and Jozure crept around the north side of the sprawling apartment complex while Kiyomasa, Ibichi and Kuroda circled southward. They kept to wedges of shadow, angling toward the dark overgrown areas. Shizuka took the point, astonishingly fast and agile in her armor. She darted quickly into and out of the spots of best cover with barely a sound. While Grant and the two Tigers stayed close to the shadow of the wall, Shizuka crept away at an oblique angle.

Grant watched her with frank admiration. He couldn't deny his attraction for the woman. She exuded self-confidence, a slightly self-deprecating sense of humor and, despite her warrior trappings, a gentleness of spirit. She was certainly more mature than Domi, both in years and behavior.

And there was something about her that penetrated his guarded reserve. He didn't know exactly what it was, but she touched his inner core in a way only one other woman had done in his life—Olivia, the only woman who'd truly claimed his heart.

A shadow suddenly shifted behind Shizuka, a shape blacker than the darkness. A Mag glided soundlessly out of the gloom, combat knife in one fist and Sin Eater in the other. He wasn't wearing his helmet and in a split second Grant understood the man's strategy.

Removing his helmet in a potential killzone was more than unforgivably stupid; it was a major breach of hard-contact protocols. Without his helmet, the Mag couldn't relay a report about an intruder. His only option was to try to take out Shizuka with the knife rather than a blaster, which would possibly alert other intruders skulking around the perimeter.

Grant started to yell a warning when Shizuka spun faster than anyone he'd ever seen, Kane included. She whirled on the ball of one foot and came up with a two-handed stroke. With a faint wet sound, the blade sliced off the Mag's right arm just below the elbow. Coming up from under his armpit without ceasing her movement, she circled back, ready to deliver a second slash if necessary.

It wasn't. The Magistrate who had just lost his arm gazed with wonder at his limb lying on the ground, the hand still holding his Sin Eater. As blood continued to pour from the stump of his arm, he fell to his knees, then on his face. He died within seconds from the double traumas of blood loss and shock.

Grant, Jozure and Odo joined Shizuka around the body. Staring at the blood-damp *katana* in wonder, Grant husked out, "What the flash-blasted hell is that sword made out of?"

"Steel, of course," Shizuka replied, reaching beneath her breastplate and taking out a scrap of silk. She carefully wiped the blood from the blade.

"Steel can't cut through Mag armor like that," Grant objected incredulously. "Or it shouldn't be able to."

"It's a new process...or rather an old one, rediscovered about twenty years ago by Lord Takaun."

Grant eyed first the *katana* then her with suspicion. "Kiyomasa said the old sciences had been lost."

"A century ago, most of them had been. But not all of them remained so." Her dark eyes peered at him, glittering through the slits in her visor. "Did Kane-san reveal everything about your Magistrates and your barons?"

Grant forced a chuckle. "Point taken."

Shizuka turned to Odo and Jozure, addressing them curtly. They took hold of the Magistrate and his severed arm, dragging both out of sight into a tangle of shrubbery. The four people then resumed their circuit around the walled courtyard.

This time Grant assumed the point position. If they encountered another sentry, the sight of a man in the black armor wouldn't instantly drive him to the attack. Their progress was achingly slow, since they had to pick their way over a scattering of broken masonry, most of it butting up against the wall.

He heard a voice call out in a hoarse whisper, "Claremont, is that you?"

Grant turned slowly, trying to pinpoint the source of the voice. A hedgerow rustled a dozen yards to his right, and a Magistrate stepped out, this one wearing his helmet. Grant didn't recognize his jawline or voice so he mumbled a monosyllabic acknowledgment.

The Mag accepted the mumble as an affirmative and strode toward him, saying, "I'm so sick of this shit. Nobody's following us, so why can't we keep moving? Do you have your canteen with you—?"

The man was so intent on venting two days' worth of accumulated frustration it wasn't until he stood nearly toe-to-toe with Grant that he realized he wasn't addressing Claremont. His litany of complaints abruptly ceased, and he opened his mouth and raised his Sin Eater simultaneously.

Grant's left fist hammered upward, catching the Magistrate under the jaw, twisting his head back brutally on his neck. The impact of the uppercut dropped the man to earth without a sound. Grant was not as fast as Kane, but he was a good deal stronger, and when he struck, he usually struck only once.

Shizuka, Jozure and Odo swiftly stepped over to him. Wryly, she said, "Your technique may be straightforward to the point of crudity, but I can't argue with the effect."

The tip of Jozure's blade lightly touched the narrow strip of flesh visible between the Mag's high-collared undersheathing and his helmet, probing for the carotid artery.

Grant snapped fiercely, "No!" and launched a kick at the *katana*. Jozure snatched it away with lightning speed, causing Grant to stagger. The Tiger of Heaven instantly assumed an offensive posture, sword positioned for a double-handed stroke.

Struggling to compose himself, Grant said sternly, "No killing of the guards unless absolutely necessary."

He felt the pressure of Shizuka's penetrating eyes upon him. She asked, "Is this a man you know?"

Grant shook his head. "He's only following orders, like Kane and I did when we were officers like him. He probably didn't want to take part in the massacre of the settlement, but he had no choice."

Directing violence against members of his former brotherhood still caused Grant pangs of guilt. He retained vividly unpleasant memories of the firefight with Cobaltville Mags when he, Kane, Domi and Brigid made their escape. They were not memories he relished.

Grant said nothing more, though he sometimes questioned himself about his reluctance to kill Magistrates when they would have no such qualms if the situation was reversed. The Magistrate Division, for all of its many faults, had been the only true home he had ever known. It was where he had grown to manhood, where his personality and identity had been formed. No matter how far away from the Division he might run, both in distance and experience, he could never completely outdistance its oaths and its disciplines. In the remote recesses of his mind, the division was his home, not Cerberus.

Bending over the unconscious man, Grant swiftly disarmed him, appropriated his Copperhead, searched through the pouches on his web belt, found the nylon cuffs that were part of standard Mag equipment and bound the man's wrists behind him.

He fashioned a gag with the man's web belt and made sure he couldn't comcall for help by removing his helmet. The Magistrate looked frighteningly young, almost like a child. And there was something vaguely familiar about his soft features. Grant dragged him deep into a brush-clogged thicket by the ankles, acutely aware of how foolish his humanitarian efforts appeared to the samurai.

Shizuka's posture telegraphed impatience. "Let us waste no more time."

Although he wanted to, Grant did not object to her autocratic tone. As he began walking again, static hissed into his ear and Kane's voice filtered through the helmet's comm-link. "We're set."

Grant whispered into the transceiver, "We're not. Stand by for my signal."

With a note of impatience in his tone, Kane responded, "Standing by."

It didn't seem likely they would come across any

more sentries before they reached the entrance to the courtyard. Pollard had obviously stationed two on the north side and two on the south. He only hoped Kiyomasa would dispatch the ones on that side efficiently and silently.

Almost as soon as the thought registered, the quiet of the night was torn apart by a scream of terror and the staccato roar of blasterfire.

Chapter 11

With infinite caution, Kane crept sideways, crouched, listened, but heard nothing. He stalked along the corridor, aware of the faint sounds of Brigid's and Domi's footfalls six feet behind him.

He kept close to the right-hand wall, and the two women walked down the center so they would have a clear field of fire. The plaster on the walls was cracked where it wasn't broken altogether, and large pieces of it were scattered on the terra-cotta-tiled floor. Despite the lack of humidity, the air tasted dank and stale, as if they were creeping through a mausoleum.

Most of the rooms on either side of the hall showed as black as pitch, but several were dimly lit by the ghostly moonlight, peeping in through rents in the roof. They were far from bare, but their contents had not withstood the merciless double team of time and the elements. They were littered with haphazard heaps of unidentifiable junk. He hoped Brigid the historian didn't feel cheated.

They reached a T junction in the hallway and paused. On the right, a flight of rickety and sagging stairs angled up into darkness. Kane heard the mutter of voices somewhere ahead of them, so he moved on, senses alert, finger lightly touching the trigger stud of his Sin Eater. They reached a point where their path was blocked by a jumbled barricade of fallen timbers and support beams, so they had to work their way over and around and through them. It was a tight squeeze, even for Domi.

Turning a corner, Kane saw the double doorway leading directly into the courtyard. Crouching, he motioned for Domi and Brigid to take up positions on either side of it. He kept his eyes fixed on Pollard, watching his every move, and opened the comm-link channel to Grant. "We're set."

Grant's whispery voice responded, "We're not. Stand by for my signal."

Impatiently, Kane replied, "Standing by."

With hand motions, Kane told Brigid and Domi to throw their Alsatex grens when he gave the word. He would follow with the canister of CS gas. The three devices weren't lethal, but they would cause the prisoners some discomfort. However, it was a far safer solution than employing the high-ex grens in his war bag. As it was, with the people below ground level in the pool, they weren't likely to be caught in a cross fire.

Kane waited for Grant's communication, barely able to stop himself from fidgeting. Like all hard-contact Magistrates, Kane hated forestalling preemptive action. The moments directly preceding action were the hardest to endure. They always felt like a long chain of interlocking eternities. But since he had spent years as a hard-contact Mag, he also knew that real violence often came without warning.

As he reflected on that concept, he heard a scream, interwoven with the crackle of a Copperhead on full-auto.

The burst was short, barely two seconds in duration, but it galvanized the Mags in the courtyard like electric shocks. Shouting, they scrambled to their feet, snatching weapons and helmets. Pollard lumbered swiftly toward the entranceway, roaring an unintelligible command.

"Shit!" Kane hissed. When the two women turned questioning faces toward him, he gestured and snapped, "Do it!"

Domi and Brigid unpinned their grens and tossed them into the compound. They bounced unnoticed over the flagstones and detonated almost simultaneously, with painfully loud thunderclaps and eardrum-compressing concussions. A pair of stars seemed to go nova, and intolerable white glares blazed, bleaching all of the shadows out of the courtyard. The building shuddered, and little flakes of plaster sifted down. Even over the echoes of the twin explosions, Kane heard the prisoners crying out in fear.

The Magistrates nearest the epicenters of the explosions were stunned and deafened, and those without their helmets were blinded, their optic nerves overwhelmed. They clapped hands over their eyes and screamed out curses. While other Mags reeled in shock, trying to bring their blasters to bear, Kane pinched the gas gren's pin and hurled the gren with a looping overarm. It passed through the doorway, trailing a little stream of acrid vapor. When it struck the flagstones, it erupted with a loud pop and spewed a billowing plume of white smoke. Almost immediately the courtyard was engulfed by clouds of roiling vapor.

Yells and shouted commands became incomprehensible as the gas seared eyes, lungs and nostrils. The Mags coughed and gagged, groping for whiffs of fresh air. Two of them opened up with their Copperheads at the doorway of the building. Kane could barely see flame wreathing the stuttering muzzles through the blinding smoke, but the bullets turned the wall behind him into a sieve. Chips of wood and plaster flew past his head, deflected from his eyes by his visor. Slugs plowed up the floor in the center of the corridor, beating a drumroll on the terra-cotta tiles.

Dark shapes shifted through the planes of gas, fanning out to approach their position inside the doorway. The chemical vapors wafted into the building, and Kane heard Brigid cough, then choke as she tried to suppress it.

"You two stay where you are," he directed the women. "Don't move!"

Kane stepped out into the center of the corridor, framing himself in the opening. He allowed himself to be seen. Just to make sure, he squeezed off a triburst from his Copperhead at the nearest black figure. As he did so, he realized the man wasn't wearing his helmet and his weeping eyes were but slits in his face. Kane also recognized him, but it was too late to alter his aim.

Three 4.85 mm steel-jacketed rounds struck Franklin in the face and neck. His features dissolved in a wet blur, blood spraying out of his throat like a fountain. As he jerked backward, something struck Kane high on the left side of his chest, just below his collarbone. He heard an explosive report and saw a spurt of flame from vapor.

Staggering from the impact, air kicked from his lungs, Kane flailed backward into the gloom of the corridor, his feet scrabbling for purchase on the floor. Though his armor had absorbed and distributed most of the high-caliber bullet's kinetic energy, he was numbed, his heart quivering from hydrostatic shock. If the round had struck his molded pectoral directly, he knew his heart would have stopped beating.

Grant's voice suddenly snarled into his ear. "What the fuck's going on?"

Kane had only enough oxygen to either run or answer. He could not do both. He glimpsed four Mags bulling through the door, gripping their Sin Eaters and Copperheads. They did not see either of the women crouched in the dark corners on either side of them. Painfully dragging air into his laboring lungs, Kane turned and ran.

As THE DOUBLE EXPLOSIONS sent tremors rolling through the night air, Grant broke into a sprint, dashing around the corner of the wall and making for the entranceway into the courtyard. He opened the commlink to Kane. ''What the fuck's going?'' He snarled out the words. There was no reply.

A Mag pushed his way through the arch, raised his Sin Eater, then checked the motion. He started to call out to Grant, but when he spotted the Tigers of Heaven running up behind him, the man tried to bring his blaster to bear again, but Grant beat him to it.

The Sin Eater and Copperhead in Grant's hands spit flame and thunder, unleashing round after round. The Mag stumbled, voicing a garbled babble of screams and profanity. The hailstorm of bullets didn't breach the armor, but the kinetic shock was sufficient to numb him and slam all the air out of his lungs. He reeled back into the courtyard.

A Magistrate came around the south corner of the wall, but he wasn't running. He stumbled dazedly, hands over his midsection. Falling to his knees, he put out his hands to catch himself. When he did so, blue-sheened intestines fell from a slash in his armor, spilling in a wet and pulsing mass to the ground.

Kiyomasa, Ibichi and Kuroda came around the corner a breath later. Kiyomasa's sword gleamed with blood. Its razor edge had sheared through the Mag from groin to chest.

On his knees, the Mag tried to scrape up his intestines and push them back into his belly through the gash in his armor. He raised his face to Grant and tried to speak.

The *katana* in Kiyomasa's hands flashed. The Magistrate's head fell from his shoulders, the mouth open and lips moving as if it had one last thing it wanted to say. Then the body slumped forward.

Kiyomasa barked, "This pig managed to get off a few shots before I could attend to him." He sounded embarrassed, not angry. "I apologize."

Grant said nothing, ignoring the quiver of nausea in his stomach. When Kiyomasa made a motion to enter the courtyard, Grant put out a restraining hand. "Wait until the gas dissipates. You'll have plenty to do out here."

Almost as soon as the words left his mouth, a quartet of Magistrates staggered out of the entranceway, their mouths opening and closing as they desperately dragged in lungfuls of fresh air. When they saw the Tigers of Heaven and Grant, they simply froze, not knowing what to do.

The samurai knew. They went into whirling attacks, their *katanas* surgically dismembering the Mags. One man's gun hand was taken off at the wrist, and in the half second he stared in disbelief at the blood-squirting stump, the edge of the sword sliced through the neck of his companion, separating it from his head. The severed neck spouted a scarlet-foaming fountain from the opened arteries.

The Mag with the amputated hand opened his mouth to drag enough air into his lungs to start screaming, but a sword blade lifted, fell and lifted in between eyeblinks. The edge clove his helmet and the skull beneath it nearly in two. Both men dropped to the ground at the same time.

The other two Magistrates screamed in soul-deep terror and broke through the samurai, racing like panicked deer for the river. The Tigers pursued them only a little way, bounding like their feline namesakes, their *katanas* licking out. Blood rushed from piercing wounds in their backs and the two men screamed hideously, turning to fight. Grant did not engage them. Neither Magistrate managed to squeeze off a single shot when four Tigers of Heaven closed in around them.

It was not a fight—it was a slaughter. Within seconds the Magistrates floated facedown in the water, blood spreading away from their bodies. Then the weight of their armor pulled them beneath the surface and out of sight. Jaw muscles bunched, Grant turned away, back toward the walled-in compound.

"You don't approve of our fighting style?" Shizuka inquired softly.

"That wasn't a fight," he said, his tone frosty with disgust. "It was butchery."

"The honorable act would have been for them to bow their heads and accept the killing punishment they earned."

Grant refused to acknowledge the woman's observation. Taking and holding a deep breath, he pushed through the archway and into the courtyard, plunging into the planes of gas. He tried to stay beneath the drifting clouds of chemical vapor, but he inhaled some of it and for a second he gagged himself blind.

Grant's breath burned in his throat, his eyes still tearing from the tainted air, but it would have been far worse without his visor. A black-armored figure came to a stop in front of him. He started to speak, then spotted Shizuka at his side. He whipped his Copperhead to his shoulder.

Grant lifted the Sin Eater first, firing a triburst, aiming for the red-tinted visor. The subsonic rounds cored through the faceplate and pushed the man's brains ahead of them in a thick wad. The Mag stumbled, rocking on his heels and hit the ground, already a dead man.

Sounding slightly surprised but gratified nonetheless, Shizuka said breathlessly, "*Ah so domo arigato.* Thank you. I didn't expect you to do that."

"I said no unnecessary killing," he replied gruffly. "He didn't give anybody a choice."

Grant moved deeper into the courtyard, squinting against the burn of CS gas hanging in the air. Footsteps pounded on the flagstones behind him. He started to whirl, and metal flashed at the periphery of his vision.

A Magistrate staggered back from Shizuka, who had her sword angled over her left shoulder. The armored man made a peculiar croaking sound, then blood bubbled up in a precise line across his torso. The cut was from the juncture of the neck just above the seventh vertebra, then through the collarbone, angling to the sternum, slicing through the cartilage and spinal column. The Mag slid wetly in two pieces to the ground.

Grant stared in amazement and revulsion. Before he could say anything, he saw more Mags racing across the courtyard. He also glimpsed Pollard waving his Copperhead and bellowing commands in the booming, aggressive voice he had learned to despise. Grant brought up both of his blasters. Whipsawing autofire raked the onrushing Magistrates in continuous steel-jacketed stream. A Mag was hit broadside and bowled off his feet.

Return fire ripped the air around Grant, tearing through it in a frenzy, like a ground-level gale. Holding down the trigger of his Copperhead, he swung the flame-belching barrel from left to right. Hot brass spewed from the ejector. He found himself subconsciously aiming for the red badges emblazoned on the left pectorals of the body armor.

Wild rounds smashed into the wall behind him, filling the air with fragments of stucco and brick. Flagstones shattered, the ricochets whining and buzzing in all directions.

The firing pins of both blasters clicked dry almost in the same second. With swift sure hands, Grant toggled the Copperhead's magazine release, then rammed a fresh one home. He shot the bolt, stripping and chambering the first round.

The thinning clouds of chemical vapor suddenly lit

up with a hot, hell-hued white flash, like heat lightning contained within the walls of the building. Chunks of debris blew out of the ground-floor windows, and as they pattered down around him, Grant instinctively lifted an arm to shield himself.

In that instant, Pollard stitched Grant across the midriff with a zipper of slugs. They bruised him, pounded him dazed and gasping to the ground.

Before Grant's body had fully settled, the air shivered with a scream of rage from Domi, followed a shaved fraction of an instant later by the ear-knocking report of her handblaster.

Chapter 12

The gren detonated only moments after the Mags raced into the building after Kane. The concussive wave crashed down the corridor, and the fog-shrouded courtyard was lit up with a bright white flare. Brigid felt the shock and the heat on the back of her head. Instinctively, she crouched in an even tighter ball, hunching her head between her shoulders. Plaster and bits of wood fell from the ceiling, pelting her and filling her hair.

An instant later, she felt the fanning of cool air on the right side of her face as Domi screamed in outrage and fired her Combat Master. The boom of the report painfully compressed her eardrum, which was still throbbing because of the detonation of the gren. She turned to Domi and shouted angrily, "Be more careful!"

Domi said nothing, her eyes fixed on the supine Grant. He climbed to his feet as they watched, but their view of him was blocked by running, shouting, shooting figures. If nothing else, Domi's reaction to Grant's dilemma proved to Brigid that her anger toward him was superficial in nature, and didn't pollute her deep wellspring of devotion.

"Bastard fucking 'forcers!" Knuckling the grit from her eyes, Domi sprang out of the shelter of the doorway like a snow leopard pouncing on prey, her Combat Master banging and spitting flame.

Brigid watched in morbid fascination as Domi sought out Magistrates. When one of them loomed out of the misty veils, pointing his Sin Eater directly at her head, Domi instantly ducked and sidestepped. She lashed out with a leg, and her foot clipped him solidly on the back of his right ankle. He went down heavily on his shoulders and back. A staccato burst from his blaster went up into the sky.

Domi cartwheeled up and onto the man, landing on his abdomen. Her right foot, with all her weight behind it, drove up and beneath his visor. The steel toe of her boot impacted like a battering ram against the bottom tip of the Mag's nose. There was a very faint, mushy crunch of cartilage. His crushed nose spewed blood as bone splinters pushed through his sinus cavities and into his brain. Scarlet streaks contrasted sharply with his black armor. The Magistrate went into convulsions, clawing at the ground, his feet kicking spasmodically.

Domi heeled away from his death throes, turned and waved for Brigid to join her. "They got nothin'!" she crowed.

Double-fisting her Iver Johnson, Brigid left the building. Smoke rolled down the corridor from the epicenter of the gren explosion. She couldn't be certain, but she doubted the Mags had thrown the gren.

More than likely Kane had done so to discourage pursuit.

A Mag appeared in the murky vapors, assuming a combat stance, Sin Eater held in both hands. Neither Domi nor Brigid could see at whom or what he was aiming, but sighting down the barrel of her blaster, Domi triggered a shot at him. A splash of blue sparks jumped from the frame of the Sin Eater, and he stumbled sideways, shaking nerve-dead fingers.

The black-helmeted head pivoted toward her, mouth opening wide to utter a shriek of pain and anger. Domi calmly shot him through his open mouth. Arms flung wide, he lifted up on his toes and fell to the flagstones, a banner of blood trailing from his mouth.

Brigid did not allow herself to feel horror. As always in a combat situation, her mind seemed to disengage from her emotions, her thoughts functioning in a matrix of reaction and analysis. She turned toward the clangor of steel and saw the blades of the Tigers of Heaven flashing and flickering.

Brigid tried to find Pollard among the drifting scraps of chemical fog and running, screaming figures, but her vision was blurred by CS-induced tears. She framed the nearest Mag in her sights and fired four rounds that smashed dead center into his red duty badge and propelled him backward in a kicking spasm. Hydrostatic shock stopped his heart, and the man was dead before he hit the ground.

She altered direction, racing toward the pool, firing

from the hip at the Mag trying to maintain a guard on the prisoners. He returned fire with his hand-blasters, and she felt a bullet pluck at her hair, ripping a few strands out by the roots.

Arms and hands reached up to latch on to the Magistrate's legs and haul him backward. He fell into the pool with an obscenity bursting from his lips.

A Tiger of Heaven materialized beside her, as if conjured out of the CS fog. When he lifted his faceplate and threw Brigid a grin, she recognized the features of Jozure. Two Mags rushed him from opposite directions, trying to get Jozure between so as to catch him in a cross fire. He danced away, the *katana* in his hands flicking back and forth, reflecting little white flares of light. The barrels of the Sin Eaters tried to follow his movements.

Jozure made a low, whirling movement, squatted, then propelled his body into the air at the exact microsecond both blasters trained on him. The bores spat twin tongues of flame, and the bullets struck the armored men in the torsos, sending them staggering.

Jozure pivoted, his *katana* cutting wheels through the fading streamers of gas. His dodging dance came to halt, no more than a yard from Pollard. The moon-faced man's lips writhed back from his stumpy teeth in a snarl of fury. He held down the trigger of his Copperhead, sending a full-auto fusillade ripping into the metal-sheathed abdomen of Jozure.

His lower torso flew apart in a greasy explosion of blood and bowels. The Tiger went over backward, and curled into a ball, the silver sword spinning from his hand, his carbine clattering across the flagstones.

Pollard swung the barrel of the subgun toward Brigid, his little eyes glinting first in recognition, then astonishment. His finger froze on the trigger for a shaved shred of a second as he tried to figure out what a convicted seditionist was doing with a group of armored, sword-wielding madmen.

Although Pollard was momentarily paralyzed by confusion, a Magistrate sprinting up from the direction of the courtyard entrance wasn't so impaired. He directed a clumsy burst from his Sin Eater in her general direction as he ran.

Brigid threw herself forward in a frantic somersault, trying to stay ahead of the deadly stream of lead. Dirt fountains erupted behind her, little slivers of stone stinging her legs. She shoulder rolled across the ground and snatched up Jozure's fallen carbine. She raised it hastily, surprised by its heavy weight. She put it to her shoulder, framed Pollard in the blade sights and squeezed the trigger. The longblaster kicked, the recoil slamming the stock painfully into her shoulder socket, the barrel pulling upward as the shot boomed.

The bullet cleaved the air well above Pollard's head. Gritting her teeth, Brigid set herself, drew another bead on the man and squeezed the trigger a second time. Nothing happened except the firing pin clicked with dry, mocking impotence against an empty chamber.

Pollard stared in astonishment, then an ugly leer twisted his lips.

Bouncing to her feet, Brigid flung the carbine out in front of her. The metal plate of the stock smashed into Pollard's forehead, sending him staggering against the Magistrate standing beside him. Both of them yelled in pain, fury and frustration, but they managed to align her running figure in front of their blasters. Then a small, metal-shelled ovoid landed between her and the Mags.

With alarmed shouts, Pollard and the other Magistrate started to run, but the flash-bang detonated with a brutal, bone-jarring thunderclap. Amid the blaze of light, sand, dirt and pieces of flagstone were flung skyward in a cloud. The concussion slammed into Brigid, picked her up and dropped her heavily. She hitched around on her left side, raking her hair out of her eyes.

Grant lunged through the eye-stinging haze. He stroked a short burst from his Copperhead, but his shots missed by fractional margins.

Pollard and the other Magistrate whirled and ran toward the building. The magazine of the Copperhead clicked empty, so Grant discarded it. He glimpsed Pollard doing the same thing, throwing his subgun aside as he and the Mag raced into the dark mouth of the double doorway.

Grant halted to one side of the opening to reload his handblaster. Taking a shuddery breath, he winced at the ache in his chest. Pins and needles burned through his torso. He coughed, and the contraction of his diaphragm muscles sparked a hot spasm of pain in his right rib cage. It took an iron will to keep from clutching at his side.

Blinking back tears of pain from his eyes, he moved into the building at once, ignoring Brigid's voice calling his name. He crept along the hall, his head swiveling back and forth to peer into shadows, cursing the fact his comm-link to Kane was not on-line.

He had gone only a few yards down the corridor when his peripheral vision caught a twinkle of light reflecting dimly from an egg-shaped object bouncing down the corridor ahead of him. He dived backward, twisting to land on his shoulder on the tiled, debris-littered floor, sliding along on his side, trying desperately to roll back to the doorway.

With an earsplitting, teeth-jarring crack, the high-ex gren erupted in a flash of orange flame and white smoke. A hell-flower bloomed, petals of flame curving and spreading outward. Spewing from the end of every petal was a rain of shrapnel, ripping into the walls and ceiling. Fragments rattled violently against the floor, and Grant felt a few sharp blows against his upraised, armored arms.

The air went on shuddering with the echoes of the explosion, as ugly black fissures spread out in a spiderweb pattern on the ceiling. The walls cracked open like overripe fruit. The ceiling split in the middle and folded downward like a double lid.

Before Grant could do more than spit "Shit!" a seething cascade of plaster, wood, insulation and broken rafters poured down. The rain of splinters, planks and steel braces half covered him.

Coughing, blinded and nearly smothered, Grant struggled against the pressure of the debris covering him from upper chest to the toes of his boots. His visor was occluded by smears of dust, and kernels of grit stung his eyes and set them to watering. His right arm, his gun arm, was trapped beneath him, the Sin Eater's barrel snagged on shards of wood and impeded by metal reinforcing rods. Frantically he tried to free himself, but the plaster broke into fragments when he secured fingerholds. He glimpsed a black-armored form sliding out of the dust-laden air, then a heavy weight landed on his rubble-covered chest, nearly driving all the air from his lungs.

"Wasn't sure it was you," the Magistrate said, stomping hard on the layers of plaster and sheet rock covering Grant's chest. "Couldn't be, I told myself. But it is, isn't it? Grant the traitor."

The man's voice rang a distant chord of recognition, and Grant cleared his dust-coated throat enough to whisper, "MacMurphy?"

"One and the same."

Grant repressed a groan. MacMurphy was a man he had served with for many years and with whom he had shared the dangers of the Mesa Verde penetration that had started the chain of events leading to his exile. He had also been forced to shoot him during his rescue of Lakesh some months ago.

"You should've chilled me in Cobaltville, Grant," MacMurphy grated, stamping again.

"I didn't try to chill you," Grant replied, trying to work his right arm loose. "The object was to discourage you."

MacMurphy uttered a snarl. "You managed to do that, you son of a bitch! After you got away, I was booted back down the ranks. I've been pulling PPD for the last six months!"

PPD was the euphemism for Pit Patrol Duty, an assignment performed only by newly badged recruits—or veterans who were being punished through humiliation.

"Could you possibly understand what that's like?" continued MacMurphy, his voice rising to a high, hoarse pitch of fury. "I was in line for an administrative transfer. I should've had it by now. But it was all taken away. *Everything!* I even have to live in the fucking barracks now!"

The man's Sin Eater slid into his hand. The hollow bore peered down at Grant like a cyclopean eye. "This mission was my one chance to redeem myself, but you fucked it up. But a traitor like you doesn't care, doesn't believe in anything, doesn't understand anything about honor, oaths or duty."

"I understand perfectly," Grant said. Then he shot MacMurphy three times between the legs. He had managed to work his blaster free of the crushing weight just enough to tilt back the barrel and fire through the slabs of debris.

The rounds tore holes in the plaster amid little puffballs of dust and pounded into MacMurphy's codpiece with all the driving impact of a series of jackhammer blows. Although they didn't penetrate the polycarbonate cup, the kinetic force pulverized his testicle sac.

MacMurphy howled, clasping at his groin. He reeled backward, his feet sliding and seeking purchase on the debris-strewed floor. Raising a shaking arm, he pointed his Sin Eater at Grant. While the air still vibrated with the sound of the agonized scream, Brigid and Domi fired in perfect synchronization.

MacMurphy's tinted visor flew away in fragments, the bullets tearing through neck ligaments, cartilage and cervical vertebrae. The man's face dissolved in a wet scarlet blur. He fell to the floor very close to Grant. As he watched, MacMurphy's struggles to cling to life ceased and he jerked in postmortem spasms.

Domi and Brigid kneeled on either side of him. "Are you all right?" Domi demanded, her high voice quavering with anxiety.

Grant coughed. "Thanks to you two."

As they helped to dig him out, Brigid tersely told him that the surviving Mags had surrendered to the Tigers of Heaven. Grant kicked his legs free, crawled back a few feet, then rose unsteadily.

"I don't know if giving up will do the Mags any

good,'' he said flatly, shambling out of the doorway. ''The Tigers don't seem inclined to take prisoners.''

''Kane told Kiyomasa he only wanted Pollard spared,'' Brigid said bleakly. ''And then only for questioning.''

Grant paused, looking down the ruin of the corridor. He could not be sure, but he thought a couple of the objects protruding from the heap of rubble were polycarbonate-shod arms or legs. ''Where the hell is Pollard, anyway?''

''More importantly,'' Brigid retorted, her eyes bright with jade glints of worry, ''where the hell is Kane?''

Chapter 13

As Kane squirmed and wriggled through the forest of fallen rafters and planks, he heard the pounding footfalls of the Magistrates sprinting down the corridor after him. The barrel of his Copperhead was jammed tight between two boards. He tugged at it, then let the weapon go.

A Sin Eater opened up and a storm of lead ripped into the barrier of wood, punching through it amid clouds of dust and sprays of splinters.

Thumping blows drove hot nails of pain into his back. The jolting impacts of the bullets impaled him from back to chest with lances of agony. However, the sledgehammer blows knocked him through the barricade. He slammed onto the floor, skidding forward a few feet on his stomach.

Gasping, his vision blurred, Kane hitched around and dug into his war bag. His hand closed around another Alsatex, and his thumb flipped away the pin. He flung the gren behind him, not really seeing where it landed, and not caring.

The sharp report of the gren's explosion pushed down the corridor like a deafening wave, and a dazzling white blaze seemed to ride the crest. Behind him, the fallen timbers, boards and stringers crashed apart. The splintery shards clattered loudly against the floor tiles.

Dragging himself to his feet, Kane glanced behind him at the boiling cloud of dust. He dared not open up with his blaster blindly for fear of hitting either Brigid or Domi.

The swirl of plaster dust and wood particles convulsed and lit up with dancing spearpoints of flame. Behind it came the steady hammering of a blaster on full-auto. Howling like a blood-mad berserker, the Mag plunged through it, the ejector port of his blaster spraying empty cartridges in a clinking rain.

Kane backpedaled as fast as his legs and throbbing torso would allow. A bullet fanned a splash of cold air on his face, another thumped into the wall near his left arm and two more brushed the sides of his helmet.

Kane wheeled and raced down the hallway, silently enduring the spasms of pain igniting in his back and chest. A storm of shots followed him, the slugs peeling long splinters from the walls on either side of him.

When he came abreast of the first open door, Kane hurled his body through it, kicking his way through the detritus of two centuries. He entered a small kitchen and vaulted over a countertop, searching for another way out. A swift look around showed him the foot of a staircase and he bounded to it. He took the steps three at a time, his left hand pressing lightly against the wall for balance. He knew he was being reckless. The risers creaked and sagged alarmingly beneath his boots, and the banister wobbled whenever he touched it.

He reached a landing, paused, saw a door hanging askew on one hinge a dozen yards down the hall and rushed for it. With a clattering crash, the floorboards gave away under his weight. As he plunged into blackness, he slapped his hands around a thick strip of ornamental molding running between the floor and the wall. He managed to insert his fingers into the narrow crack between it and the floor. Below him, falling pieces of board clacked and banged against each other.

With his breath gasping through locked teeth, Kane kicked out with his legs, seeking purchase for his feet. The toes of his boots struck an interior cross brace, and for a moment he was able to relieve some of the tendon-tearing strain on his hands and wrists. Muscles quivering with the strain, he pulled his body up to chin level with the edge of the hole. Drifting in from outside the building was the racket of a fusillade, with at least a dozen guns blasting all at once. A few seconds later came the thunderclap crack of an Alsatex.

Desperately, he muscled himself upward. All feeling drained from his fingers, but he managed to get his elbows atop the sheared-away floorboards. Behind him came the creak of the stairs beneath booted feet.

With a frantic heave, Kane dragged his body clear of the opening, the splintered ends of the boards scraping against his body armor. If he hadn't been wearing armor, his belly and chest would have been severely lacerated. More of the flooring broke away, but he lunged and rolled into the hallway.

Staggering to his feet, he ran to the door. With a single wrench he pulled it loose from its hinge and entered a small room cluttered with the remnants of mops, buckets and push broom. Metal ladderlike stairs climbed the far wall, leading to a square wooden hatch in the ceiling.

Kane swarmed up the rungs and thrust the trapdoor aside. The ladder extended up a square shaft to the cupola housing of the bell tower. To his right was the faint gleam of aluminum air conditioning ductwork inside a maintenance accessway, elevated mere inches above the ceiling panel by rafters and supported by wooden chocks.

Kane briefly inspected the interlocking ceiling panels, then he clambered into the crawl space. There were small crosspieces of two-by-fours joining heavy rafters. He crawled along these, putting his weight on the wood. When the sound of creaking wood and footsteps was audible, he stretched out on a rafter and carefully tugged aside a corner of a panel.

As he had figured, the pursuing Magistrate had jumped over the gaping hole in the floor and was almost directly below his position. Kane inserted the barrel of his Sin Eater into the small space between the tiles. He made sure his body was shielded by the rafter before he squeezed the trigger.

Over the rattling roar and the clink of ejected cartridges, Kane heard cries of shock, pain and anger. Return fire raked the ceiling, showering him with panel chips and splinters.

He withdrew the blaster and shifted position. He felt the rafter beneath him shudder as a couple of rounds nicked it. He slid back, weathering the storm of bullets that chewed up the panels only a few inches below him.

The autofire ceased, to be replaced by the rapid scuff and scutter of running feet. Clinging to the rafter with one arm, Kane kicked out several bullet-blasted panels and swung down, hanging above the floor.

The Mag was running down the corridor, back toward the stairwell. Kane leveled his pistol, preparing to shoot when the Mag paused at the edge of the split in the floorboards.

Then the entire building seemed to jump up several inches before sinking. The walls rocked. A terrific explosion erupted from the ground floor, a sound Kane instantly recognized as being caused by a hi-ex gren. Smoldering wreckage spouted up the stairway. The weak floorboards split beneath the Magistrate to let out spurts of smoke and flame. Boards burst upward, then the entire floor collapsed with a rumbling crash. The Mag plunged feet first into smoke-spewing darkness.

Kane clung to the rafter tightly. His eardrums, strained by the initial concussion of the explosion, registered the clatter and thump of wreckage falling to the ground floor. The gren had virtually annihilated the lower section. He wondered who had been responsible for tossing a gren into the building, and with a stab of anxiety he hoped Brigid and Domi weren't still hunkered down by the doorway.

Dust and smoke from the explosion whirled up in a great pall. Coughing, Kane pulled himself up into the crawl space and squirmed back to the ladder in the small room. He could not go down, so he went up, climbing to the open cupola. Looking down into the courtyard below, he saw bodies strewed across the flagstones, lying twisted in pools of blood and body parts. Most of them were Magistrates. Because of the smoke, he could not see much, but he did spot a couple of Tigers of Heaven. Brigid, Domi and Grant were nowhere within his range of vision.

Hearing the creak of wood and metal below, Kane peered through the trapdoor. A black-armored figure was climbing the ladder, doing his utmost to be stealthy. His head turned from side to side, and Kane caught the blaze of wild, panicked eyes.

Pollard grasped a splintery two-by-four in his right hand, and it shook with the intensity of his emotion. He trembled in either terror or rage or a combination. His Sin Eater was snugged in its holster and since Kane didn't see his Copperhead, he guessed the man had expended all the ammo for both blasters. He had evidently lost his combat knife somewhere, as well.

Kane crept to the opposite side of the bell tower, walking on the balls of his feet. He crouched in a smear of shadow and waited until Pollard's bulky body pushed through the hatch. He cautiously moved to the open side of the cupola and peered out. As he stared into the courtyard below, his blunt-featured face contorted in a mask of horror. Most of the sounds of conflict had faded, replaced now with moans and gasping pleas for mercy.

Kane stepped closer to him, and a chunk of brick crunched beneath his boot. Pollard whirled, drawing in a sharp breath. He held the length of wood in a two-fisted grip. Blood streamed from a shallow cut on his forehead, bisected by the bridge of his nose. He squinted in Kane's direction and although he made out the Mag armor he didn't relax. "Don't move."

Kane obeyed him.

Pollard squinted even tighter. "What are you doing up here? What the fuck is your name?"

"Take a guess," Kane replied quietly, slipping a taunting note into his voice. "Down to only a stick, Polly?"

Pollard's entire body jerked in reaction to Kane's voice as if he had received a kick to the groin. He froze, staring in incredulous wonder. His lips worked, and when he was finally able to speak, his voice was a half-gasped bleat. "Kane?"

"One and the same. I haven't seen you since that little field trip of yours into the Darks. How was your stroll back to Cobaltville? I don't imagine Abrams helped you make good time, not walking on that lame leg I gave him."

He paused and added, "You're looking good,

though. Especially after the way Grant kicked the shit out of you in the Admin Monolith.''

Pollard's flesh-bagged eyes bulged. ''You were there, in the Darks?''

Kane grinned coldly, showing only the edge of his teeth. ''I was driving the war wag, Polly. Pretty funny when you think about it—your mission was to find me and Grant, and there we were, right within arm's length all the time. And you were too donkey-shit dumb to know it.''

Pollard began to tremble violently, his eyelids flickering, spittle collecting at the corners of his mouth. His shoulders quaked as if he were suffering from a seizure. Then he threw back his head and screamed, a howl of agony, terror and maddened fury ripped from the roots of his soul. Saliva spraying from his mouth, he dropped the two-by-four and charged Kane headlong.

Kane waited for his attack with lips creased in a tight smile. As the man rushed in, he stepped close and delivered a double hammer blow to Pollard's face. His nose flattened beneath the heels of his hands, scarlet spraying from his nostrils.

The man made no effort to ward off his blows but locked his arms around Kane's body, pinioning him. Pollard's arms were like steel bands, and despite his armor, pain shot up and down Kane's spine. The Magistrate rammed the crown of his head savagely against Kane's chin, and little multicolored spirals erupted behind his eyes.

Play The **Lucky Hearts** Game

and get...

FREE BOOKS & a FREE GIFT...
YOURS to KEEP!

yes! I have scratched off the silver card. Please send me my **2 FREE BOOKS** and **FREE MYSTERY GIFT**. I understand that I am under no obligation to purchase any books as explained on the back of this card.

Scratch Here!
then look below to see
what your cards get you...

The Gold Eagle Reader Service™ — Here's how it works:

Accepting your 2 free books and gift places you under no obligation to buy anything. You may keep the books and gift and return the shipping statement marked "cancel." If you do not cancel, about a month later we'll send you 6 additional novels and bill you just $26.70* — that's a saving of 15% off the cover price of all 6 books! And there's no extra charge for shipping! You may cancel at any time, but if you choose to continue, every other month we'll send you 6 more books, which you may either purchase at the discount price or return to us and cancel your subscription.

*Terms and prices subject to change without notice. Sales tax applicable in N.Y. Canadian residents will be charged applicable provincial taxes and GST.

If offer card is missing write to: Gold Eagle Reader Service, 3010 Walden Ave., P.O. Box 1867, Buffalo NY 14240-1867

BUSINESS REPLY MAIL
FIRST-CLASS MAIL   PERMIT NO. 717   BUFFALO, NY

POSTAGE WILL BE PAID BY ADDRESSEE

GOLD EAGLE READER SERVICE
3010 WALDEN AVE
PO BOX 1867
BUFFALO NY 14240-9952

NO POSTAGE
NECESSARY
IF MAILED
IN THE
UNITED STATES

Pollard grunted, snarled and growled in blood-thirsty gratification. "They told me you were *dead!*"

Kane jabbed his thumbs into the sides of Pollard's neck, seeking out the nerve centers. But all of Pollard's tendons and muscles were tense with the fury of his intention to snap Kane's spine. He writhed in pain but held on, tightening his arms until Kane's breath blew hoarsely out of his mouth. He tried gouging for the man's eyes, but he ducked his head, pressing his face against Kane's breastplate, forcing his upper body to bend over his encircling arms. Despite the armor, Kane knew Pollard's fury-fueled strength could break his back.

Although tempted, Kane did not shoot him. He used the barrel of his Sin Eater as a bludgeon, clubbing and battering the back of Pollard's skull. Caught in the grip of insane blood-lust, Pollard did not react to the crashing blows.

Kane allowed his legs to go slack and limp. He let every ounce of his 180 pounds sag upon Pollard's arms. The man stumbled forward, thrown off balance by the sudden, unexpected deadweight. They lurched drunkenly across the bell tower, and his grip loosened. Kane turned, strained, kicked and fought his way out of Pollard's murderous embrace.

Pollard could have stiff-armed Kane through the open wall, but he showed no interest in escaping. He was intent only upon killing him. He flung himself upon Kane and seized his throat, squeezing it as if wringing out a towel. He pressed with his thumbs against his larynx. Kane did not waste time trying to pry the man's fingers off his neck. He had always known Pollard was an exceptionally strong man, but now his murderous hatred had pumped up his strength to superhuman levels.

Falling backward with Pollard atop him, Kane doubled up his knees and planted his feet against the man's midsection. He straightened his legs like steel springs. The soles of his boots pushed solidly against Pollard's belly and propelled him up. The man flew backward, his stranglehold broken. Strips of skin peeled away from Kane's neck under Pollard's clawing fingers.

Pollard staggered the length of the cupola, his arms windmilling wildly. The backs of his thighs struck a dry-rotted wooden sill, and it crumbled beneath his weight.

With a gargling cry, Pollard tottered and tipped backward, slapping both hands on the molding of the frame. Kane reeled to his feet, lunging out to grab him. The ancient wood turned to powder under Pollard's fingers, and he plunged through the opening.

Arms and legs flailing and flopping like those of a stringless puppet, he plummeted straight down to the floor of the courtyard some fifty feet below. He struck the flagstones with a sound like a bag of rocks dropping into mud. A puff of grit-laden dust mushroomed up around his polycarbonate-enclosed body.

Kane leaned against the window, trying to drag air back into his lungs and wincing at the deep boring pain in the center of his back. He watched as Pollard stirred fitfully. His twitchings reminded him of those made by the mutie scorpion when its black carapace had been crushed. That memory seemed a year old now.

He saw Brigid, Domi and Grant surround Pollard's body, and he gusted out a sigh of relief. He tried to call to them, but his punished throat muscles and windpipe could produce only a strangling sound, like a dog coughing up a piece of bone. Still, they heard him, looked up, saw him and Domi raised her Combat Master. Kane brought his index finger to his nose and snapped it away to let them know the armored man in the bell tower was him.

Brigid kneeled beside Pollard, peeled back an eyelid and tilted her head back, turning her face toward Kane. She called up grimly, "If you want to question him, I suggest you do so very soon."

Chapter 14

Except for the need to interrogate Pollard, Kane was in no great hurry to find a way down from the bell tower. He knew what would happen once the prisoners were freed. Even he, with all the combat he had participated in and the bloodshed he had seen, had no stomach for what lay in store for the few surviving Magistrates.

But there was no stopping it, not unless he cared to pit himself and his friends against the prisoners and the Tigers of Heaven. He only hoped Grant and Brigid could protect Pollard long enough so he could wring some information out of him.

After a couple of minutes of searching, Kane found a fire escape and climbed down to the courtyard. His companions were uninjured, although Grant suffered various bruises. The same could not be said for the Tigers. Kiyomasa grimly informed him that Jozure was dead, killed by none other than Pollard. Ibichi had a gunshot wound to his leg, which would impede their travel back to Port Morninglight.

He did not seem impressed when Kane told him he and his samurai had gotten off lucky compared to the Magistrates. Only a few remained essentially unhurt.

Several of the wounded would die of their injuries before dawn. Their former prisoners were in no rush to put them out of their misery. In fact, they preferred to prolong it. They would make sure the killers of their friends and family felt every second of agony before they died.

If not for Grant and Brigid, the people of Port Morninglight would have dragged Pollard down into the swimming pool to be tortured. They had joyfully transformed their holding pen to a torture pit, using knives given to them by the Tigers.

Brigid and Grant kneeled protectively on either side of Pollard, with Kiyomasa and Shizuka hovering just within the reach of their *katanas*. Kiyomasa's posture in particular put Kane in mind of a ravening tiger, straining at a leash. He glimpsed Domi standing at the rim of the pool, apparently taking a keen clinical interest in the bloody proceedings going on below.

Pollard was conscious, but just barely. Despite the measure of protection provided by his armor, many bones in his body had been broken and he suffered from internal injuries. His ugly face was white and glistening with sweat. He panted through gaping, dry lips. Brigid tipped a canteen over his mouth, moistening his lips.

When Kane leaned over him, his eyelids fluttered and he wheezed, "Unlucky bastard to the last."

Kane took off his helmet and squatted beside him.

"That's probably the truest thing you've ever said, Polly."

Pollard managed a grin, his lips peeling back over red-filmed teeth. "I wouldn't be in your boots...not when the baron gets hold of you."

"Now that you've brought him up," Grant said, "why did he order you into Baron Snakefish's territory?"

Pollard cast his gaze toward him. "How'd you know about that? Preservationist spies in the division?"

Decades before, when Lakesh concocted his underground resistance movement to oppose the barons, he wove the myth of the Preservationist menace, presenting a false trail made by a nonexistent enemy for the barons to pursue and fear. He created the Preservationists to be straw adversaries, allegedly an underground movement whose members pledged to deliver the hidden history of the world to a humanity in bondage.

Even Kane had been surprised to learn the Preservationists were a fabrication, so he didn't bother trying to explain it to Pollard. "Yeah, that's right. Preservationist spies. Why are you taking prisoners here? Where are you taking them? Cobaltville?"

Pollard tried to shake his head and produced the dry crunching of fractured neck vertebrae. He squeezed his eyes shut, his face screwing up in an attempt to control the pain. "Hurt too much to think...give me something..."

Kiyomasa uttered a scornful snort at Pollard's admission. Although they had left the medical kit behind in the riverbed, part of the standard complement of Mag equipment were items to practice field medicine. Grant unsnapped a pouch on his belt and took from it a small squeeze hypodermic. It contained a pain reliever and metabolic stabilizer developed by the medics at the Mag Division. He undid the seals on Pollard's left gauntlet, tugged it off and injected the ampoule's liquid contents into the vein of the man's upper wrist.

All of them saw the string of digits written in blue ink on his flesh, though a couple of the numbers were blurred due to perspiration. Eyes narrowing, Brigid pulled up the sleeve of his Kevlar undergarment so she could see the entire sequence. "What are those numbers?"

Pollard coughed, a rattling hack. He turned his head and spit a glob of bright pink, frothy saliva on the flagstones. None of them said anything, but they knew by the color of the sputum the man's lungs were punctured.

"What do you think those numbers are, whore?" he husked out, curling his lips in a contemptuous sneer.

Kane's eyes flashed in anger, and he reflexively drew back his hand to cuff Pollard's face. Although her lips were compressed, Brigid shook her head at him and he checked the movement. She leaned closer to Pollard's sweat-pebbled face and stated confidently, "I think they're the destination-lock codes for a gateway."

Pollard's piggish eyes widened in surprise, a silent affirmation her opinion was correct.

"But," she went on crisply, "they don't correspond to the unit in Cobaltville, the one in the Admin Monolith on the baron's level." Two lines of concentration appeared on either side of her nose bridge. Her lips moved slightly as she impressed the numerical sequence into her eidetic memory. She added, "In fact, they're not the destination-access codes to any of the units we've ever used."

The last was directed more toward Grant and Kane than Pollard. Neither man doubted her declaration, since she had proved time and again her power of total and accurate recall was infallible.

"So, Polly," Kane said, "when you returned to the redoubt with the prisoners, you weren't going to transport back to Cobaltville?"

A smile tugged at the corners of Pollard's mouth. The drug coursing through his bloodstream not only masked the pain but produced a temporary euphoria. "We were," he said dreamily. "Not the slaggers. Gonna send them someplace else. With them numbers."

"Why are they written on your arm?" Grant demanded.

"So's I'd remember 'em, why else?"

"Yeah," Kane muttered. "Why else?"

"Where is the location of the unit you were sending the prisoners?'' Brigid inquired, lowering her voice and softening her tone, trying to sound friendly.

"Dunno," came the mumbled response. "Griffin didn't tell me, and I didn't ask."

"Griffin?" Grant echoed in surprise. "Why would Griffin assign you this mission?"

"He's the Division administrator."

"That paper-pushing jack counter? Since when?"

Pollard's brow furrowed as he dredged his narcotic-fogged memory. "A couple, three months, mebbe. Since Abrams was removed, I guess."

Brigid said curtly, "Let's get back to the matter at hand. Gossip about the old gang back home can wait."

Both Grant and Kane gave her hard stares but said nothing more. Leaning closer to Pollard, she asked, "What were Griffin's specific orders?"

Pollard's eyes had acquired a glassy sheen. Brigid dribbled a little more water into his mouth and repeated the question. As if by rote, he answered, "To march to Port Morninglight. To round up as many healthy outlanders as we could find and take them prisoner. Chill the rest. Make sure we left nothing to connect Mags to it."

"Why?" Kane snapped. "There are plenty of outlanders in Baron Cobalt's own territory."

"Mebbe there is," Pollard murmured faintly. "Mebbe there ain't. Once we marched 'em back to the redoubt, I was supposed to shove 'em in that mattrans thing, input the numbers on my arm on the comp controls and send them someplace. Then we were ordered to return to Cobaltville.''

Grant's face tightened in a scowl. "This doesn't make a whole lot of sense."

"It just might," Brigid intoned dolefully.

"Kane..." Pollard's voice was now no more than a hoarse rustle.

Kane leaned closer. "Yeah?"

Pollard lifted a trembling hand, his forefinger tracing the outline of the red duty badge affixed to Kane's armored chest. "You're a fucking traitor, but you still wear that? How can you live with yourself?" He shifted his gaze to Grant. "Both of you, fucking traitors."

Grant's jaw muscles knotted. "Watch your mouth."

Pollard forced a slurringly soft laugh. "What are you going to do, chill me? I just want to understand you. We served together for years, flash-blastin' slaggers and Dregs and outlanders. And you threw it all away—and for what?"

"You wouldn't understand, Polly," Kane snapped.

Pollard swallowed, wincing in pain. "Salvo didn't understand, either. Drove him crazy. Then I was told he was working with you all the time, that he was just as much of a traitor as you three. Is that true?"

Kane, Grant and Brigid silently exchanged glances. With a shrug, Kane said, "No, it wasn't. Salvo wasn't a traitor. He was a scheming, lying sack of shit, a backstabbing murderer and probably insane, but he wasn't a traitor." He paused and added, "I hope that makes you feel better."

Pollard nodded, his lips writhing to form a caricature of a satisfied smile. "It really does. What happened to him?"

"He's dead."

"When?"

Kane wasn't inclined to explain how he had shot Salvo atop a Manhattan rooftop on New Year's Eve 2000 in an alternate-past timeline. He had lived through the experience and barely understood it himself, so he said simply, "A long, long time ago."

Gruffly, Grant demanded, "Is that all you know?"

"Yeah, that's it," Pollard answered. "I'm just a grunt, always an unlucky bastard, operating on a need-to-know basis…just like you used to do…." Pollard's voice trailed off into incomprehensible murmurings.

Grant arose swiftly, stiffly and stalked away, shouldering between Shizuka and Kiyomasa. Shizuka hesitated, then followed him. Kane gazed after Grant, able to guess at the kind of thoughts wheeling through his head. An old guilt returned, making Kane's belly churn with the sickness of self-loathing for a moment. More than a year before, when he had turned against Salvo and broken his lifetime of conditioning, it had resulted in the convictions of Grant and Brigid as his accomplices.

He could have dealt with the consequences of his actions if they had landed solely on his shoulders, but he'd dragged two good, innocent people into exile with him. There was no way he could ever make it up to them, especially to Grant. He had hoped the man had come to terms with his exile, his criminal status after all this time.

True, the peeling away of their Mag identities had been a gradual process and hard to endure, especially during the first three months in Cerberus. Now, when Kane thought of his years as a Magistrate, it brought only an ache, a sense of remorse over wasted years.

Superficially, Grant had handled his exile better than Kane, but the man was always stoic in the face of physical and emotional pain. Grant had followed Brigid's lead, who was the most adaptable of the three of them, and he seemed devoted to the new work Cerberus offered.

But old Mag habits died very hard. Kane managed to push most of them to the back of his mind, storing them with his memories of all the other things that were past and he wasn't particularly anxious to think about.

Except when he collided head-on with a reminder like Pollard, and then they swarmed out like bugs from beneath a lifted rock.

A full-throated scream suddenly cut across the courtyard, piercing and full of torment. It terminated in a wet, ghastly gurgling as of a man choking to death on his own blood. A ragged cheer burst from within the swimming pool.

Pollard's glazed eyes snapped wide at the sound. "Are you going to let 'em do that to me?"

"Why not?" Kane asked coldly. "You deserve it more than your men. You led them, ordered them."

"Just following my own orders, Kane. You know how that is. You haven't forgotten what it's like."

"No," Kane affirmed darkly. "I haven't, no matter how much I wish I could. But being a good soldier doesn't justify a massacre."

Pollard clutched at his forearm, at his holstered Sin Eater. "Chill me yourself, then. Just put your blaster to my head and pull the trigger. Don't let me die like that. It's not right, not for a Magistrate."

Kane gazed down steadily into the man's damp face for a long, contemplative moment. *A Magistrate is virtuous in the performance of his duty.* The panegyric phrase drifted through his mind. The duties and obligations that came with his badge and blaster were drilled into him—all Magistrates, for that matter—from the day they first entered the academy. The oath was a part of their every action and reaction—a justification and a reason to live, a moral sword and a shield for the work they performed in service to maintain order, in service to the baron. And as Kane and Grant learned, in service to a lie, a conspiracy hatched hundreds of years before any of them were born.

Kane glanced up into the immobile face of Kiyomasa, then back down at Pollard. Quietly, he said, "It's not up to me. You chilled a man's woman and his child she carried. Even if you didn't do it yourself, you commanded it to be done or you didn't stop it. Someone else will decide how and when you'll die. Not me."

He pulled away from Pollard's grasp. "If it means anything, I'm sorry."

"It doesn't," Pollard said in a gasping snarl. "Fuck you, traitor."

Kane rose to his feet, automatically dusting his hands as if they were dirty. After a moment, Brigid stood. Another scream cut through the night air and pimpled Kane's flesh beneath his armor. Brigid glanced toward the pool with slitted eyes, then turned smartly on a heel, marching away into the shadows until it was over. Kane knew it would be several hours before the last of the screams stopped.

Facing Kiyomasa, he said lowly, "I would be in your debt if you can see your way to stopping the torture."

Kiyomasa sighed. "Torture is not our way, either, Kane-san. But the people whom these men abused, whose families they murdered, whose homes they burned have earned the right to balance the scales." He paused, hefting his *katana*. "As have I. Please do not interfere with what I must do so the spirits of my woman and baby can rest easily."

"Can you at least promise to make Pollard's end swift?"

Softly, apologetically, he answered, "Forgive me, Kane-san, but I can promise nothing of the sort."

Kane stared into the man's expressionless face, as

impassive as if it were carved from ivory. He nodded in resignation and turned to walk away, to find Brigid. He had taken only two steps when he heard a scuff and scutter behind him and a sobbing laugh.

A jarring, stunning blow against the back of his head caused multicolored pinwheels to spin behind his eyes. He fell sprawling face first against the flagstones, nearly driving all the wind from his lungs. As he went down, he heard Kiyomasa blurt in angry surprise, then a peculiar swish of sound.

With his left hand, Kane heaved himself onto his back, his Sin Eater slapping into his right palm. Pollard towered over him, one boot lifted as if preparing to stomp the back of his head. Temples throbbing, Kane leveled his blaster, ready to fire. Pollard did not lower his foot. He simply stood there, looking ludicrous while he balanced himself on one foot.

Then light glittered dully from the flat silver spur projecting from the junction of Pollard's right shoulder and neck. Kiyomasa stood behind him, his face set in a grim mask. He had slid his sword with apparent ease through armor, flesh and bones, moving the blade up at a thirty-degree angle until the point broke free of Pollard's body. Then, with a whipping motion, Kiyomasa pulled the *katana* free of the man's polycarbonate-encased torso and lifted it high.

Kane wasn't sure he even saw the downstroke. One second Kiyomasa's sword was in the air above his head, then it was down in a slashing blur and coming back up, the razor edge shearing through Pollard from groin to chest.

Pollard dropped to his knees, his intestines streaming out of his body cavity. His eyes were wide, and his mouth worked as if trying to cast one last curse at Kane. Then his body toppled forward, scarlet spreading in a widening pool around him.

Before Kane could climb to his feet, there was another flashing sweep of Kiyomasa's *katana*. By the time he stood, Kiyomasa held Pollard's head aloft by his hair.

Bitterly, he asked, "Was his end swift enough for you, Kane-san?"

Chapter 15

Grant strode deliberately out of the confines of the walled courtyard, past the eviscerated and decapitated bodies of several Magistrates and into the surrounding darkness. He was glad when he could no longer taste the chemical tang of lingering CS gas, but he did not stop to take in the fresher air.

He continued walking, entering a tangle of undergrowth. He came to a halt when he heard a muffled whimper at his feet. The Mag he had rendered unconscious lay where Grant had dumped him, his jaws still distended by the makeshift gag. Ambient moonlight gleamed on his terror-wide eyes. Grant reached down for him, but he cringed, a whine bubbling around the tough fabric of the web belt in his mouth.

"Shut up," Grant told him in a fierce whisper, sliding his hands under the man's armpits. He dragged him to his feet. "If I wanted to chill you, I'd have done it twenty minutes ago."

The Mag trembled violently, his knees quivering, saliva drooling down his chin from beneath the gag. His face was pallid, drained of all color, his eyelids fluttering like the wings of a crazed butterfly.

Spinning him, Grant unsheathed his combat knife

and slashed through the nylon cuffs. "I'm not going to hurt you, understand?"

A prolonged, liquidy scream arose from the compound, and the Magistrate jerked in reaction to the sound. His teeth tried to chatter around the strip of leather and cloth in his mouth, and he clawed at his gag, managing to pull it down around his neck.

"Think you can find your way back to the installation in the mountains?" Grant asked quietly.

The young man did not answer for a moment. His eyes darted from Grant to the direction of the courtyard. Tersely, impatiently, Grant continued, "I'm not going to chill you. Can you get back to the redoubt or not?"

The youthful Magistrate had lived the past half hour in such intense terror it could not be easily allayed. He managed to choke out, "I think so. Yes. Yes, sir."

Grant gave him a shove out of the thicket. "Then prove it."

The man stumbled forward and regarded him fearfully over his shoulder. Once again Grant was struck by how familiar his features seemed. "What's your name, boy?"

"Mace," he stammered.

"You have a brother in the division?"

"Had a brother. He's dead, over a year ago now."

"How?"

"He was blasted down in Tartarus, trying to arrest terrorists."

Grant managed to conceal his reaction. The man's brother had been in the force of Magistrates led by Salvo to apprehend him, Brigid and Kane. He had always known the furious firefight that ensued had claimed the lives of at least three Mags, possibly more.

"Get going," Grant ordered.

Mace hesitated. "I don't know if I can operate that—that—"

"Gateway?" Grant supplied.

He nodded, a spasmodic bobbing of his head. "That thing that brought us here. Don't know if I can work it."

"If you get back to the redoubt alive and can't figure the gateway out, just wait for me. I'll send you back home."

Mace said in an aspirated whisper, "Thank you, sir," and began a shambling run into the darkness.

Grant waited until he disappeared into the gloom and left the tangle of thorns and vines. He removed his helmet and saw with a twinge of anger the tremor in his hands. He told himself it was the aftereffect of combat, of adrenaline, but he wasn't able to convince himself.

He knew on a deep gut level he wasn't just disgusted with the slaughter and the torture, but was also profoundly shaken by it. He had no idea why. In his twenty-odd years as a hard-contact Magistrate, he had not only witnessed but participated in events of such bloody carnage that even a swampie would have nightmares.

A month or so previous, Grant had realized the simplest answer was that he was getting old—too old to take violence in stride anymore, too old to simply shove scenes of horror away in a dark, cobwebby corner of his mind.

The last five years he spent as a Magistrate had been fairly routine. He had looked forward to a transfer to a deskbound administrative position, and the prospect of hanging up his blaster and putting his armor in storage hadn't disquieted him at all.

When he sacrificed all of that to join Kane in exile, he had harbored the secret hope, one he'd never spoken of, that his involvement in bloodshed would be minimal. Instead, it was far worse than even his first few years as a Mag. The irony weighed on his mind, no matter how many mental tricks he employed to either justify it or not think of it.

When they first joined the Cerberus exiles, Grant made a concerted effort to get to know the other personnel. They were brilliant and wayward members of different divisions in other villes who, through Lakesh's machinations, had fallen afoul of baronial laws in one fashion or another. Again through Lakesh's machinations, they ended up in Cerberus as insurrectionists rather than facing executions.

Grant had tried to view them as fellow expatriates, comrades-in-arms, all joined together to throw off the heel of an oppressor. But the ingrained habits of a lifetime couldn't be cast aside in the course of a year. On occasion, he still thought of his fellow exiles as slaggers, as criminals, and of Lakesh as a dangerous subversive.

Another agonized scream floated from the courtyard, and he reflexively turned his head in that direction. Shizuka padded up to him, her elaborate helmet tucked under an arm. Her face was begrimed with a sprinkling of dried blood on the graceful column of her neck. She gazed into his face searchingly. "Are you all right, Grant-san? You don't require medical attention?"

He shook his head. "As long as I can walk, I'm fine."

She smiled at him slyly. "Spoken like a true samurai. You fought very well, very bravely."

"It's what I do."

"As do your friends, particularly the little ghost girl."

"She tends to get carried away."

Shizuka stepped closer, her penetrating dark eyes fixed unblinkingly on his face. "Is she yours?"

Grant felt his heartbeat speed up. "No," he said frankly.

"So you don't get carried away?"

A dismissive retort leaped to Grant's tongue, but he swallowed it before he could utter it. "Not like that I don't."

She gestured to the darkness. "So that is why you

freed one of the killers.'' Her voice was flat, holding no particular emotion.

Grant narrowed his eyes, glowering down at her. Tilting her head back, she met his stare unflinchingly. He asked, ''Why didn't you stop him? Mince him up with that supersharp sword of yours?''

She shook her head. ''It was not my place. His life was yours to do with as you willed. The captain may not have approved, but he wouldn't have interfered, either.''

''It's good to learn your samurai code makes some allowances for individual actions—like mercy.'' He didn't bother softening the sarcasm in his voice.

Shizuka did not seem to be offended. ''The *otoko no michi* is complex and multifaceted. Do not make snap judgments until you learn more about it and us.''

He felt a twinge of shame at the quiet note of reproach in her voice. Falteringly, he said, ''I would like to learn more about New Edo, about you.''

''I am of a samurai family and to learn about me is to learn about New Edo.''

''I'd like to see it one day.''

She nodded. ''Mayhaps you shall. It is not far off the coast or hard to find.'' She smiled impishly. ''If you know where to look, that is.''

Shizuka's smile was replaced by a troubled expression. ''But like this country it is torn by disagreement. I fear that after this day's atrocities committed against our allies, the disagreement may explode into actual strife.''

"Why so?" Grant inquired.

Shizuka sighed heavily, sweeping her hair back from her high forehead. "I should not speak of it. You are gaijin, an outsider. Yet I feel I can trust you."

Grant waited silently and with another sigh, Shizuka said in a breathy whisper, "Captain Kiyomasa and my daimyo, Takaun, disagree about the path the future of New Edo should embark upon. Lord Takaun wishes to remain isolated, as self-sufficient as we can manage."

"And Captain Kiyomasa doesn't see it the same way?"

"He does not. He wishes to expand our influence into the mainland, over this section of the Pacific coast. He seeks trade agreements, mutual nonaggression and protection pacts with settlements. He wants to establish a sovereign colony here."

"The barons may have a little something to say about that," Grant interjected wryly.

Shizuka's lips quirked in a fleeting smile. "That is Lord Takaun's main objection, inasmuch as we have precious little intelligence about the military might of your baronies."

"I see." Grant cleared his throat. "I can tell you one thing about them—they won't come at you with World War II–vintage longblasters loaded with only one round."

She acknowledged the comment with a self-conscious chuckle. "Very true," she admitted. "Our armament is not what you would call state-of-the-art, not even by the standards of the year of the holocaust. Ammunition is expensive and hard to come by. We don't have the natural resources to manufacture much of it ourselves.''

''So why only one bullet per gun?''

''Actually,'' she answered, ''only Jozure had one bullet. As the poorest marksman, that's all the captain felt he deserved.''

Recalling her remarkable prowess with the bow, Grant said, ''Then why didn't he give you a long-blaster with a full clip to carry?''

''Captain Kiyomasa did not feel I was worthy of one.'' Seeing the skeptical expression crossing his face, she added, ''It's a misconception that an archer's skill can be applied to firearms. Besides, none of us—including the captain—have had sufficient ammunition with which to practice. Our daimyo prefers we hoard it until we face a genuine emergency.''

''In that case,'' Grant said, ''even if you manage to plant a colony here, the barons will take it away from you, burn you out, just like the Mags did to Port Morninglight.''

''Perhaps.'' Shizuka's voice lowered in volume to a husky whisper. ''But if we have allies who might be inclined to trade guns, bullets and training with us...'' Her words trailed off.

Grant perceived her line of thought and picked it up. ''What can New Edo provide in exchange?''

"Some of the science and technology that we have revived."

"Like how you can hone a blade so sharp it cuts through anything?"

"Much of that is due to training," she responded. "But yes, that and much more."

Grant fingered his chin contemplatively. "I'm not much on making business deals, especially in circumstances like these. But your proposal has a lot of merit. First we'd have to see your tech, which means we'd have to visit New Edo."

"I'm sure that can be arranged. If we leave at daybreak, we could be back there by this time tomorrow evening."

He shook his head. "We've got our own mission to complete."

She cocked her head quizzically. "I presumed you had completed it. You questioned that man Pollard—"

"And learned very damn little," he broke in. "We know what he was doing but not the why. He didn't know, either, so we have to return to our home base and make further plans."

Shizuka ducked her head and in a genuinely regretful tone said, "That saddens me, Grant-san. I looked forward to your visit."

"Why?" he asked bluntly.

Slowly, Shizuka raised her face. In a voice so low he had to strain to hear it, she said, "There is something magnificent in your spirit, Grant-san...it is compatible with my own.'' She placed a hand on his cheek. Despite her gloves, her touch was warm and electric. ''I know you feel the same way. I see it in your eyes, hear it in your voice when you speak to me.''

Grant's throat constricted to an almost painful degree. He felt his body responding to the woman's proximity. Tentatively, he lifted his left hand and cupped the woman's cheek. In a gravelly whisper he said, ''Shizuka—''

As soon as he spoke her name, she raised herself on tiptoes, dropping her helmet at her feet. She put her arms around him, one hand at the back of his neck, forcing his head down. Grant bent and touched his lips to hers, and she responded hungrily, with an urgent, burning passion.

Almost without volition, Grant caught her up in his arms, crushing her slim figure to him, and kissed her fiercely on eyes, cheeks, lips and throat. Shizuka returned his kisses with those as tempestuous as a storm wind.

Grant had no idea how long they stood there, locked in a passionate embrace. But when he heard a faint crunch of feet on dry leaves, he reluctantly pushed her away, lifting his face from hers. At first he saw nothing, then he detected a movement in a wedge of shadow, a blurred glimpse of a white-haired head.

Tension knotted in his stomach like a length of rope, and he gusted out a groaning sigh. Perplexed and a little cross, Shizuka asked breathlessly, "What is it?"

Carefully, Grant disengaged himself from the woman. "I think it's time we get back to the others."

Bending to pick up her helmet from where she dropped it, Shizuka said tonelessly, "I heard her, too. You said she wasn't yours."

"She isn't," Grant replied defensively. "But she thinks I'm hers."

He started to explain further, but Shizuka said "Oh" in such a way he knew no explanations were necessary. She understood perfectly as only a woman could.

They returned to the courtyard, Grant keeping a surreptitious eye out for Domi. Although he knew Shizuka's martial skills were more than adequate to protect her from a wild attack from the girl, he wouldn't have been surprised to find his own throat on the receiving end of her knife blade.

KANE HAD NO INTENTION of remaining in the town until the last Magistrate was permitted to die. Already two of the former prisoners had inflicted so much torture they were exhausted. They sat on the edge of the pool, tired, disheveled, faces drained, blood drenched from fingertips to elbows. He wasn't certain what they had done to the Mags, but he knew sharpened stakes and knives heated to red-hot over a fire played prominent roles.

He had no idea of where Grant had disappeared to.

Unable to raise him on the comm-link, he sent Domi to find him and fetch him back. He sought out Brigid and found her in a far corner, on the opposite side of the courtyard from the pool. She sat on a crumbling concrete bench, looking very wan and not a little sick.

"I think we should pull out as soon as possible, Baptiste," he said. "It'll be easier to cross the desert at night. The water and concentrated food in the kit will get us back to the redoubt if we ration them." When she didn't immediately respond, he added, "If you feel up to it, that is."

She did not look at him. Her emerald eyes were dulled with fatigue, her face smudged by dirt. "Oh, I'm up to it," she said listlessly. "We've learned all we're likely to learn here."

"Which is precisely shit," he said, sitting beside her, revolving his helmet in his hands.

She ran her fingers through her tousled red-gold mane. "That's not quite so."

"Explain."

Drawing in a long breath, she held it and released it slowly. "I can only speculate and extrapolate, but given what we know of Baron Cobalt's activities over the past few months, I think he's more concerned with saving himself than maintaining the oligarchy as a whole."

Kane frowned at her. "I'm not going to argue about that. So, what do you think—since we made the Dulce facility useless to the barons, Cobalt is scrambling around trying to find fresh genetic material only for himself?''

She nodded. ''Exactly. In my opinion, he's preoccupied with consolidating his power base and in order to do that, he has to stay healthy.''

Kane mused, ''That may explain why he never sent another Mag squad into the Darks to avenge Abrams's defeat. Revenge is taking a back seat to plain old survival.''

''More than that,'' Brigid replied. ''Certainly, he needs to sustain himself, just like all the other barons. But it's possible he's doing so at the expense of his brother barons. He may be waiting for them to sicken and start dying off so he can conquer their villes.''

''Mebbe,'' Kane conceded doubtfully. ''But making ambitious moves like that is a pretty blasphemous thing for a baron to do. He'd be spitting not only on the unification program but on the Archon Directorate itself. One of the reasons the barons have observed a balance of power for so long is their fear that the Archons will get pissed and blow the world up again.''

Brigid massaged her temples. ''I know. But that presupposes the barons—or Cobalt at least—actually believe in the Archon Directorate anymore. Perhaps they never did.''

Kane noticed her wincing, but he didn't inquire about why. ''For the sake of argument,'' he said, ''let's say Baron Cobalt is doing what you say. But where is he processing the raw genetic material for his own private treatments? We know it's not the Anthill, and it's for damn sure not that Nazi pesthole in Antarctica. None of the villes have the necessary kind of medical facilities or know-how to perform the advanced genetic therapy the barons need to stay alive. Only Dulce had that."

"The gateway codes Pollard had on him are probably the answer," Brigid said a touch impatiently.

Thoughtfully, Kane replied, "I suppose we can input them into the controls when we get back to Redoubt Charlie and see where we end up—"

Brigid made a snorting, spitting sound of disdain. "And maybe jump into a platoon of Mags or a nest of hybrids. Use your head, Kane."

"What's your suggestion, then?" Kane shot back.

"Once we've returned to Cerberus, I'll see if I can match up the code with the index in the Cerberus network database. If we have a redoubt designation, we'll have a location and an idea of what to expect there. That's what I suggest—a modicum of preliminary investigation and planning."

Kane realized he couldn't argue with her reasoned response, and he felt slightly embarrassed. When he noticed she still rubbed the sides of her head, he asked, "Head hurt?"

"Like hell," she answered. "But it's controllable. DeFore said I was likely to experience headaches for a couple of months, particularly after periods of exertion. It'll pass."

"I tried to get you to sit this op out."

"I've been convalescing long enough." Her tone had an edge to it, and Kane dropped the subject.

Once again he silently marveled at Brigid Baptiste's stamina. She was one of the toughest people he had ever met. For a woman who had been trained to be an academic, a scholar and had never strayed more than ten miles from the sheltering walls of Cobaltville, her resiliency and resourcefulness never failed to impress him. Over the past year, she had left her tracks in the most distant and alien of climes and walked in very deep, very dangerous waters.

Both of them had come a very long way—in distances that could not be measured in mere miles—from the night of their first meeting in the residential Enclaves.

Kane gazed across the courtyard where the Tigers of Heaven prepared a litter for the wounded Ibichi. "What do you think of our new friends?" he asked. "Pretty amazing how their swords cut through armor."

Brigid shrugged. "They've probably laser sharpened the edges to only a few molecules thick. It's an old technique." She angled a questioning eyebrow at him. "Besides, don't you think it's a little premature to call them friends?"

"They helped us."

"Only because we could help them. Pretty much an alliance of convenience all the way around."

"Sometimes," he declared, "that's how friendships are forged. I think you and I are the perfect examples of that.''

Brigid smiled for the first time since they entered the ruins of the town, a lopsided lifting of a corner of her mouth. ''Whatever you say, Kane.''

Domi reappeared, stalking with a stiff-legged stride beneath the arch over the entranceway. ''Did you find him?'' Kane called out to her.

She didn't answer or even deign to look in his direction. She only gestured behind her, a snapping, almost dismissive wave of one arm. ''What the hell is going on with her now?'' Kane wondered aloud.

When Grant entered the courtyard with Shizuka at his side, Brigid nodded toward them. ''You should probably ask them.''

Repressing an exasperated groan, Kane pushed himself to his feet and crossed the courtyard to meet the pair. Brigid followed a moment later. ''We're ready to move out,'' Kane said, without preamble.

Shizuka regarded him in mild surprise. ''Now? A night march?''

''Why not? Easier to walk at night wearing this armor than in the heat of the day.''

''What about the stuff we left in the riverbed?'' Grant asked.

''Leave it,'' Kane replied. ''I don't feel like backtracking, especially through the field of snakes again.''

The big man nodded. ''I guess crossing the desert

at night makes sense." He didn't sound happy about it, however.

Kiyomasa sauntered over to them. His foul humor over killing Pollard quickly rather than shoving red-hot coals in his mouth followed by his testicles seemed to have disappeared. Politely, he said, "We thank you for your help in bringing these murderers to judgment and for rescuing our friends from slavery."

They rescued them from a fate worse than slavery, Kane thought but he said only, "Our pleasure."

Kiyomasa hesitated, then said in a burst, "New Edo would be most interested in striking an official alliance with you and the powers you represent, Kane-san. Now that you are aware of our existence, perhaps we may be of some service to each other in the future."

Kane smiled wryly. "I was thinking along much the same lines. But how do we reach New Edo?"

From inside his breastplate, Kiyomasa produced a folded square of yellow parchment. "I wrote this down a few minutes ago. It is the longitudinal coordinates of our island." He handed it to Brigid, saying, "It is Japanese, but I'm sure you can translate the ideograms, since you show such a facility with our language."

Brigid wasn't sure if she was being mocked, so she opted to bow and reply, *"Ah domo arigato."*

All of the Tigers of Heaven assembled around the three outlanders, Ibichi included, leaning on a crutch made from a piece of broken rafter. They bowed deeply, murmuring *"Arigato"* and *"Sayonara."*

Domi wasn't interested in taking part in the formal farewells. She had already stalked to the courtyard entrance and stood beneath the arch, her eyes snapping with impatience.

"If the winds of fate wish it to be so, they will blow us to each other very soon," Shizuka whispered to Grant.

"If the winds of fate will it," he responded in the same low voice. He cast a sideways glance toward Domi, making sure both her blaster and knife were securely leathered. "Among other things."

Chapter 16

Front Royal, a ville in Virginia, was not greatly changed since the time of the inaugural Council of Front Royal nearly a century before. Siege damage had been repaired long ago to the ville, restoring its former appearance of a medieval castle. The towers and turrets and observation eyries overlooked a wide, green valley. The weathered bricks and blocks were clean of vines and lichens. The main building, the keep, rose above the walls in a defiant thrust of chiseled stone, stained-glass windows and forged steel.

The ville was enclosed by walls nearly half a mile in circumference and fifty feet tall, offering flat buttresses of impregnable fortifications. The walls in turn were surrounded by a river with only a single bridge that crossed it into a central, cobblestoned plaza.

As one of the concessions to modern times, powerful halogen spotlights were mounted both on the walls and atop the turrets. Projecting from each corner of the walls were Vulcan-Phalanx gun towers, the heavy weapons ready and waiting to fend off any sort of attack.

Front Royal was not occupied except by a skeleton maintenance staff and a garrison consisting of twenty soldiers. It was not a ville in the conventional sense, but more of a neutral zone, a place where the barons could meet on equal terms. It was the birthplace of the Program of Unification when the nine most powerful barons from across the Deathlands put aside their differences and regional jealousies in order to consolidate their collective strength and unite the nation under their control. A mysterious emissary named Thrush issued an ultimatum to the barons: either they would agree to the principles of the unification program or they would face devastation on a scale unrivaled since the nukecaust. In exchange for their agreement, the barons would have access to predark technology and techniques of social engineering that would further extend their control over an unsuspecting populace.

In Erica van Sloan's opinion, Front Royal was not much of a substitute for Camp David. That the barons preferred to maintain its quaint, Old World architecture, as fake as it was, in lieu of redesigning it to resemble the Administrative Monoliths in the villes was not much of an improvement. The main hall of the keep was immense. Its heavy-beamed ceiling and waxed, oak-paneled walls always danced with the light of a hundred false electric candles in the wrought-iron chandelier.

The floor was of polished marble in swirling, indefinable patterns. At the far end was a hearth big enough to comfortably sleep four barons and two of the security staff. A yard-long electric log always glowed there.

Despite its tasteful furnishings, the place was so obviously faux it almost reached the point of being funny. Erica van Sloan could not help but be reminded of theme parks built to emulate King Arthur's Camelot or some other place that probably never existed outside of the imagination.

As far as she knew, none of the barons objected to the installation of a mat-trans unit within a shielded cubicle, complete with stripped-down control room, on the opposite side of the main hall. Erica did not think the six-sided elevated chamber with its sky-blue armaglass walls added or detracted from the Old World feel of the big room. It simply stood there, at the far end of the control room, like an ugly conversation piece.

Sitting in her wheelchair in the control room, she tensed—or made an attempt to—when she heard the characteristic high-pitched drone exuding from the emitter array within the platform. The sound was an electronic synthesis between a hurricane howl and bee-swarm hum, dropping to inaudibility as the mat-trans unit cycled through another materialization.

The noise was nerve-racking, but she didn't bother trying to make out the vague shape shifting on the other side of the translucent armaglass shielding. She knew who would be standing there within the walls, and so she saw no need to sit and wait for the delegates to arrive one by one. She was sure the matter-stream and destination codes were locked on their automatic settings.

Blowing into the air-pipe control, Erica turned her wheelchair from the comp station and rolled toward the conference room. She resolutely avoided looking in the direction of the monitor screens, glass-encased control boards or anything that might reflect her appearance. Behind her she heard the click of solenoids as the heavy slab of armaglass that served as the chamber's door swung open on counterbalanced hinges.

She knew mist swirled thickly within with thready static electricity discharges arcing within the billowing mass. The mist was simply a byproduct of the quantum interface, a plasma wave form that only resembled vapor. Before she reached the corridor, the low-pitched hum arose again.

Born in 1974 by the old calendar, Erica van Sloan still viewed the matter-transfer machines more akin to magic than science, like leftover props from the science-fiction films and TV shows she had enjoyed as a child. Unlike similar devices in celluloid fiction, the gateway units had never been responsible for ghastly accidents, like transposing a human subject's head with that of a fly's, or splitting a man into his positive and negative halves. At least as far as she knew.

She really didn't know the entire history of the quantum interphase mat-trans inducers despite being assigned to Operation Chronos, the sister subdivision of Project Cerberus. As a cybernetic specialist, she understood in theory how the quantum energies released by the gateways transformed organic and inorganic matter to digital information, transmitted it along a hyperdimensional pathway and reassembled it in a receiver unit.

To accomplish this, the mat-trans units required an inestimable number of maddeningly intricate electronic procedures, all occurring within milliseconds of one another, to minimize the margins for error. The actual matter-to-energy conversion process was sequenced by an array of computers and microprocessors, with a number of separate but overlapping operational cycles.

With another exhalation of breath into the control stem, the wheelchair turned right with a squeaking of rubber tires and the buzz of an electric motor. As per the established policy, she encountered no one else. All of the servants and guards were forbidden to enter the bottom level of the keep, particularly when the barons were present.

Erica entered a room that seemed to stretch for a mile. The floor, the walls, the ceiling, all were made of a slick, slightly reflective vanadium alloy. Not only was the sheathing for security purposes, but also it provided protection just in case a Roamer or a Preservationist—or even Kane and Grant—fired a LAW rocket at the keep.

At the far end was a conference table, a highly polished twelve-foot-diameter oval of rare and expensive teak. Erica rolled past the nine chairs around the table, noting expressionlessly that one of the chairs would remain vacant. Another puff of air brought her chair to a halt near the head of the table, where she waited and remembered.

Dr. Erica van Sloan was of half Latino and half British extraction. She had inherited her dark hair and eyes from her Brazilian mother, but she possessed her father's tall frame and long, solid legs. God only knew from which side of her family her 200 point IQ derived, but she knew she received her beautiful singing voice from her mother.

At eighteen years of age, the haughty, beautiful and more than a trifle arrogant Erica earned her Ph.D. in cybernetics and computer science. She wanted to pursue a singing career, but within days of her graduation from Cal Tech she went to work for a major Silicon Valley hardware producer as a models and systems analyst.

Eight months later, she left her six-figure annual salary to accept a position with a government-sponsored ultra-top-secret undertaking known as Overproject Whisper. Only much later did she realize Whisper was a major division of something called the Totality Concept, and she was assigned to one of its subdivisions, Operation Chronos. In the vast installation beneath a mesa in Dulce, New Mexico, she served as the subordinate, lover and occasional victim of a man who made her own officious personality seem mousy and shy by comparison.

Torrence Silas Burr was brilliant, stylish, waspish and nasty. He excelled at using his enormous intellect and equally enormous ego to fuel his cruel sense of humor. He delighted in belittling and degrading not just her, but other scientists assigned to Overproject Whisper. The one scientist he could not deride was Mohandas Lakesh Singh, the genius responsible for the final technological breakthrough of Project Cerberus, which permitted Operation Chronos to finally make some headway.

Although the Totality Concept projects were rarely coordinated, the techs of Operation Chronos used Singh's mat-trans discoveries to spin off their own innovations and achieve their own successes. Operation Chronos dealt in the mechanics of time travel, forcing temporal breaches in an attempt to enter "probability gaps" between one interval of time and another. Inasmuch as Project Cerberus utilized quantum events to reduce organic and inorganic material to digital information and transmit it through hyperdimensional space, Operation Chronos built on that same principle to peep into other timelines and even "trawl" living matter from the past and the future.

Although more than one hapless human being was snatched from the past and brought forward into the present, there had been only one proved success with a trawling subject, who arrived in the twentieth century sane in mind and sound of body. After many failures, his subdivision successfully retrieved a living subject from a past timeline, a scientist from the nineteenth century. However, the subject proved so very troublesome he was finally removed from Dulce.

Not too long after that, a series of sweeping policy changes came into play, which created something far beyond the scientific ambitions of the Totality Concept staff. Other government agencies became involved, as well as other countries.

With the advent of the Cerberus success, the redoubts were built, linked to each other by gateway units. Though the Continuity of Government facilities and the redoubt scientific enclaves were not part of the same program, there was an almost continuous trade-off of design specifications, technology and personnel. Many of the Totality Concept's subdivisions and spin-off researches were relocated to COG redoubts. Operation Chronos was moved to Chicago and Project Cerberus was moved to Montana.

The most ambitious COG facility was code-named the Anthill because of its resemblance in layout to an ant colony. It was a vast complex, with a railway, stores, theaters and even a sports arena. Supplies of foodstuffs, weapons and anything of value were stockpiled.

Because of its size, the Anthill was built inside Mount Rushmore, using tunneling and digging machines. The entire mountain was honeycombed with interconnected levels, passageways and chambers.

Erica learned that once construction on the Anthill was completed, the entire Totality Concept program would be moved into it. She could not understand why, and when she spoke to Burr of her confusion, he spoke cryptically of the "Jamais vous principle," referring to a time-perception disorder.

He spoke darkly of a probability-wave dysfunction that Operation Chronos had triggered when it disrupted the chronon structure. He claimed they had inadvertently created an alternate-future scenario for humanity, and it wasn't one he cared to live in.

Burr hinted that the frenzied construction of the redoubts was due to his report of the dysfunction, and if the Totality Concept researches had been left to molder in old military intelligence files at the end of World War II, the alternate-future scenario would never have come into existence. There was no stopping it, there was only surviving it and he wasn't very sanguine about humanity's chances.

He declared vehemently he had no intention of voluntarily imprisoning himself in the Anthill. He would make his own plans, utilizing the Jamais vous principle he had created. Erica only saw him once more after that, secretly removing files and computer diskettes from his office. It was Christmas Eve, 2000. She could have wished him the season's greetings or she could have logged in the security violation and had him executed, but by then she was too emotionally wrung out to do either.

She did not miss Burr once she arrived in the Anthill to begin her new duties. There were far more immediate concerns to attend to than the fate of her former boss and lover, whom she despised anyway.

When the world blew out on noon of January 20, 2001, she ceased to think about him at all. Like everyone else in the installation, she prayed the safety measures would kick in as they were designed to. But despite all of their precautions, radiation still trickled in. Bomb-triggered earthquakes caused extensive damage.

Since the military and government personnel in charge had no choice but to remain in the facility, it took them awhile to realize they were just as much victims of the nukecaust as those whom they referred to as the "useless eaters" of the world. Erica van Sloan could not help but laugh to herself over the grim irony. She remembered how a fringe movement called survivalism had gained popularity, primarily among ex-military and rural people with various political axes to grind.

They trained and indoctrinated themselves so thoroughly to survive Armageddon, some of them actually began to look forward to it. They deluded themselves into believing a postholocaust world would be better than the one they lived in. They aspired to have a world where the romance of the frontier spirit would be revived, free of government regulations, laws and moral obligations, where a human being's worth would be measured only in how willing he or she was to kill a child for a crumb of food.

Most of the government people in the Anthill viewed survivalists as brain-damaged paranoids. But as the second anniversary of the nukecaust passed, it became patently obvious the men who knew in advance about the atomic megacull were just as stupendously ill-informed as the survivalists at whom they had once sneered.

Like their less educated counterparts, they had no real grasp of the scope of the global devastation. None of their painstaking calculations regarding acceptable losses, destruction ratios and the length of the nuclear winter bore any resemblance to the terrifying reality.

When this select few, this powerful elite, finally did come to terms with reality, it was too late to do much about it. They had assumed that after five years or less of waiting inside the Anthill, a new world order would be in place. Now the schedule appeared to be closer to twenty. Erica recalled how General Kettridge would rant about how "they" had lied to them, about how "they" had deceived them. But Kettridge tended to rant and rave at the slightest pretext anyway, so she suppressed her curiosity about the identities of "they."

The prolonged nuclear winter changed ideas about a new world order. Even if the personnel managed to outlast the big freeze, the skydark, they would still sicken and die, either from radiation sickness or simply old age.

So they embarked on a radical and daring plan. Cybernetic technology had made great leaps in the latter part of the twentieth century, and Erica herself had made some small contributions to those advances. General Kettridge ordered operations to be performed

on everyone living in the Anthill, making use of the
new techniques in organ transplants and medical technology, as well as in cybernetics.

Over a period of years, everyone living inside
Mount Rushmore was turned into cyborgs, hybridi-
zations of human and machine. Radiation-burned
flesh was replaced by synthetic skin, limbs with can-
cerous marrows were changed out for ones made of
plastic, Dacron and Teflon. With less energy to expend on maintaining the body, the cyborganized subjects ate less and therefore extended the stockpile of
foodstuffs by several years.

Since the main difficulty in constructing interfaces
between mechanical-electric and organic systems was
the wiring, Erica oversaw the implantation of super-
conducting quantum interface devices or SQUIDs, directly into the brain. One-hundredth of a micron
across, SQUIDs facilitated the subject's control over
the new prostheses.

Although Erica herself had designed the implants
and oversaw the early operations, she certainly did
not care for the process being performed on her. She
knew that SQUIDs could be used to electronically
control their subjects, and she wasn't fond of being
turned into a biomechanical drone. However, she was
even less fond of the alternative—euthanasia.

Of course, the transformations did not solve all of
the Anthill's survival issues. Compensation for the
natural aging process of organs and tissues had to be
taken into account. The Anthill personnel needed a

supply of fresh organs, preferably those of young people, but obviously the supply was severely limited. So General Kettridge, now calling himself the Commander in Chief, came up with a solution—cryogenics, or a variation thereof.

Kettridge was inspired by the method of keeping organic materials fresh by pumping a hermetically sealed vault full of dry nitrogen gas and lowering the temperature to below freezing. He ordered the internal temperatures inside the installation to be lowered just enough to preserve the tissues but not low enough to damage the organs.

Other scientific disciplines were blended. The interior of the entire facility was permeated with low-level electrostatic fields of the kind hospitals experimented with to maintain the sterility of operating rooms. The form of cryogenesis employed at the installation was not the standard freezing process relying on immersing a subject in liquid nitrogen and the removal of blood and organs.

Rather, it utilized a technology that employed a stasis screen tied in with the electrostatic sterilizing fields, which for all intents and purposes turned the Anthill complex into an encapsulated deep-storage vault. This process created a form of active suspended animation, almost as if the personnel were enclosed by an impenetrable bubble of space and time, slowing to a crawl all metabolic processes. The people achieved a form of immortality, but one completely dependent on technology.

Erica never wondered aloud where the stasis technology came from, but she assumed it derived from the mysterious "they" whom Kettridge accused of betrayal.

However, even those measures were temporary. Erica volunteered to enter a stasis canister for a period of time, to be resurrected at some future date when the sun shone again and the world was secure.

When Erica awakened, more than a century had passed. During her long slumber, the Anthill installation suffered near catastrophic damage. General Kettridge was killed and a number of stasis units malfunctioned, including her canister.

Due to that malfunction, her SQUIDs device had inflicted neurological damage on her body, and she was resurrected as a cripple. Worse than finding out her long, shapely legs were little more than withered sticks was learning the plans made for her while she slept.

Erica was briefed on the Program of Unification and the baronial oligarchy, and the true identities of Kettridge's "they" were finally revealed. Or at least, they were given a name—Archons. She was told that to be of optimal use to the Archon Directorate and their hybrid plenipotentiaries, the barons, she needed to be as fit as it was possible for a human in her physical condition and chronological age. Moreover, Erica was informed she was only one of several preholocaust humans, known as "freezies" in current vernacular, resurrected to serve the baronies and she should consider herself fortunate to be among their number.

In other words, she was not to grieve, mourn, weep or otherwise feel sorry for herself. She was to concentrate only on what her technological skills could contribute to the furtherance of the Program of Unification. Otherwise, she would be put out of her misery.

Erica was not assigned to any particular ville for any length of time. She was given quarters in Front Royal, and from there she traveled from barony to barony, setting up their computer systems, training personnel in their operation and in troubleshooting procedures. The systems, although in absolutely pristine order, were not state-of-the art, certainly not by the standards of the first year of the twenty-first century.

None of the mainframes employed the biochip developments that would have been commonplace if the nukecaust had been averted. Most of the software, hardware and support systems were fairly basic, as well. Erica could not help but suspect that the truly advanced predark tech was being deliberately suppressed. She could only assume it was done out of fear of the new postnuke society becoming just as dependent on technology as the old one.

Whatever the real reason, she learned quickly not to question. Over the years of Erica's long life, due to the creativity and skills of her intellect, she had undergone many organ transplants so as to extend her value to the united baronies. Despite the pain and suffering that had accompanied each successive operation, Erica never regained the use of her legs, and the neurological degeneration grew so acute she became a complete cripple.

The cost of every one of those years of agony showed in her face, and so she always tried to avert her eyes from a reflective surface, even the highly polished tabletop. Erica had never grown accustomed to the craggy, seamed face staring back at her from mirrors or even windows. Her hair, though still as black as the night, was so thin and straggly she usually wore it pulled back in a tight knot at the nape of her wattled neck.

She wore a nondescript gray coverall, which was baggy on her small and scrawny frame. Only her jet-black eyes seemed to show any life, blazing in her deeply lined face, glinting with impatience.

Erica was anxious for the session to begin. Since cybernetic principles were applied to management and organizational theory, she always had much to offer in the way of streamlining ville government. Just as everything that occurred in the universe could be reduced to cause-and-effect chains, the chains themselves could be used to build organizational models.

Now, months after the disaster at the Dulce site, a new model urgently needed to be constructed, and so Erica sat in the council chamber and waited for the barons to arrive. They needed her input, not simply so they could determine a course of action, but also to stay alive. She was less a moderator of the meeting than a mother figure.

Erica repressed a bleak smile and wondered what she should tell them.

Chapter 17

The baronial council was in full session, with all eight surviving barons in attendance. They filed into the room, moving with a bizarrely beautiful, danceresque grace.

All of them were dressed identically in the ceremonial garb of the baronial oligarchy—flowing, bell-sleeved robes of gold brocade and tall, conical, crested headpieces, ringed by nine rows of tiny pearls.

No one, not even the humans who had advised them for years like Erica van Sloan, knew from whence the tradition of ceremonial attire sprang. She always presumed the design had something to do with Archon culture, whatever that might be. Baron Thulia's adviser, a man named Bakshmi, had told her in an unguarded moment that there was a marked similarity between the barons' garb and that of Tibetan high lamas. If indeed the entities called Archons had influenced humanity since the dawn of time, then it stood to reason they had interacted with Tibetans.

Not only was the barons' mode of dress identical, but they were also so similar in appearance they might have been born from the same mother and father. In many ways, they had been.

Their builds were small, slender and gracile. All of their faces had sharp planes, with finely complexioned skin stretched tight over prominent shelves of cheekbones. The craniums were very high and smooth, the ears small and set low on the head. Their backslanting eyes were large, shadowed by sweeping, supraorbital ridges. Only hair, eye color and slight differences in height differentiated them.

Baron Beausoleil was the only female of the oligarchy, but she, too, had the same wispy hair the texture of duck down, although hers was dark with reddish highlights.

All in all, they were a beautiful people, almost too perfect to be real. But their eyes glittered under the muted lights with wariness or suspicion, or a combination of both. Baron Sharpe's eyes, the clear blue color of mountain meltwater, held another spark, a glint that in a human being might have been interpreted as a sign of dementia.

Even their expressions were markedly similar—a vast pride, a diffident superiority, authority and even ruthlessness. They were the barons, and as such, they were the avatars of the new humans who would inherit the Earth.

Before they seated themselves at the table, they faced one another and moved with a swaying motion, like reeds before a breeze. The movements were very precise, very ritualistic, and Erica knew it was a form of a ceremonial greeting. It seemed a behavior instinctive rather than learned, perhaps encoded in their hybridized genes.

After they had taken their chairs, Erica spoke first in a hoarse, dry croak not much above a whisper. Her most recent vocal cord transplants had worn out a decade ago. "This, my lord barons, is a historic first."

Cobalt's eyes flashed a quick acknowledgment of her opening statement. The big irises were a beautiful yellowish-brown in color, only a few shades darker than his complexion. "We are here to make sure it is not a historic last, Adviser Sloan." His voice was musical, like a melody played on a flute.

Baron Thulia snorted through delicate nostrils. He was much like the atmosphere of the extreme Northeastern territories he claimed—impenetrable. A white wisp of a man, his thin, feathered hair resembled a patina of early-morning frost, and his movements reminded Erica of the shifting of mist. "Let us dispense with the amenities and fripperies, then. We all know why we are here."

Without preamble, Erica said flatly, "I've completed the calculations. By the model I constructed, all of you have a maximum of three months of relative health and vitality left to you. After that, I can only approximate the degree of deterioration. That depends upon your individual metabolisms. Regardless, your autoimmune systems will definitely fail. I believe it is safe to say that inside of eight months, the entire oligarchy will be dead."

None of the barons spoke for a long time. A high,

wild tittering from Baron Sharpe broke the silence. He put his fingers to his mouth as if to cram the giggling back in. "Pardon me," he murmured, then he giggled again.

The barons ignored the outburst. Of all the oligarchy, Sharpe displayed the most human range of emotional characteristics, all of them unstable. He was driven by capricious whims and ridiculous impulses. They all knew of his bizarre delusion that he had died before and crossed back and was therefore immortal. He was further distinguished by the fact he was the only baron other than Cobalt who had faced off against Kane.

"The Dulce facility is beyond repair?" Baron Beausoleil inquired.

The woman's black hair, pulled back from a pronounced widow's peak on her high forehead, fell down her back as straight as a frozen flow of India ink. Her teardrop-shaped face was of marble whiteness, and her slanting eyes were a deep violet in color. Those eyes, rich with suspicion, flicked back and forth between Cobalt and Sharpe.

Erica had wondered a time or two why Beausoleil had not taken the title of baroness, but she supposed it had something to do with the patriarchal tradition of the ruling class. More than likely, only her personal staff in her ville knew she was female.

Samarium answered her question. "The damage is, for all intents and purposes, total."

"How do you know?" Baron Palladium inquired.

He had a languid, scholarly manner about him, but there was nothing relaxed in his gimlet hard green eyes. He was frightened.

"Brother Sharpe and I toured it a short time ago. The nursery and gestation facilities are completely unusable and unrepairable. Therefore, it is far more logical to relocate what can be salvaged to a new installation."

Rather heavyset for a hybrid, Baron Mande shifted in his chair. The expression on his face was one of perpetual disapproval. "If one exists. None of the redoubts in our territories has the necessary equipment to begin immediate treatment. And then there is the lack of material with which to work—"

"Yes," Baron Snakefish broke in. "That is another subject with which we must deal." Long hair as yellow as flax was tied back with a coil of silver, and his piercing silver-gray eyes bored in on Cobalt. "The limited supply of genetic material stored in Dulce was destroyed. Even if we located another properly outfitted installation in any of our territories, we no longer have an efficient method by which to harvest and transport replacement merchandise."

He employed the old euphemism for raw human tissue and organs. Snakefish dropped his voice to a ghostly, sepulchral croon as he addressed Baron Cobalt. "However, there are inefficient ways. For example, two days ago I received a strange report from my Outlands territories. A seaside settlement had been completely wiped out. Massacred. Oddly, only the infirm and the old were killed.

"Further investigation deeper into the zone turned up a number of dead Magistrates. Curiously, several of them carried ville scrip." The man paused and added almost nonchalantly, "Cobaltville scrip."

One by one, the eyes of the assembled barons turned toward Cobalt, who sat with his slender arms crossed over his chest. His face acquired an expression of detached amusement.

"So," Baron Snakefish continued, "if you were wondering when your troops would return, allow me to set your mind at rest. They will never come back. Whoever killed them made certain of that."

"My lord, I believe your family is waiting for some kind of explanation," Erica van Sloan ventured.

Baron Cobalt's brow ridges arched. "I owe no one an explanation, Adviser. However, for the sake of discussion, let us assume for the nonce I dispatched a squad of Magistrates to brother Snakefish's territory."

"If so," Baron Palladium intoned, his voice silky soft and menacing, "let us assume you intentionally violated the treaty."

"Treaties made nearly a century ago did not take into account matters of survival," Cobalt retorted coldly. "Each and every one of us has the right to defend their villes. And to do so we must stay alive. And to stay alive, we must take drastic action."

He nodded, tilting his crested headpiece in the direction of the one vacant chair. "Consider what has happened to the late brother Ragnar's ville since his unfortunate assassination. All the decision and policy making is in the hands of his staff and his division administrators. All of them humans.''

The last word passed his lips like a drop of venom. ''Word has leaked out the baron is dead. Riots in the Pits are daily occurrences, chaos runs unchecked. Do we wish the same fate for our own villes? A return to the anarchy of the Deathlands?''

''It is not our place to violate the treaty, regardless of the cause,'' Beausoleil snapped. ''Such crises are within the purview of the Archon Directorate.''

Cobalt chuckled, but the sound did not warm the blood. It was a low, dry rustle of contempt. ''I am both shocked and saddened that any of you still subscribe to that pathetic belief. You are like human children praying to a savior for deliverance. There is no Archon Directorate. I doubt if ever there was. Keep in mind that everything we were led to believe about the Directorate was conveyed to us by—'' he cut his eyes over to Erica ''—humans.''

Erica felt paralyzed by shock, but she was able to mask it. She had never totally accepted the hard reality of the so-called Archons, regardless of what she had been told upon her resurrection. She had focused on the hybrid barons themselves, their physiology, linguistic modes and social patterns.

Whatever they really were, mutants or the final phase of a genetic experiment, they were intrinsically superior to man, but less effective, as well. Without the supervision of the Archon Directorate, the superior qualities of the barons would eventually breed superior ambition, even though none of them had ever displayed such behavior before.

Never had it occurred to her that any of the barons would ever doubt the existence of the Archons. With a sinking sensation in the pit of her stomach, she realized that regardless of their indoctrination, not even the nine barons really knew who the Archons were or where they came from.

Eventually it would occur to them how they actually knew little more than the same dogma they shared with members of the Trust, the inner circle of their respective villes. However, she was less disquieted by Baron Cobalt's sneering dismissal than by the lack of outraged reaction to it among the others. She then understood all of them had reached the same conclusion as he had.

"With all due respect, my lord," Erica rasped, "if you are not a bridge between the Archons and humanity, then what are you? From whence do you come?"

Cobalt's eyes blazed with haughty, imperious anger. "Why ask me, Adviser?" he hissed. "You should know the answer to that better than I, better than any of us."

Erica did not reply and decided to say nothing more. As an adviser, her authority was purely informal. She was not safe from the wrath of any of the barons.

Cobalt returned his attention to the assembly. "In the past few months we've witnessed the most blatant examples of violence against the baronies since the institution of the unification program. Where are the Archons?"

Everyone elected to remain silent.

"I believe all of you have suspected the same thing as I," Baron Cobalt declared. "As the baronial hierarchy acts the control mechanism for the human race, the myth of the all-seeing, all-powerful Archon Directorate acted as the control mechanism for the barons. Our belief in them curbed our individual initiative."

"That is what you call covertly sending your troops to my territory—individual initiative?" Baron Snakefish snapped.

"No," Cobalt retorted. "I call it insuring my survival."

Thulia eyed him distrustfully. "How? Even if you abducted the healthy people from the settlement, without processing facilities your actions are pointless and unconscionable. If the rest of us so desire, we can interpret such an incursion as an act of war."

Baron Cobalt favored him with a thin, smug smile. "Declaring war on the one man who can save you— all of you—would be the pointless act, my brother."

That self-confident, arrogant pronouncement elicited a scandalized reaction from the barons at the conference table. The babble of suspicious questions, demands for clarification and aspersions on Cobalt's sanity reached a point where all of them spoke at once. Although Erica felt it was her duty to restore some kind of order, her voice was not strong enough to be heard over the cacophony. Besides, she wasn't inclined to draw attention to herself.

Baron Cobalt sat through it all, smiling his coldly aloof smile. Finally, when the questions and insults trailed away, he declared, "Unlike the rest of you, once I learned of the destruction of the Dulce facility, I did not enter into a state of denial or wait for the Archon Directorate to save me. I embarked on a search for an alternative."

"As did we all," Samarium growled.

"Unlike you," Cobalt continued, "I found one."

Baron Mande leaned forward, his eyes wide. "Where?" he demanded skeptically. "Not the Anthill."

"No. My scouts reported that place would be useless to our needs."

Snakefish's lips twisted in anger. "You sent scouts there?"

Erica van Sloan understood his anger. The Anthill was the one place forbidden to the barons, shrouded in so much secrecy it became a taboo. Since all the villes were standardized, equally matched in terms of technology and firepower to maintain a perfect balance of power, none of the barons dared mention what unclaimed wonders might still lie within Mount Rushmore.

Even a word of wonder about it might be construed

as a tendency toward ambition, something strictly forbidden by the tenets of the Program of Unification.

"Why shouldn't I?" Baron Cobalt shot back. "The installation is within my territorial jurisdiction, is it not? So, yes, I sent scouts not just there, but to all redoubts on record that were connected to bioengineering research."

"And?" Beausoleil inquired, a challenging edge to her voice.

Cobalt fluttered a dismissive hand. "Useless, all useless. During unification, everything of value was moved out of them and into Dulce. However, I managed to locate one facility that played host to a number of Totality Concept–related projects at one time or another—including Excalibur.

"Although its medical equipment is not as advanced as that in Dulce, and will require some additional work, the place will adequately serve our needs."

"Where is it?" Palladium demanded. "How did you find it?"

"To answer your questions in reverse order," Baron Cobalt replied smoothly, "I simply knew where to look. My former high adviser was senior archivist in the Historical Division. He was an antiquarian of unchallenged erudition and knew the location of every major secret base of predark America.

"After he disappeared from the ville, I had all of his personal papers and computer files analyzed. It took quite a bit of time, but that's how I found it. As for where it is—'' the cold smile stretched into an equally cold grin of malicious triumph ''—that you will only learn if you meet my terms.''

He surveyed the high-planed aristocratic faces staring at him, now all contorted in expressions of shock, fury and incredulity. Baron Sharpe laughed as if Cobalt had just reached the punchline of a particularly clever joke. ''Well played, brother!''

Cobalt's grin vanished. ''It's no game. The rule of the barons has reached a crossroads, a crisis undreamed-of by the drafters of the unification articles. All the established procedures, laws and protocols are meaningless. We cannot appeal to a higher authority, inasmuch as we all seem to be in agreement that the Archon Directorate does not exist. Therefore, an entirely new set of rules must be developed and applied if we are to continue to hold the reins of power.''

''What do you propose?'' Baron Thulia demanded.

Leaning back in his chair, Cobalt steepled his inhumanly long fingers beneath his pointed chin. ''I propose we adopt and adapt lessons from ancient history. The Roman Empire was governed by a senate but ruled by an emperor. I propose we revive that system.''

''With you,'' inquired Beausoleil darkly, ''as the imperator?''

Cobalt nodded gravely. ''I shall serve as the final arbiter in matters pertaining to ville government. Before, we always acted interdependently, unified in name only. Now we will establish a central consortium.''

Face suffused with the blood of rage, Palladium said, ''You suggest we become your viceroys, plenipotentiaries in our own territories?''

''Is that so onerous? You were content to serve as plenipotentiaries for the Archon Directorate, were you not? This is no different, except now you know exactly who is the guiding authority.'' Cobalt paused, then added gently, ''And since a slow, painful and more than likely a disgusting death is your only alternative, I think you can learn to accept it.''

The barons exchanged silent, wary glances. They looked toward Erica expectantly.

''Her input is unimportant. She has nothing to do with us,'' Cobalt snapped.

''We must have proof of your claims,'' Mande said.

''I realize that. I shall provide it—but only after I receive your assurances of cooperation.''

Beausoleil cleared her throat. ''A vote must be taken.''

''Then do so,'' Baron Cobalt said impatiently. ''A show of hands or a secret ballot will suffice. Just get on with—''

His lips suddenly writhed back over his small, perfect teeth, and a cry of pain burst from his mouth. Voice high and wild, he said, ''Get out of my head—''

As the barons and Erica van Sloan watched,

shocked into speechlessness, Cobalt fell forward onto
the table, his headpiece rolling off and falling to the
floor. He clasped the sides of his head as if he feared
his skull would break apart. Blue veins throbbed in
his temples. His "Stop it!" was a pleading cry of
agony.

A voice spoke, a hoarse, scratchy whisper. "A vote
will not be necessary."

All heads turned toward the doorway. Erica puffed
air into the control to turn her chair. Every eye was
glued to the pair of figures framed in the doorway,
backlit by the muted lighting of the corridor. Neither
figure was tall, but both of them carried a palpable
aura of otherworldliness.

Both of their bodies were draped in flowing robes
of a yellow saffron hue, almost identical to those
worn by the barons. They did not wear headpieces;
hooded cowls cast their faces in deep shadow.

The two figures stepped into the council room, the
taller of the pair holding the hand of the smaller as if
he were a toddler. He wasn't much larger than a five-
year-old child. Erica, dimly aware that her hair was
standing up stiffly on the scalp, noticed how they
walked with the same kind of bizarrely beautiful danceresque grace possessed by the barons.

Baron Snakefish was the first to recover a modicum
of his emotional equilibrium and a trace of his arrogance. "How dare you interrupt this conference?
Who are you?"

The taller figure lifted a slender arm. Six long, spidery fingers, all nearly the same length, pushed back the cowl. A low cry came from Baron Cobalt's lips when the head was revealed.

The figure's high, domed cranium narrowed to an elongated chin. His skin bore a faint grayish-pink cast, stretched drum-tight over a structure of facial bones that seemed all cheek and brow, with little in between but two great upslanting eyes like black pools. His nose was vestigial, and his small mouth only a tight, lipless slash. The huge, tear-shaped dark eyes regarded them alertly. His slit of a mouth parted. A voice issued from it, a faint, strained whisper.

"I am Balam," he said. "I am here to answer your questions about the Archon Directorate…and settle the matter of who shall lead you."

Chapter 18

The sky was a heavy, leaden gray. The snow flurries had stopped, but the wind still whipped around the high peaks, gusting over the plateau and rattling the scraps of chain-link fence. It blew over the cracked tarmac, sluicing the drifts over the far edge and down into a hell-deep abyss.

The snow sifted in thin blankets over the two gravesites on the slope at the opposite side of the plateau. The headstones glistened damply in the diffuse sunlight. Brigid stood between the two sites, her back to Beth-Li's grave. The fabricated markers bore only their last names, Cotta and Rouch. There were no other inscriptions, no birth or death dates, no poetry. She wondered briefly how many more such austere markers Farrell would fashion in the redoubt's workshop before their work was done.

When Brigid first awakened from her coma, she did not recall that Cotta was dead despite the fact she had witnessed his dismemberment in Antarctica by the mind-controlled Jacko. Curiously, though, she remembered Beth-Li Rouch was dead, even though she had not seen Domi drown her in the swimming pool.

Swallowing a sigh, she tucked her hands in the

pockets of her leather jacket and slowly surveyed the plateau. Recessed within the rock face of the mountain peak, vanadium alloy gleamed beneath peeling camo paint.

Redoubt Bravo, as it was officially designated, was from outward appearances only a sec door within stone. Surrounded by a wilderness of trees, house-sized boulders and grass, it seemed no more than a broad, wind-scoured plateau enclosed by the remains of a fence and rusted-out metal stanchions that had once been steel guardrails.

A narrow road looped and curved away from the plateau, twisting down like a path cut by a broken-backed snake writhing in its death throes. One side of the road butted up against the great, overhanging crags, and the other bordered sheer cliffs, formed when acres of mountainside collapsed during the nuke-triggered earthquakes of nearly two centuries ago.

The Montana mountain range once known as the Bitterroots but now known as the Darks was technically within Cobaltville's territorial jurisdiction, but the wilderness area was virtually unpopulated. The nearest settlement was roughly a hundred miles away and consisted of a small band of Indians, Sioux and Cheyenne. They held in superstitious regard the mountain range, believing ferocious storms and evil spirits lurked in the mountain passes, ready to devour body and soul.

Although it could not be noticed from the road, the

air or even from the plateau itself, an elaborate system of heat-sensing warning devices, night-vision scopes, vid cameras and motion sensors surrounded the perimeter of the mountain peak in triple depth. Planted within rocky clefts and concealed by camouflage netting were the uplinks with an orbiting Vela-class reconnaissance satellite and a Comsat.

Brigid was no longer impressed by the predark tech to which Cerberus had access. She had already learned its limitations. In the three days since returning from California, neither she, Bry nor Lakesh had found a mat-trans destination code that corresponded to the sequence written on Pollard's arm.

Although Lakesh reassured her that was not particularly unusual given the number of unindexed modular gateway units that were shipped all over the world, Brigid wondered if her own memory was the true culprit. She had not spoken of her fear that her memory might be failing her after the concussion she suffered, not even to DeFore. But the fact she had to be reminded of Cotta's bloody death, which had occurred right before her eyes, scared her. She tried to convince herself she had been so traumatized that her conscious mind blanked out the memory, but that explanation did not sit well.

Another gust of icy wind caused her to shiver. Although it was still autumn in the flatlands, winter came early to such high altitudes. Still, she preferred to be outside, rather than spending another futile five hours planted before a computer terminal, staring at columns of scrolling numbers.

Brigid heard a clanking, rumbling sound and she turned to see the sec door opening. The massive, multiton vanadium alloy sec gate was one of only two ways to enter the redoubt. Operated by a punched-in code and a hidden lever control, the gate opened like an accordion, one monstrously dense section folding over another.

She was slightly surprised to see Lakesh step through the door and cross the tarmac toward her. His head was hunched between the padded shoulders of the long coat flapping around his skinny shanks, his hands thrust deep into the pockets. He had been born in the tropical climate of Kashmir, India, more than two hundred years before, and he claimed his internal thermostat was still stuck there. He had been a scientist then, with a doctorate in cybernetics and quantum mechanics at age nineteen. He had worked for premiere institutions before being recruited to work at the Project Cerberus site in Dulce, New Mexico, eventually achieving the post of project overseer.

In early January of 2001, most of the Cerberus staff was evacuated to the Anthill complex. After a year or so there, Lakesh elected to spend a century and a half in cryonic stasis, and though he conceded it made no real scientific sense, he had been very vulnerable to cold ever since.

Upon his revival from stasis, he had undergone several operations in order to prolong his life and his usefulness to the Program of Unification. His brown, glaucoma-afflicted eyes were replaced with new blue ones, his malfunctioning old heart exchanged for a sound new one and his lungs changed out. Although his wrinkled, liver-spotted skin made him look exceptionally old, his physiology was that of a fifty-year-old man's.

Calcified arthritic joints in his shoulders and legs were removed and built with ones made of polyethylene. None of the reconstructive surgeries or physiological enhancements had been performed out of samaritan impulses. His life and health had been prolonged so he could serve the Program of Unification and the baronies.

As Lakesh struggled up the slope toward her, the breeze tousled his thin hair, the color and texture of ash. He took a misstep and stumbled. He uttered a breathless curse as he paused to adjust the thick-lensed eyeglasses with the hearing aid attached to the right eyepiece, seating them firmly on his long nose.

By the time Lakesh reached her, he was panting, his breath pluming in front of his face and fogging his glasses. "Dearest Brigid," he wheezed, "I thought I might find you out here."

"Were you looking for me?"

"In a way, yes. I thought we might continue the destination-code search with an ancillary database."

Brigid sighed. "Yes, we might. But I'm starting to wonder just how important this is. It might be more of a long-run benefit to translate the coordinates Kiyomasa gave me to find New Edo.''

Lakesh regarded her keenly over the rims of his spectacles. ''If Baron Cobalt is embarking upon his own personal organ harvest by making an incursion into another baron's territory, it means he's leaving himself vulnerable for dire repercussions…providing we can discover where he's sending the merchandise.''

Brigid winced at his use of the term. ''And then what do we do? Rat him out to his brother barons? For all we know, he's colluding with others.''

''As you said, for all we know. We need to know exactly what he's up to. And why.'' When she did not respond, he continued, ''I've reconsidered our approach to this problem. Instead of fixating on the wheat, we should concentrate more on the chaff.''

Brigid frowned at him. ''A process of elimination?''

''Precisely.''

''In other words, we should focus on where the individual unit isn't.''

Lakesh bobbed his head on his wattled neck. ''Yes. If nothing else, we would narrow the search parameters and save ourselves time. Even though we don't have records of where all the modular gateway units were shipped, we know there are only a finite number of places they can be…at least in this hemisphere.''

Thoughtfully, Brigid replied, ''Makes sense. We've

already exhausted all of the Totality Concept–related redoubts and the indexed Cerberus network.''

Another gust of wind blew swirling snowflakes in front of Lakesh's face. He flinched, shivered and asked through chattering teeth, ''Then may we get back to it?''

The two people left the slope, went across the plateau and entered the partially open sec door. Lakesh pulled down the green lever on the wall to close it completely. Just below the control, rendered in garish primary colors, was a large illustration of a froth-mouthed black hound. Three snarling heads grew out of a single, exaggeratedly muscled neck, their jaws spewing flame and blood between great fangs. Three pairs of crimson eyes blazed malevolently. Underneath the image, in an ornate Gothic script, was written the single word Cerberus.

The mythological guardian of the gateway to Hades was an appropriate totem for the installation that was dedicated to ripping open gateways in the quantum stream.

The Cerberus redoubt was a subterranean labyrinth of corridors, offices, laboratories and chambers that had been built within the mountain. The main corridor, twenty feet wide, was made of softly gleaming vanadium alloy and shaped like a square with an arch on top. Great curving ribs of metal and massive girders supported the high rock roof.

From the main corridor, side passages and elevators led to a well-equipped armory, bunk rooms, a cafeteria, a decontamination center, an infirmary, a gymnasium with a pool, and a detention area.

The redoubt had been constructed to provide a comfortable home for well over a hundred people. There were far, far fewer than that now, and for most of the dozen permanent residents who labored there, time was measured by the controlled dimming and brightening of lights to simulate sunrise and sunset.

When Lakesh had reactivated the installation some thirty years before, the repairs he made had been primarily cosmetic in nature. He had been forced to work in secret and completely alone, so the upgrades had taken several years to complete. Still a masterpiece of impenetrability even after two centuries, the Cerberus redoubt had weathered the nukecaust and skydark, and all the subsequent changes. Its radiation shielding was still intact, and its nuclear generators on the bottom level still provided an almost eternal source of power.

The nerve center of the installation was the central operations complex. A long room with high, vaulted ceilings, it was lined by consoles of dials and switches, and divided by an aisle of computer stations. A huge Mercator relief map of the world spanned one wall. Pinpoints of light shone steadily in almost every country and were connected by a thin pattern of glowing lines. They represented the Cerberus network, the locations of all indexed functioning gateway units across the planet.

On the far side of the center was an anteroom, and

on the far side of that stood a mat-trans unit, the first fully functional, debugged gateway in the Project Cerberus network. The jump chamber was enclosed on all sides by eight-foot-high slabs of translucent, brown-tinted armaglass.

Bry and Wegmann stood beside the biolink telemetric monitor, making adjustments on it. Bry nodded his copper-curled head in a greeting. A round-shouldered man of small stature, his white bodysuit bagged on him. He served as something of Lakesh's apprentice.

Wegmann paid no attention to Brigid and Lakesh at all as they passed by, which was not unusual. In his mid-thirties, he was no more than five and a half feet tall, weighing maybe 140 pounds, which made him the smallest exile, except for Domi.

Brigid knew despite his unprepossessing physical appearance he was a scrapper and a mechanical genius. He also was something of a misanthrope, preferring the company of the nuke generators to his fellow exiles. But no one took his loner traits seriously, not after the way he risked his life to expose and to thwart a conspiracy to kill Brigid, Grant and Kane.

The biolink medical monitor they worked on was tied into the subcutaneous transponders every person in the redoubt carried within their bodies. The transponders were nonharmful radioactive chemicals that fit themselves into the human body, and allowed the monitoring of heart rates, brain-wave patterns and blood counts. Lakesh had ordered all of the Cerberus redoubt personnel to be injected with them. Based on organic nanotechnology developed by Overproject Excalibur, the transponders fed information through the Comsat relay satellite when personnel were out in the field.

The computer systems recorded every byte of data sent to the Comsat and directed it to the redoubt's hidden antenna array. Sophisticated scanning filters combed through the telemetry, and the digital data stream was then routed to the console before which Wegmann and Bry stood. The data was then run through the locational program to precisely isolate the team's present position in time and space.

Shrugging out of her coat and draping it over the back of her chair, Brigid sat at the master ops console, turning on the comp. It juiced up quickly, the big VGA monitor screen flashing to life. The central control complex had five dedicated and eight shared subprocessors, all linked to the mainframe behind the far wall. Two hundred years ago, it had been the most advanced model ever built, carrying experimental, error-correcting microchips of such a tiny size that they even reacted to quantum fluctuations. Biochip technology had been employed in its construction, using protein molecules sandwiched between microscopic glass-and-metal circuits.

The information contained in the main database may not have been the sum total of all humankind's knowledge, but not for lack of trying. Any bit, byte or shred of information that had ever been digitized was only a few keystrokes and mouse clicks away.

As an archivist in the Cobaltville Historical Division, Brigid Baptiste knew the primary duty of archivists was not to record predark history, but to revise, rewrite and often times completely disguise it. The Cerberus memory banks contained unedited and unexpurgated data, and having access to it was one of the few perks Brigid found in her life as an exile.

As she enabled the search-and-collation program, she heard Kane's voice murmuring a monosyllabic greeting to Bry and Wegmann. Brigid felt his presence behind her chair, and she said irritably, "You know how I hate it when you hover behind me like that."

With a laugh, Kane shifted position, stepping into her field of vision. Unlike the rest of the personnel, he wasn't wearing the white bodysuit that was the unofficial uniform of Cerberus. She saw he had dipped into the articles of predark clothing stored in the redoubt again. He wore a pair of baggy, unflattering warm-up pants, running shoes and a black T-shirt. The legend imprinted on it was nearly illegible, but she managed to make it out. It read I'm With Stupid.

"What's the status of the search?" he asked.

"Ongoing, friend Kane," Lakesh replied a bit stiffly.

A thin, slightly mocking smile lifted a corner of Kane's mouth. "Funny," he said with such a studied nonchalance Brigid knew sarcasm was sure to follow. "I was led to believe that computers were the great liberators of predark days. They did things human beings couldn't possibly accomplish on their own, far faster and a lot more efficiently."

As triple columns of digits appeared on the screen, Brigid slipped on her spectacles. "Don't be obtuse, Kane," she said coldly. "A computer is limited by the way data is stored in its memory. That doesn't mean the information isn't there. It means you have to know *how* to find it."

She raised her gaze, her emerald eyes narrowed and challenging. "If you think you can do it better, by all means take over. I'll be more than happy to step aside. My neck hurts like hell, and I'm developing carpal tunnel syndrome."

"Leave the experts to their field of expertise," Lakesh said sternly. "We don't tell you how to shoot someone."

Brigid instantly felt the electric tension spring up between the two men, a continuation of the conflict that went back to the day of Kane's arrival at the redoubt. Up until a few months ago, Lakesh made all the decisions in Cerberus, from policy to diet. Now decisions were no longer within his exclusive purview. The minicoup staged by Kane, Brigid and Grant a short time before had seen to that.

Lakesh had not been unseated from his position of authority, but he was now answerable to a more democratic process. At first he bitterly resented what he construed as the usurping of his power, but he had no choice but to come to terms with it since Kane, Grant and Brigid were privy to his secret recruitment program.

Almost every exile in the redoubt had arrived as a convicted criminal—after being framed by Lakesh for crimes against their respective villes. He had admitted it was a cruel, heartless plan with a barely acceptable risk factor, but it was the only way to spirit them out of their villes, turn them against the barons and make them feel indebted to him.

This bit of explosive and potentially fatal knowledge had not been shared with the other exiles in the redoubt. Now Brigid wondered if Lakesh's acceptance of the new democratic order was feigned, as resentment toward the sword they held over him grew.

However, much to her surprise and relief, Kane did not fire back with an insult or a veiled threat. He said wryly, "Reprimand accepted. But if I'm not tromping on your expert toes, I've been thinking about why you can't find the gateway that matches the code."

Without waiting for either Brigid or Lakesh to say whether they wanted to hear what he had to say, Kane declared, "If Baron Cobalt has found a new place to process genetic material that is already equipped with a mat-trans unit, more than likely it's within or not too far from his own sphere of influence."

Brigid raised a questioning eyebrow. "Why do you say that?"

"Simple psychology. The barons aren't conditioned to care about much beyond their own territorial borders. If we assume Baron Cobalt is engaged in his own secret search for a substitute for Dulce, I think he'd expand it out from Cobaltville, progressively going farther afield."

Sounding intrigued, Lakesh said, "A fairly reasonable hypothesis, friend Kane. But what would he use as his search resource?"

"What both of you used in the course of your jobs in the ville. The archives in the Historical Division."

A vast amount of predark historical information had survived the nukecaust, particularly documents stored in underground vaults. Tons of it, in fact, everything from novels to encyclopedias, to magazines printed on coated stock, which survived just about anything. Much more data was digitized and stored on computer diskettes, usually government documents.

"So," Kane continued, "if you narrowed the search radius for any place in the Western and Southwestern states that might have had a use for a gateway unit in predark days—Totality Concept related or not—you might come across several possible sites. In the event you do, we can program Pollard's coordinates into our own gateway and see if we get an active jump line."

He pointed to the Mercator map. "If we do, it may be registered there. And that'll give us a good idea of the site's location and what it might be."

Brigid turned her head, exchanged a look with Lakesh, then shrugged. "It's worth a try."

As her fingers clattered over the keyboard, she murmured, "Not bad, Kane."

"I have my moments," he admitted.

"They're so few and far between," she replied, "I tend to forget you have any at all." She threw him a smile to let him know she was joking and no offense was meant.

For a long time at the beginning of their relationship, it was very difficult for Kane and Brigid not to give offense to each other. Both people had their gifts. Kane's strengths were his survival skills, his ability to prevail in the face of adversity and cunning against enemies. But he could also be reckless, high-strung to the point of instability and given to fits of rage.

Brigid, on the other hand, was compulsively tidy and ordered, with a brilliant analytical mind. However, her clinical nature, the cool scientific detachment upon which she prided herself, sometimes blocked an understanding of the obvious human factor in any given situation.

Regardless of their contrasting personalities, Kane and Brigid worked very well as a team, playing on each other's strengths rather than contributing to their individual weaknesses.

The computer beeped, signaling it had completed the search. Lakesh and Kane leaned down, staring over Brigid's shoulders at the results.

"These are only possibilities," she said, nodding

toward the three lines of copy glowing amber against black. "Defined within a thousand miles of Cobaltville in all directions."

Kane read aloud, "'NORAD Command, Cheyenne Mountain, Wyoming.'"

"Forget that place," Lakesh murmured, "it was a first-strike target."

"'Kirtland AFB, New Mexico,'" Kane continued. "What about that one?"

Lakesh shook his head. "Possibly parts of it survived somewhat intact, but I doubt it."

"'Nellis AFB Bombing and Gunnery Range—'"

Before Kane finished reading, Lakesh jerked up and back, his eyes widening behind his spectacles. He uttered a few words in a language Kane had heard him speak a few times under moments of stress.

Swiveling her chair, Brigid stared at him keenly. "What is it?"

The old man did not answer for a moment. His lips worked as if he were dragging information out of the dim, dark recesses of his mind.

"Lakesh?" Brigid's voice held a challenging edge.

Dry-scrubbing his thin hair with gnarled fingers, Lakesh said in a distracted, husky whisper, "I know how Baron Cobalt found the place—my fault, my fault. I didn't have time to delete the files...."

Harshly, sharply, Kane snapped, "Talk sense."

Lakesh swallowed, squaring his shoulders. "I know where Baron Cobalt has established a new processing center. The Nellis Air Force Base in Groom Lake, Nevada.''

He paused to inhale a deep, shuddery breath. ''Dreamland. Area 51.''

Chapter 19

It was impossible for the barons' eyes to widen, but they stared wide and unblinking as Balam glided farther into the room, leading the smaller figure by the hand.

The eight barons did nothing but gape in stupefied shock. Their bodies, their vocal cords and minds seemed paralyzed. Erica van Sloan watched their faces as they gazed at Balam, reminding her of babies trying to reason out the intricacies of a mirror. They saw their own reflections in Balam's blank, masklike face at once familiar and terrifyingly alien.

The barons were Balam and Balam was the barons. His fathomless black eyes surveyed them, and power seemed to pour forth, a naked strength far greater than the barons, the elite of the world, could ever aspire to achieve. It was a power that had seen epochs come and go, mighty empires rise and fall into ruins. In his eyes Erica saw the scorn, and a pride so old that the imperial dreams of the barons were but infantile fantasies beside it.

Balam came to a stop, yet somehow he continued to move. His huge eyes seemed to leap from his head and enter Erica's mind, enter all of their minds. Staring transfixed, she heard faint, agonized cries, and distantly she knew it had been torn from not only her lips, but those of the barons, as well.

An unreasoning, undiluted terror filled her, as if her consciousness were an empty cup. After a long, tormented moment of anticipation, a nonvoice insinuated itself into her brain. The voice was neither male nor female, young nor old, neither high nor deep.

You have squandered all that was given to you, came the words. *Created to unify the Earth, to mingle my race's blood with that of humanity, to forge a tribe greater than the sum of its parts, you cast aside your legacy in favor of petty dreams and ambitions.*

Faced with a crisis as are all races, you have bent your intellects to seeking individual advantage over your brethren. You are not a unified whole—you have fragmented yourselves, you scheme and plot. It is no wonder that you are now at the mercy of the humans you claim you rule. I propose to deal with the matter decisively and at once.

The image of the eyes withdrew, receded from Erica's mind, but she still felt Balam's presence there. All of the barons were gasping, their faces slick with sweat, their eyes glassy. The psionic address had shaken them severely. She recoiled from the sensation of queasiness awakening in her belly, and the sudden twinge of pain stabbing between her eyes. Judging by Balam's voice, his vocal cords were weak, if not atrophied, so it was no wonder he preferred telepathic communication. She shivered, her skin prickling as if ants crawled over it.

Erica dredged her memory for what she had been told about the Archons after her resurrection. She recalled how twentieth-century exobiologists had postulated that all Archons were anchored to one another through hyperspatial filaments of psionic energy, much like the hive mind of certain insect species.

Despite the fact she was still mentally reeling, not just from the telepathic communication but the sheer shock of actually being in the same room with Balam, she remembered more and more of those briefings—and the underlying reasons for creating hybrids. Theorists had argued about the insurmountable problems standing in the way of communicating with extraterrestrials. They had claimed that human beings would have nothing in common with alien life-forms, no matter how intelligent.

The theoreticians had overlooked the pivotal possibility that aliens would acknowledge the same problem and take measures to correct it. The Archons' solution was a long-range hybridization program, combining the genetic material of humankind with their own race to construct a biological bridge. From what Erica remembered, and the little she understood at the time, the program had been instituted hundreds of years ago, long before the nukecaust.

For that matter, it was still an open question long after the nukecaust. Were the Archons truly aliens, a species apart from humanity, or simply different? No one knew for certain if they had their origins on another planet, in another dimension or even another time plane.

Erica could only imagine the thoughts careening and colliding within the oversized craniums of the barons. For the entirety of their artificially prolonged lives, the barons believed they served the will of the Archons—or they convinced themselves they were the Directorate's servants, and therefore any action they undertook to safeguard their positions as the overlords of humankind was justified.

But their probing intelligence needed proof, and without it, doubt inevitably ate away the belief structure. With the events of the past year, the foundation had been weakened to the point of complete collapse. Although none of the barons spoke of it, they had ceased to subscribe to the belief in the Archons. In which case, they were no longer content with their roles as the plenipotentiaries of a higher, grander authority.

They had reached this conclusion tentatively, by degrees over a period of time. When they finally did, they were as absolutely certain of it as they had been certain of the existence of the Archon Directorate. Now, dealing with the appearance of Balam, their minds were in utter turmoil, fears, desires and thoughts all crashing into one another.

In other words, Erica reflected, trying to repress a sour smile, Daddy came home and found the house in a mess.

Baron Cobalt was the first to speak, gasping out a defense. "We have squandered nothing. We have the right to defend ourselves by any means we deem necessary."

Balam turned his immobile face to Cobalt. The baron struggled visibly to reclaim his dignity and choke down his fright. "I attempted only to restore our unity, to salvage something of what you had given us. It requires a single, strong vision, and that was mine."

Balam's lips did not move, but the thready nonvoice said, *The concept you proposed of a single governing power is a sound one. Yet a creature who schemes as you did, to make your brethren beggars at their own demise, to doom their dynasties, shall not serve as that power, as the imperator.*

"I cannot be blamed for taking action."

You can be held responsible for putting a price on the lives of your brethren and therefore upon unity. Balam's expression did not alter, his facial muscles so much as twitch, yet Erica winced at the ferocity of his response, cringed from the contempt woven through it. *You have allowed yourself to be corrupted by the very creatures you claim threaten you.*

Baron Thulia spoke, his voice timid and trembling. He shivered violently. Not in fear, but from an awe so deep it was almost a religious ecstasy. "Has the Directorate returned to punish the human insurgents, to avenge what the oligarchy has suffered at their vile hands?"

Revenge is the province of the human insurgents you despise, not of you. You were bred to allow logic to dictate your actions, not visceral emotion. Any emotion, particularly vengeance, leads only to a weakening of the will and infirmity of purpose.

Acts of rebellion and savagery are to be expected from the humans. You should not hate them because of it. If a wild animal chews off its own leg to free itself from a trap, you cannot blame the animal for acting like an animal. You cannot blame humans for behaving as humans.

Balam paused and added, *But* you *can be blamed for behaving as humans.*

Baron Cobalt's golden skin flushed dark, from either anger or humiliation. In a low, quaking voice he demanded, "How do you propose to deal with the matter?"

I do not propose, came the wispy retort. *It is done.*

Balam gently pulled the small, hooded figure forward, and with one six-fingered hand pulled down his cowl. The revealed face was not anything like they expected. Though he was childlike in size, Erica had not seriously considered the figure was actually a child.

The boy looked to be about seven years of age, but the cherubic face beaming at them all was so androgynous Erica could not be sure if the child's sex was truly male. His skin was smooth, alabaster in hue, and his thick hair was pure warm silver, framing his full-cheeked face like the edges of a summertime cloud.

His big eyes seemed to shift with all colors like the dawn sky. They were old in his childish face, wise and sad in their wisdom. When he smiled upon Erica, his smile was more compassionate than if he shed tears.

In a soft, lisping voice, he said, "Hello. My name is Sam. I'm happy to meet you all, my brothers and sister."

Baron Sharpe stared goggle-eyed, then threw back his head and burst into a peal of high-pitched, nearly hysterical laughter. "A human child who calls us brothers! A human child will lead them!"

Baron Cobalt got to his feet in a rush, his face contorting in fury, foam flecking his lips. "Is this a joke?" he screeched. "You propose to place us beneath the rule of this apeling, this…this *human?*"

He spoke the last word as though uttering the most obscene blasphemy ever conceived.

Unperturbed by Cobalt's outburst, Sam pulled out the vacant chair and tried to climb into it. He required Balam's help to do so. He looked ludicrous sitting there, his upper body barely visible above the rim of the table, like an infant in a high chair. In his lisping voice, Sam said, "Sit down, Baron Cobalt."

The baron tilted his head at an arrogant, challenging angle. Affecting to ignore Sam altogether, he directed his gaze toward Balam. "This is more than an insult, it is heresy to the doctrine of unification. You cannot possibly expect—"

Sam's eyes suddenly flared as if lightning flashed behind them. His lips parted. *"Sit down."*

The two words seemed to roll through the air like the brazen chime of a gong, echoing from the high ceiling and bouncing from corner to corner. Erica fancied she felt the vibrations in her bones.

Baron Cobalt's tirade clogged in his throat. He did not so much sit down in his chair as fall clumsily into it, as if he had been shoved. A glint of fear replaced the outrage, the arrogance in his eyes.

Calmly, Sam said, "I find the title of 'Imperator' rather archaic and a bit distasteful, but I will accept it only for the psychological weight it carries."

He smiled almost shyly and when he spoke again, his voice was different. Distantly, Erica realized he was manipulating the timbre and pitch so the vibrations would resonant sympathetically to the inner ear and stimulate the neuroenergy system.

"I recognize and appreciate all of your efforts to maintain order and stem the chaos. Some of the unfortunate events of the past year could not be foreseen—others were out of your control entirely. Whether by accident or design, the actions taken by a small group of rebels impacted directly on your limitations, and therefore you could only assume a reactive posture. All that will change."

Erica understood the implications of Sam's analysis. The barons, bred for brilliance, had emotional limitations placed upon their enormous intellects. They were captives of a remorseless mind-set that did not carry with it the simple comprehension of the importance to humans of individual liberty.

Smug in their hybrid arrogance, the barons did not understand that indoctrination and conditioning could be spread only so far among humans. Their inborn, inbred pride would not allow them to acknowledge this flaw in their reasoning.

"Order and security will be restored," Sam continued, "not just to the villes, but to the world. It is a task that I was born to undertake and fulfill. It is not unification I speak of, but *reunification*. However, I am not so idealistic as to expect your complete support, at least not right away. But, by the same token, I will require your cooperation."

The last seemed to be directed solely at Baron Cobalt.

"I know all of you are consumed with curiosity about me, who I am and where I came from. All that you will learn in time. Until you prove yourselves trustworthy, suffice it to say that while the barons, as hybrids, were envisioned as the bridge between the old and new human, I symbolize what lies on the other side."

Silence settled on the council room like a heavy, sound-absorbent cloak. Sam, with Balam at his side, smiled disarmingly into the faces of the barons. One by one, hesitantly and a trifle fearfully, they returned the smile. As they did so, Sam nodded to each one in turn. When the smile reached Baron Cobalt, it was met with a sneer.

"Tell us, Imperator," Baron Cobalt said in a tone liquid with contempt, "the repercussions of any of us withholding our support and cooperation. Hypothetically speaking, of course."

Sam's smile remained in place on his angelic face. "Obviously, those barons will not partake in the rich rewards that will be available after the program of reunification is complete. Hypothetically speaking, of course."

"You will take no action against dissenting baronies?" he added dryly.

"I didn't say that. In order for the program to succeed, there can be no dissension, no independent or individual agendas. As you said earlier, this is a matter of survival. There is an old human bromide that I find applicable— 'If we do not hang together, we shall surely hang separately.'"

"Ah." Baron Cobalt nodded in satisfaction as if he now comprehended everything. "We are either with you or against you, with no middle ground?"

"A bit more simplistic than I would have phrased it, but I can't argue with the substance."

Baron Cobalt pushed himself away from the table, standing in a swift, smooth motion. His eyes swept over the assembled barons. "All of you are fools if you grovel before this child, this human child, regardless of his mind tricks."

He pointed at Balam in accusation. "You seek to use us for some hidden purpose, like puppets or tools.

If you truly represented the Directorate, you would not resort to this kind of subterfuge.

"And if you do indeed represent the Directorate as you would have us believe, your reappearance at this juncture in our history is irrelevant. The barons have maintained order and kept the peace for nearly a hundred years.

"We hold the power. The people of the villes are conditioned to obey *us*. They are indoctrinated from the day of their birth to uphold the principles of unification set forth in the first council of Front Royal."

He slapped his chest. "*We* guide the destiny of humanity. *We* hold the reins of power, not you and not some mutant child."

Neither Balam nor Sam reacted. The barons averted their eyes. Baron Cobalt stalked imperiously around the table and toward the doorway. Without glancing behind him, he proclaimed, "I am not with you— therefore by your own definition, I am against you. If it is to be war, let it be so."

After he strode out into the corridor, the seven barons remained sitting, not speaking, their eyes fixed on their hands, their laps, the tabletop, anywhere but in the direction of Sam and Balam.

The boy broke the silence by saying blandly, "I expected brother Cobalt to be a problem. He can be dealt with, never fear."

Slowly, the barons lifted their gazes. When Sam held their attention once more he said quietly, "I don't blame him, not really. If I were in his place—

in all of your places, for that matter—I would demand some sort of proof that I am qualified to make policy. A pity he left us before that proof could be offered.''

Sam wriggled off the chair and approached Erica, his little feet kicking at the hem of his robe. He extended an arm, one tiny hand reaching out from the belled sleeve of his robe. She noticed the unusual deep creases crisscrossing the pink palm. She also noticed a faint, overlapping pebbled pattern between the fingers, like a suggestion of scales. Erica tried to cringe, but all she achieved was spasmodic jerk of her head.

''What are you doing?'' she croaked.

The boy smiled at her encouragingly. ''Don't be afraid, Erica, not of me. Empty your heart and mind of fear.''

His voice seemed to echo and vibrate around her skull. Instead of feeling fear or anger, she felt a chill of dread as she sat helpless, watching as the open pink hand reached for her. But there was no threat, no malice in the blank beauty of Sam's face. Only an aching pity and sadness shone in his eyes.

''Don't be afraid,'' he intoned. ''As I will restore order, I will restore you.''

His words echoed repeatedly, like the toll of a bell. She felt her soul being drawn out by his eyes, pulling into him, joining, intermingling, entwining it with his own spirit. There was a sensation of all sanity and stability crumbling beneath her.

The boy laid his open hand against Erica's chest,

between her sagging, flaccid breasts. From it seeped a tingling warmth. The tingling swiftly built into a pins-and-needles sensation that spread out from her chest in waves, creeping into her limbs. She felt his mind fondle hers, a caress far more intimate than the touch of his hand.

Living, healing energy rippled through Erica's body, a vibrant, buoyant web suffusing every separate cell and atom, throbbing and pulsing through and around her.

Breath seizing in her throat, her vision clouded. She was only dimly aware of thrashing convulsively, her hands fitfully opening and closing on the arms of her wheelchair. Her consciousness felt as if it were sucked into a maelstrom, a whirlpool made of glittering, golden dust motes.

She heard the ragged sob of her labored respiration, the pounding of her own blood in her ears. Then slowly, comfortably, the spinning sensation ebbed away. Gulping in air, Erica felt perspiration sliding from the roots of her hair. She wiped it away, then stared dumbfounded and disbelieving at the hand with a dew of moisture glistening on the fingertips.

Wild elation lifted, engulfed her, scattering all rational thoughts like a flock of birds. She was no longer entombed in her own flesh; her body was no longer dead. She could not repress a cry as she held out her hands and stared at them. The prominent ropy veins of old age had sunk back into smooth, unlined flesh. She used her hands to touch the hard muscles of her legs, her flat belly and the firm swell of her breasts straining at the fabric of her coverall.

Up the unseamed throat the wondering, wandering fingers went, to caress smooth cheeks, lips without a dewlap. She realized her gums hurt and were swollen. With the tip of her tongue, she touched the tiny, hard teeth shoving through the flesh.

Erica patted the thick lustrous hair framing her face and explored the growth of bristles sprouting from her scalp where her hair had thinned. Her eyes darted to the tabletop, and in its polished surface she saw a face she had not seen in well over a century. It was a face of youth, beauty and vitality.

A sob broke from her, but it turned into a wail of joy. Erica fell from the wheelchair and embraced the boy, hugging him tight about the waist. The barons' faces were frozen masks of awe, their eyes rapt and shining.

Erica, her voice shaking with the intensity of her gratitude, her eyes blurred with tears, said, "Whoever you really are, whatever you are, anything you want of me, I'll give to you."

She heard herself saying it, and she meant every word. Her voice was no longer a dry, crackling rasp but was as full and melodic as it had been in her twenties.

Sam stroked her hair and said softly, "I only ask you make your font of knowledge available to me…"

"Yes!" Erica cried, embracing him even tighter.

"And that you seek out and contact one of your

own, a man whose knowledge can always be of use to me.''

Drawing in a breath, trying to steady her trembling limbs and slow the frantic pace of her heart, she asked, "One of my own? I don't understand. Who is he?"

Sam placed a gentle hand beneath her chin and lifted her face so he looked directly, lovingly into her eyes. "His name is Mohandas Lakesh Singh."

Chapter 20

The Cerberus redoubt had an officially designated briefing room on the third level, with a high ceiling, blue walls and ten rows of theater-type chairs facing a raised speaking dais, and a rear-projection screen.

It was never used except to watch old movies on DVD and laser disks in storage. The library was well-stocked and extremely eclectic, ranging from animated feature films such as *Snow White* to truly esoteric works like *Wild Strawberries* and *Glen or Glenda.*

The Cerberus personnel found most of the films fascinating, others simply silly, but by and large the overall reaction was one of confusion. Without a cultural touchstone, cinematic stories about the single life or supposed comedies about a British secret agent with bad teeth simply disturbed them.

Most of the briefings were instead held in the cafeteria on the second floor. The briefings rarely involved more than a handful of people, so it made more sense to convene them in the cafeteria. Lakesh, Brigid, Domi, Grant and Kane sat around a table, sharing a pot of coffee. Access to genuine coffee was one of the inarguable benefits of living as an exile in the redoubt. Real coffee had virtually vanished after the skydark, since all of the plantations in South and Central America had been destroyed.

An unsatisfactory, synthetic gruel known as "sub" replaced it. Cerberus had tons of freeze-dried packages of the authentic article in storage, as well as sugar and powdered milk.

Lakesh and Brigid sat together on one side of the table, while Grant and Domi occupied either end. Neither of them seemed particularly anxious to attend the briefing when they were apprised of it. Or, Kane reflected when he noted how they avoided eye contact, they were not anxious to be with each other. For once, Domi was modestly attired in a white bodysuit instead of her usual formfitting and abbreviated regalia.

Another first was how neither Brigid nor Lakesh arrived loaded down with sheaves of computer printout, maps, diagrams or other visual aids. No one sat beside Kane, and he wondered if it had something to do with the legend imprinted on his T-shirt.

"What are we here for?" Grant demanded gruffly. "You said you found where Pollard was supposed to transport the outlanders?"

"We found the most likely place," Brigid answered. "We won't be sure until we make a hands-on recce."

"Where the hell is it?"

Lakesh's face was deeply creased in consternation. "I shall give you the whole works verbally, since next to nothing is contained in the database about Area 51 except for very old and unhelpful aerial photographs.''

"Area what?" Domi asked.

"Area 51," Lakesh replied. "Also known as Dreamland, the Ranch and the Skunk Works. Very little was known about it except for unsubstantiated rumors.''

He peered over the rims of his spectacles first at Grant, then at Kane. "You may stop me if I dwell on anything you know already.''

Idly stirring powdered creamer into his coffee, Kane said, "Count on it.''

Lakesh's eyes flashed in momentary irritation. He stated, "Area 51 was, in the latter years of the twentieth century, a place as fabulous to Americans as Avalon had been to Britons a thousand years earlier. This particular Avalon, however, was very real and financed by the government. Located almost ninety miles northwest of Las Vegas, on the northern perimeter of the Nellis Air Force Base, it was the ideal location because of two concealing mountain ranges in the dry lake bed area, Groom Lake. There was only one, heavily guarded road into the area.''

Sounding a little perplexed and annoyed because of it, Domi asked, "Ideal location for what? What was so special about this place?''

"It was an above-top-secret facility equipped with hangars half the size of small towns, enormous parabolic antennas and the world's longest runway across the dry lake bed.''

"That still doesn't explain a hell of a lot," Kane commented.

Lakesh said patiently, "Area 51 was part of the Dreamland complex, where America's most advanced weaponry and aircraft were under development. Some of America's most top secret aircraft were rolled from the hidden hangars of the Area 51 complex, the Aurora being one of them...which I'm sure you and Brigid both remember."

Neither Kane nor Brigid responded, assuming Lakesh's comment to be strictly rhetorical. Kane didn't need Brigid's mnemonic powers to instantly recall the sequence of events that led them on a nightmarish foray into the Anthill complex in South Dakota. He, Lakesh and Brigid had been lured there by the mad Sindri as part of scheme to appropriate an Aurora stealth aircraft.

Although Grant had downed a small, prototypical version of the Aurora at the Archuleta Mesa site, a far larger and more deadly craft had been kept in deep storage beneath Mount Rushmore.

"The entire Dreamland complex was mainly underground to prevent any unauthorized observation from satellites," Lakesh continued, "or overflights, or individuals hiking in the surrounding mountains. It was guarded by a small army of military and intelligence services personnel, as well as a reputed handpicked squad of ex-servicemen who served in the Navy's counterterrorism forces. Deadly force was authorized for use on any trespassers."

A rueful grin creased Lakesh's face. "Area 51 was often compared to a terrestrial black hole into which billions of tax dollars disappeared each day without a word of explanation from the military or the government."

Grant shifted in his chair impatiently, knitting his heavy brows. "What's that got to do with—?"

Lakesh raised a peremptory hand. "I'm getting to that, friend Grant. The Area 51 portion of the vast desert facility was where it was claimed that the U.S. government examined all UFOs that had been either crash-landed or captured. These spacecraft and their occupants were said to have undergone intensive examination by top specialists in the medical, metallurgical and propulsion fields. And more pertinent to us, Area 51 was first coded Mission Snowbird."

All of them knew that Mission Snowbird and Project Sigma, two subdivisions of the Totality Concept's Overproject Majestic, were the only ones that dealt directly with the so-called Archon Directorate and its technology.

"It is believed," Lakesh went on, "that Snowbird's main mission was to test-fly retro-engineered alien spacecraft. The Aurora, for example, was popularly believed to have employed alien technology. That was only one of the hundreds of rumors that abounded about the place, and how the aliens influenced it. Some reports had them actually living there as consultants in special compounds.

"They allegedly took a more hands-on approach

after a disaster occurred when scientists attempted to cut into a spacecraft's power-plant reactor with a chain saw, and triggered some kind of nuclear or antimatter explosion.

"Later, diplomatic relations broke down between the human personnel of the base and the aliens, which resulted in an altercation between the two factions. A military policeman tried to take a firearm into the aliens' area, and he was wounded fatally. That incident turned into a pitched battle in which over sixty security people were killed."

Lakesh paused, then added, "Supposedly."

"When you say aliens, are we talking the Archons here?" Grant asked. "Balam's people?"

Lakesh shrugged his knobby shoulders. "Who can say with any degree of certainty? Most of what I told you is nothing but unsupported rumor. It could be completely true or it could be overblown fable."

"The Aurora was real enough," Brigid pointed out.

"If the aliens referred to were Balam's people," Lakesh declared, "then the medical facilities that may exist in Area 51 would be of great use to the barons. They would already be designed for their metabolisms. Baron Cobalt could reactivate them, turn them into a processing and treatment center without having to rebuild from scratch. He could have transferred the medical personnel from the Dulce facility."

"How would Baron Cobalt learn about it in the first place?" Kane asked, fixing his gaze on Lakesh.

"A little while ago you said something about 'my fault.' Actually, you said it twice."

Lakesh's lips pursed as if he tasted something exceptionally sour. He did not squirm in discomfort beneath Kane's stare, but he fidgeted. "As you know, I took advantage of my position as senior archivist in the Historical Division to compile as much information as I could pertaining to military or other sites that could have potential use to me. Although most of the data I copied to disk and brought here, some of it remained accessible on my computer in Cobaltville.

"A couple of months before I was forced to leave the ville, I'd been researching all documents that mentioned Area 51, but since the information was so spotty, so fragmented, so fanciful, I didn't make it a priority to encrypt it or delete it from my machine's memory. That's what I meant about it being my fault."

Kane grinned. "I won't hold that one against you, old man."

Lakesh threw him a fleeting, appreciative smile. "That would be a welcome change in attitude."

Lakesh tended to blame himself for many things, and for a long time, Kane gleefully helped him do so. As a project overseer for the Totality Concept, then as an adviser and even something of an architect of the unification program, Lakesh had helped to bring about the tyranny of the barons.

Much later, far too late as far as Kane was concerned, he turned against the hybrids, betraying them and even stealing from them to build his resistance movement. Lakesh found no true sin in betraying betrayers or stealing from thieves. He could not think of the hybrid barons in any other way, despite their own preference for the term *new human.*

Lakesh then tried his hand at creating his own new humans. Some forty years before, when he first decided to resist the baronies, he rifled the genetic records on file to find the qualifications he deemed the most desirable. He used the unification program's own fixation with genetic purity against them. By his own confession, he was a physicist cast in the role of an archivist, pretending to be a geneticist, manipulating a political system that was still in a state of flux.

Kane was one such example of that political and genetic manipulation, and when he learned about Lakesh's involvement in his birth, he had very nearly killed him.

"In the months following your disappearance," Brigid remarked, "the baron searched for any clues to your whereabouts, including your computer files." Her eyes narrowed as a sudden thought occurred to her. "How did he find out a mat-trans unit was there, not to mention its destination-lock codes?"

Lakesh knuckled his deeply furrowed forehead. "I can only postulate, but it's reasonable to assume the baron picked up the Area 51 reference and followed its thread to other files, ones that very well might have contained that information—not just about aircraft but about the medical facilities perhaps used to treat Archons."

"If that's what the son of a bitch did," Grant growled, "it seems pretty apparent he's concerned only for himself, or he wouldn't be raiding Baron Snakefish's territory for merchandise."

Lakesh regarded him stonily. "Does that make any difference?"

"It makes a big one to me. Sounds like Baron Cobalt is willing to let the other barons sicken and die, or he wouldn't be sneaking around. He's doing our job for us."

Tugging at his long nose, Lakesh said severely, "You're too inclined to view things in black and white, friend Grant. Our war against the baronies is like a monster game of chess, and we're always trying to think nine moves ahead—or eight since the demise of Baron Ragnar. One would think that by now you'd understand the real reason for any move by the barons, Cobalt in particular, is never what it appears to be on the surface."

Domi, her head propped up on a fist, grinned wolfishly at Lakesh's admonishment. Ignoring her, Grant intoned in a low, deadly voice, "We don't know if the destination codes are for a gateway in this Area 51 place or in East Asshole, Slovenia."

"Yes," Lakesh agreed, "it's still only conjecture. That's why we'll try them out and see where they take us."

"'Us'?" Grant repeated darkly. "You're going, too?"

Before Lakesh could respond, Brigid broke in. "If the codes do lead to Area 51, and if Baron Cobalt has reactivated the medical wing, the place will be crawling with sec forces."

"More than likely," Kane agreed uneasily. "In which case, we can't afford to make a scouting jump, a recce. We should go there under the assumption that we'll find exactly what we think we may find."

"And," Grant questioned, "bringing everything we need to light the place up?"

Lakesh's eyes widened in alarm. "Let us not make these rushes to judgment, gentlemen. It could be the site will be of more use to us than the barons."

Domi straightened in her chair, saying vehemently, "If fuckin' barons are there, if fuckin' hybrids are there, we chill 'em! They'd do the same to us. We got blamed for chillin' Baron Ragnar even though we didn't. We're *owed* a baron chillin'!"

The bloodthirsty blaze in the girl's eyes caused Kane's belly to turn a cold flip-flop. Lakesh, who was extremely fond of her, stared at her in dismay. Haltingly, he said, "Darlingest Domi, simply executing the barons as we find them won't solve the larger problem. It's not that I'm against such a tactic, mind you, but there are other considerations—"

"'Other considerations,'" Domi mimicked in disgust, imitating his lilting East Indian accent. "For a year now, that's all we hear. You jabber and blow about this being a war for human survival, but whenever we can do something to shorten the war, mebbe even end it, you turn pussy-hearted.''

Domi surveyed the people at the table with a crimson, challenging stare. She fastened her gaze on Grant's face and between clenched teeth hissed, ''Tired of this. Sick of this shit. If we're not in a war to win it, then it's not a war.''

Grant met her steady glare with brow-shadowed eyes. She did not avert her face or appear to be in the least intimidated. In the past, all that was required to quell one of Domi's outbursts was either a stern look or stern word from Grant. Whatever influence he had exerted on the girl was now a thing of the past.

Regardless of its true motivation, Domi's blunt, straightforward diatribe contained more than a few nuggets of truth. No one at the table could deny that, even if they cared to do so.

Kane exhaled a long breath. ''Domi has a point. When we destroyed the Archuleta Mesa complex, we pretty much destroyed the hybrids' ability to reproduce and to keep themselves healthy. It would be absolutely the most idiotic tactic to allow the barons to pick up and start over somewhere else. To use your chess-game analogy, Lakesh, a strategy like that isn't even a competition, much less a war.''

Lakesh opened his mouth, but Brigid interposed hastily, ''As much as I don't want to, I must agree with Domi and Kane. We simply don't have the personnel to take Area 51 from the barons and occupy it ourselves. Our only option is to make it useless to them in much the same way we did the Dulce installation. And if that option makes it useless to us, as well—" she shrugged "—c'est le guerre."

Even Kane knew she meant "fortunes of war."

After a contemplative moment, Lakesh murmured in sad resignation, "You're right. But allow me to contribute something to the strategy. If the four of you intend to jump there, I suggest you do so in pairs and at staggered intervals. The gateway unit could very well be heavily guarded, and there is no reason for all of you to be captured—or worse—in one fell swoop."

Kane exchanged swift, questioning glances with Domi, Brigid and Grant. When none of them voiced an objection, he announced, "Agreed. I volunteer to be on the first tour group. Who wants to go with me?"

"Me," Domi stated in a tone that brooked no debate.

Kane eyed her dispassionately, on the verge of refusing her offer. But the first action that needed to be undertaken once they reached the site would be to secure the immediate area. Domi, swift and stealthy of foot, would be more helpful at achieving that objective than either Brigid or Grant.

He recalled the time when he partnered up with the albino girl in order to join Trader Chapman's ore caravan. Despite a couple of incidents that in retrospect were more annoying than risky, she had proved exceptionally capable of handling herself in a killzone.

Grant fingered his chin. "I guess that makes me and Brigid the B team again."

"If you have any objections, now's the time to put them on the table."

Brigid smiled wanly. "I have plenty. But none hold any water."

Consulting his wrist chron, Kane said, "Let's schedule the jump for 0400 hours. If the gateway is guarded, it'll be the graveyard shift, and the sentries posted there are less liable to be at the top of their game. That'll give us time choose our ordnance, eat and catch some sleep."

"How long should we wait before jumping in after you?" Grant asked.

"A couple of hours should probably be long enough for us to make the initial recce and lock down the immediate area—or get captured or chilled."

"If it's only hybrids and barons there," Domi declared, her teeth flashing in a vulpine grin, "they'll be the ones chilled."

They left the dining hall. Lakesh, Kane, Grant and Brigid took the elevator up to the first level, while Domi stayed on the second floor for a swim in the pool. Brigid and Lakesh returned to the ops center, and Kane walked to the armory, with Grant beside him.

"I guess you have a strategy in mind," the big man remarked.

"Until we get the lay of the land, there's not much I can do. I'll go in hard, armored up. If there are any Mags there, they might think I'm one of Pollard's squad bringing in merchandise. That should buy me some time."

Grant nodded, but it was a very distracted nod.

They strode down the corridor past the vehicle depot and workroom and entered an open doorway. Kane flicked up the flat toggle switch on the doorframe, and the overhead fluorescent fixtures blazed on, flooding the armory with a white, sterile light.

The big square room was stacked nearly to the ceiling with wooden crates and boxes. Many of the crates were stenciled with the legend Property U.S. Army. Glass-fronted gun cases lined the four walls, containing automatic assault rifles, many makes and models of subguns and dozens of semiautomatic blasters. On the north wall were bazookas, tripod-mounted M-249 machine guns, mortars and rocket launchers.

All of the ordnance was of predark manufacture. Caches of matériel had been laid down in hermetically sealed Continuity of Government installations before the nukecaust. Protected from the ravages of the outraged environment, nearly every piece of munitions and hardware was as pristine as the day it had rolled off the assembly line. Most of the items in the arsenal had been taken by Lakesh from the Anthill over a period of years.

Grant hung back near the door, while Kane went

to an open case of grens. The man seemed uncomfortable and not a little embarrassed.

"Something on your mind?" Kane asked as he selected an incendiary gren from its cushion of foam rubber.

Passing a hand over his forehead, Grant shifted from one foot to the other and mumbled, "As a matter of fact, there is. I want to ask you something."

"Go ahead."

"Something..." Grant's voice trailed off, and then he blurted in an almost desperate burst, "Something personal."

Kane was startled into speechlessness, so astonished he nearly dropped the gren. He stared at Grant, nonplussed by the very concept of the man even hinting about making a personal confidence. He could think of nothing to say but to repeat, "Go ahead."

Lowering his voice to just above a whisper, resolutely not looking in Kane's direction, Grant said, "At any time over the past few weeks, have you...I mean has Domi...have you and her—"

Grant broke off, heaved a deep sigh and stated matter-of-factly, "Has Domi come to you, in your quarters, or have you gone to hers?"

Kane felt his eyebrows crawling toward his hairline. "What?"

"You heard me."

"Oh, I heard you. I just can't believe my ears." Kane felt a quiver of embarrassment mixed in with a little guilt. During the Utah mission, he and Domi had shared a room and she made it clear she would not be adverse to sharing more than that with him. He had dashed cold water on her amorous advance by reminding her of her devotion to Grant. That had been the end of it, but he never mentioned the incident to anyone, not to Brigid and certainly not to Grant.

Wearily, Grant said, "Just answer me, will you?"

"No, she didn't and no, we haven't." Kane cocked his head toward him. "Why do you ask?"

"I have my reasons."

"I'm sure you do. I'd like to hear them."

Grant shook his head and murmured, "Domi is tired of waiting."

"Waiting for what?"

"Waiting for me, waiting for us to get together. She accused me of being impotent, and then threatened to go to the other men here. You included."

Kane's eyebrows arched even higher, and with a conscious effort, he lowered them. Now he understood the reasons behind the bitterness and tension between the two people. "Domi didn't include me, and as far as I know she hasn't gone to the other men. You'd know about it if she had."

Grant swallowed, his face screwed up in misery. "Yeah, that's what I figured."

The two men shared an awkward, uneasy silence for a long moment. Kane finally ventured, "Maybe it's time you were more honest with her, about your feelings. Have you ever spoken to her about Olivia?"

Grant's head swung up, his lips compressed tightly.

"No, I haven't. It's none of her business. Or yours, either."

Kane bristled at Grant's tone but didn't respond to it. For the past year he had wondered if his friend had tired of resisting the albino girl's charms and surrendered to them, and now he knew. Furthermore, he had suspected the emotional wounds inflicted by his ruined affair with Olivia years ago in Cobaltville had yet to fully heal. Until now, Kane had never asked Grant about Olivia. The two men had observed an unspoken understanding that it was a forbidden topic.

Kane raised conciliatory hands. "All right, all right. I've told you what you wanted to know."

As he returned his attention to the crate of grens, Grant intoned, "There's something else."

"What is it?"

"I let one of Pollard's Mags go. I didn't allow the Tigers to chill him. I tied him up, and when it was all over I set him free."

Kane blinked at him surprise. "Why?"

"His name was Mace…brother to the man we chilled in Cobaltville."

For a long tense stretch of seconds, Kane said nothing, searching his memory for the face of the man. He nodded shortly. "It's done. You did what you thought was right."

"Mebbe." Grant's tone was dubious. "I didn't see any sign of him in Redoubt Charlie. That means he either didn't make it back, or he returned to Cobaltville and reported what happened. And if he did that,

Baron Cobalt will sure as hell put two and two together.''

Kane exhaled noisily. "And he'll know we're on to him, and he might be expecting us.''

"Yeah.''

Kane thought for a moment, then stated, "There's nothing that can be done. We'll have to take our chances.''

Hesitantly, Grant said, "There's one more thing.''

Kane angled an eyebrow at him. "I'm listening.''

Squaring his broad shoulders as if steeling himself to perform an unpleasant task, he declared, "You remember Shizuka.''

Kane snorted. "Yes, I remember Shizuka.'' His voice acquired a tone of patronizing weariness. "Even if it hadn't been only three days since I last saw her, she's a little on the unforgettable side.''

A ghost of a smile tugged at the corners of Grant's mouth. "She sure is that.''

"What about her?''

The smile vanished. "Domi saw us.''

Kane's eyes slitted in confusion. "Domi saw you? What do you mean? She saw you and Shizuka...''

"Me and Shizuka.'' Grant gestured helplessly. "We were only kissing, but Domi may think we'd gone further. And we might have if she hadn't shown up. Anyhow, Domi saw us together.''

Kane groaned inwardly, then aloud. Grant continued speaking, faster and faster as if in a great hurry to get the words out of his mouth. "After the way

Shizuka defeated Domi, humiliated her, really, even though she started it, it was probably the worst thing she could've seen. Especially with what's been going on between us. Or not been going on.''

He shook his head frustration. ''It's not like I owe Domi anything. She's just a child as far as I'm concerned, but I don't want to her hurt her. Or have her do a Guana on me one night.''

''I don't know if she'd go that far.'' Kane made a wordless utterance of irritation. ''This is *all* we need. We finally get the Beth-Li issue settled, and here you are, dragging it back in, breathing new life into it.''

''It's not the same thing at all,'' Grant said hotly, defensively.

''The hell it isn't,'' Kane argued.

More than a year before, Lakesh had concocted a plan to turn Cerberus from a sanctuary to a colony. To that end, babies needed to be born, ones with superior genes. Making a unilateral decision, he arranged for Beth-Li Rouch to be brought into the redoubt to mate with Kane, to insure that his superior abilities were passed on to offspring.

Kane had refused to cooperate for a variety of reasons, primarily because he felt the plan was a continuation of sinister elements that had brought about the nukecaust and the tyranny of the villes. His refusal had tragic consequences. Only a thirst for revenge and a conspiracy to murder had been birthed within the walls of the redoubt, not children.

Kane inhaled a calming breath. ''Out of all the

women you've met in the past year—Domi, Mother Fand, DeFore—why choose Shizuka to break your celibate streak?''

"How the hell should I know?" Grant snapped. "I didn't plan it. How can you explain mutual attraction? For one thing, she's closer to my own age and a hell of lot more mature than Domi.''

Kane wagged his head in disbelief. "If Domi fuses out on me during the op, at least I'll know the reason why.''

He leaned against the gren crate and smiled sourly. "You beat everything, you know that? You turn down Domi and God only knows how many other women, then at the worst possible time you decide to lock lips with a samurai—and not just any run-of-the-mill samurai, either, but one that made a fool out of Domi. You really beat everything.''

Grant took it all without a flicker of emotion. He probably wasn't hearing anything he had not already thought over before. Contritely, he muttered, "Yeah, I guess I do.''

Chapter 21

Kane flexed his fingers, brushing them against the interlocking metal hexagons that composed the floor of the mat-trans chamber. He felt the pins-and-needles static discharge from the polished plates even through his gloves.

They had already lost their silvery shimmer, and the last wisps of spark-shot mist disappeared even as he looked at it. Lakesh claimed that the vapor was not really a mist at all, but a plasma wave form brought into existence by the inducer's "quincux effect." Beneath the platform, he heard the emitter array's characteristic hurricane howl fading away to a high-pitched whine.

He lay on his back, his stomach spasming, his head swimming. He took slow deep breaths, trying to speed his recovery. The vertigo was routine by now, a customary side effect of rematerialization. The nausea seeped away, but he knew better than to sit up until the dizziness went away completely.

All things considered, temporary queasiness and light-headedness were small prices to pay in exchange for traveling hundreds, sometimes thousands of miles in a handful of minutes. Occasionally, the toll exacted was terrible, as when he, Brigid and Grant jumped to a malfunctioning unit in Russia. The matter-stream modulations could not be synchronized with the destination lock, and all of them suffered a severe case of debilitating jump sickness that included hallucinations, weakness and vomiting.

Brigid had told him of the accounts written by Dr. Mildred Wyeth regarding gateway transits. She described the symptoms of jump sickness, the pain and nightmares she and her comrades had suffered while traversing the Deathlands via the mat-trans units.

Wyeth and the others who followed the legendary Ryan Cawdor had been forced to jump blind, without the knowledge of how to program a specific destination. As a result, they were subjected to physical and mental tortures that would have tormented the damned.

Hearing a rustle of cloth beside him, Kane slowly and carefully eased himself up on one polycarbonate-shod elbow. Domi stirred from her prone position on the platform, then sat up, blinking at the armaglass walls enclosing the jump chamber. Their pale green hue told her they had completed a transit from the brown-walled chamber in the Cerberus redoubt. The six-sided units in the Cerberus mat-trans network were color-coded so authorized jumpers could tell at a glance into which redoubt they had materialized.

It seemed an inefficient method of differentiating one installation from another, but Lakesh had once explained that before the nukecaust, only personnel holding color-coded security clearances were allowed to make use of the system. Inasmuch as their use was restricted to a select few of the units, it was fairly easy for them to memorize which color designated what redoubt.

Rising to his feet, Kane made a swift visual inspection of his armor, making sure all the sections and joints were sealed. Domi stood, swaying for a moment on unsteady legs. Whether it was due to dizziness or because of the weight she carried, Kane had no way of knowing.

"Where do you think we are?" Domi asked. The small albino girl was dressed to kill—literally. She wore a padded bulletproof vest over black coveralls, the pouches and pockets bulging with extra magazines for her Combat Master snugged in a thigh holster.

A kit bag containing three flash-bangs, two high-ex V-60 minigrens, four incends and two CS grens hung from her left shoulder. Her serrated knife was sheathed outside the top of her right boot. A black knit balaclava was pulled down around her throat. She could tug it up to conceal her hair and most of her face within a couple of seconds.

Kane gestured to the armaglass walls. "We're someplace else, that's all I can tell you. How are you feeling?"

"Never better," she responded breezily. "You?"

"I'm grand." Lifting his left wrist, Kane turned toward the door. Strapped around it was a small device made of molded black plastic and stamped metal. A liquid crystal display window exuded a faint glow. The motion detector showed no movement within the radius of its invisible sensor beams.

"It appears no one knows we've arrived," he said.

"Arrived where?" Domi asked irritably.

He did not bother to answer. Gripping the handle placed in the center of the door, Kane heaved up on it. With a click, the door of dense, semitranslucent material swung outward on counterbalanced hinges. Manufactured in the last decades of the twentieth century, armaglass was a special compound combining the properties of steel and glass. It was used as walls in the jump chambers to confine quantum-energy overspills.

Kane cautiously shouldered the door aside, fairly certain in advance of what he would he would see. Most of the jump chambers opened onto to small anterooms, which in turn led to the control rooms. He was not disappointed.

Sin Eater unleathered and in hand, he padded softly through the antechamber, walking heel to toe. Domi followed him at a distance of six feet. There was a quiet hum of machinery in the air, as well as the slight hiss of filtered oxygen being pushed through ventilation grilles high up on the walls.

Just before he stepped through the open door, Kane came to a halt, indicating for Domi to take up position on the opposite side of the frame. She did so, and just barely managed to bite back a gasp.

The control room was immense, far, far larger than any they had seen in any redoubt. Kane guessed that it measured out to be eighty by a hundred feet, which made it even larger than the ops center in Cerberus. Three aisles of computer stations lined the walls. He surveyed the banks and consoles of electronics for a moment, knowing all of the equipment was not there just to monitor and manage the gateway systems.

He strode to a nearby instrument panel bearing the blank screens of a closed-circuit vid system. When he thumbed a row of toggle switches, pale black-and-white images appeared, most of them displaying empty, dimly lit corridors. They could be anywhere, he reflected, much less Groom Lake, Nevada.

One screen lit up with an exterior view, a rolling plain of desert terrain, the landscape silvered by the moon. It butted up against jagged hills and ridgelines. The area looked quiet and almost hauntingly peaceful. He touched another switch, and the view changed, showing what appeared to be at least a mile's worth of ruins, all laid out against an extremely long runway. A line of compacted rubble still stood above ground. The only descriptive adjective that came to Kane's mind was *godforsaken*.

"Where are the hybrids, the guards?" Domi's voice was hushed as she looked around uneasily. "The power is on, so somebody has to be here."

"Not necessarily," Kane replied. "All the controls are locked on automatic settings, powered by the nuke generators."

"I just wish we knew where the fuck we are," Domi said angrily.

"We could be in Area 51 or even that East Asshole place Grant mentioned."

Almost as soon the last word passed his lips he spied a square notebook on a shelf beneath the vid screens. He tugged it out. Embossed on the plastic cover was a deep blue insignia, an eagle with outspread, upcurving wings. Beneath it were the words United States Air Force Base, Nellis Reservation. Site S-4 Security Protocols, Authorized Personnel Only. MJ-Green Clearance Required. The notebook was sealed with a tiny combination lock.

"That answers our question," he said flatly. "We're in Area 51."

Domi did not seem particularly relieved to hear it, but she said nothing. Kane returned the notebook to the shelf and looked around. He saw an open doorway on the opposite end of the chamber. To Domi he said, "Stay here."

He crossed the huge room, sidling between the comp terminals. The square doorway opened up on an expanse of featureless corridor. The overhead light strips shed a pale illumination on the dusty linoleum floor. The hall was only twenty feet long and deadened against the sealed doors of an elevator shaft. Apparently, the elevator was the only way to and from the control room.

Kane weighed his options for a moment, then returned to Domi. "You're going back."

Her eyes flashed and her back stiffened. "Why?"

"To fetch Grant and Baptiste. The objective was to secure the immediate area, and we've done that."

"Why me?" she demanded. "Why not you?"

"Because you agreed to follow my orders on this op. If you're reneging, then just jump your ass back to Cerberus and don't bother to come back with the others."

Domi's jaw muscles bunched, but she only nodded tersely.

They went back to the mat-trans unit, and Domi stepped into the chamber, pulling the door closed to initiate the jump sequence. Solenoids clicked with a solid, satisfying *chock*.

Stepping back, Kane waited for the subsonic hum to begin, for the hexagonal disks to exude their familiar glow. He waited. And waited. And nothing happened.

Domi opened the armaglass door, her brow furrowed in puzzlement. She pulled it firmly shut again. Nothing happened—no whine, no glow, no spark-shot mist.

Kane opened the door, carefully inspecting the circuitry actuator on the lock, making certain full contact was achieved. He slammed it closed and stood silently in baffled anger. After a few seconds, Domi opened the door from the inside. "What's going on?"

Kane's reply was grimly to the point. "We were expected. It's a one-way conduit."

Fear shone in the girl's eyes. "How were we expected?"

Kane did not tell her about Grant and the consequences his streak of mercy may have wrought.

"We're trapped?" Her voice hit a shrill note.

Kane nodded. "That's the general concept I was trying to convey."

Chapter 22

Hearts trip-hammering within their chests, Kane and Domi went back through the control room and into the corridor. He fought off the creeping fingers of panic that clutched at his mind, refusing to conjecture on how the mat-trans unit had been reprogrammed.

When they reached the elevator, he unsheathed his combat knife and jammed the heavy blade between the doors, prying at it, working it back and forth.

"Where are we going?" Domi demanded in a fierce whisper.

"Anywhere but here," he grunted, applying more pressure to the knife's handle. "I don't want to be penned up in there."

He heaved back on the knife, and there was a grating sound as the panels separated a bit. Domi worked her small hand into the crack to help with the leverage. Something snapped loudly on the other side of the doors, and they rolled open smoothly and without resistance, rocking Kane back on his heels.

The car was large, with polished chrome handrails. There was only one button on the exterior wall, imprinted with an arrow pointing upward. Kane used the point of his knife to depress it, but the doors did not slide shut, nor did the car ascend. Domi pointed to the square hatch on the ceiling, so Kane boosted her up. She pushed it open and crawled through. She whispered down, ''Ladder here.''

Kane jumped up and grabbed the edge of the open hatch, and chinned himself through it. Because of his armor, the fit was tight, but after a moment of muscle-straining effort and a couple of breathless curses, he wriggled onto the roof of the elevator car. The illumination was weak, but Domi's sensitive eyes were sharp even in semidarkness, and Kane's image enhancer and visor made the most of all available light to provide him with limited night vision.

The square shaft rose above them. Paralleling the cables and extending up one wall were the metal rungs of a ladder. About fifty feet above shone a faint rectangle of light.

Domi stepped onto the ladder and began to climb. Kane followed, hand over hand, until they came to an opening. Elevator doors were partially ajar and led to another expanse of featureless corridor, the walls made of mortared, unpainted concrete blocks. They passed several closed, electronic-lock-equipped doors, each one bearing the circular yellow-and-black radiation warning symbol. Beneath the symbols were plastic signs emblazoned with red block lettering: Radiation Hazard Beyond This Point! Entry Forbidden To Personnel Not Wearing Anticontaminate Clothing!

Kane took the warnings seriously and decided not to investigate. When they came to a T-branching intersection, he saw a door without the symbol or the warnings, although it was locked electronically, with a small keypad instead of a knob. The face of the door held a small plaque that read Purity Control Orientation. He paused, recalling what Lakesh had said regarding the basis of ville class distinctions.

They were based primarily on eugenics, and this was determined by the Directorate, or rather Balam. He had access to the findings of the Human Genome Project, so everyone granted full ville citizenship and the privilege to reproduce had to meet a strict criteria. The actual reason, though concealed, was simple: the purer the quality of individual genetic characteristics, the purer the quality of the hybrid. The practice was called Purity Control.

Kane turned to Domi, holding out his hand. "Give me the Syne."

She dipped her hand into her kit bag and produced a small metal device shaped like an elongated circle. The Mnemosyne—or Syne, as it was casually called—was an electronic lock decrypter. Kane placed the Mnemosyne against the keypad, thumbed a stud on its surface and initialized the decryption mechanism. It emitted a faint, very high-pitched whine. The tight-band, high-power microwave frequency overrode the lock's microprocessors, and with a snap of metal, the locking bolts clicked aside.

Carefully, he toed the door open and, leading with his blaster, stepped inside. After a moment of groping, he found a wall switch and flicked it up. They stepped into a medium-sized office suite, with six partition-enclosed desks, all of them equipped with computer terminals. Two steel-gray filing cabinets stood in a corner.

Tacked on the wall, faded and yellowed with age, were large full-color illustrations arranged in a sequence that ran nearly the entire length of the wall. The pictures displayed images of a naked human male and female, superimposed over twisting DNA molecules.

The next illustration showed the strands of the helix separated, then moved back together in a new chain configuration. Another image showed egg cells being opened by microscalpels so their dark nuclei could be replaced with new ones.

The final picture showed the male and female holding the hands of a baby standing between them. The baby possessed a very high forehead and domed cranium, beneath pronounced brow arches overhanging big, slanting staring, eyes.

"What's that supposed to be about?" Domi murmured.

"Hybridization 101," Kane replied in the same muted tone. "How to make monstrosities in three easy lessons."

On the right-hand wall a slab of steel was set tightly in the concrete blocks, a wheel lock jutting from the rivet-studded, cross-beamed mass. To their left, a hallway stretched into the distance.

Kane went to the door. He put his hands on the

wheel lock and gave it a counterclockwise twist. It did not budge. Taking and holding a deep breath, he threw all of his weight and upper-body strength against the lock.

With a tortured screech of solenoids, the wheel turned, slowly and resistantly at first, then Kane was able to get a hand-over-hand spin going.

He threw his shoulder against the steel door, and there was the sticky sucking sound of rubber seals separating. The door opened inward. He stepped forward, Sin Eater filling his hand. Domi followed him, alert and watchful, Combat Master at the ready. Both of them stopped and stared. A light strip flickered overhead with a yellow glare.

They were in a large, low-ceilinged room with a dozen desks, most of them covered with computer terminals and keyboards. A control console ran the length of the right-hand wall, consisting primarily of plastic-encased readouts and gauges. The left wall was composed of panes of glass, beaded with condensation. The smell of disinfectant and chemicals cut into their nostrils. Kane's eyes took in at a glance the heavy tables loaded down with a complicated network of glass tubes, beakers and retorts.

On a long, black-topped lab table were glass cases and fluid-filled jars. Floating inside them were human internal organs—livers, hearts, loops of intestines. Domi made a gagging sound. Kane stepped to the left wall, peering through one of the sheets of glass.

Beyond it, in a cubicle, he saw the naked body of

a man. His complexion was ruddy, his hair straight and dark. He was attached to a metal framework, his arms and legs spread-eagled, secured to steel struts by gleaming, heavy-gauge wire. His genitals had been removed and his eyes were missing. Only dark, red-rimmed hollows stared back at Kane.

From a shallow console at the bottom of the window frame protruded a black knob. Kane touched it, turning it to the right. The metal framework slowly revolved, turning the man's back to the glass. His rectum had been cored out in a surgically precise manner. There was no sign of blood.

Domi moved to his side, stared and whirled away, covering her mouth with one hand. Kane felt bile rising in his own throat, but he didn't recoil. He knew that genetic engineering, DNA manipulation and splicing formed only part of hybridization process. There were also surgeries, transplants of tissues and organs. Domi's own people had been rounded up and butchered like cattle, and their eviscerated corpses left to rot.

He forced himself to step to the next pane of glass. When he saw what lay beyond it, he instinctively recoiled, his finger tensing over the trigger stud of his Sin Eater. Beyond the glass was a transparent sac filled with a semiliquid amber gel, attached to a ceiling rack. A small figure, curled in a fetal position, floated within its gelid contents. The misshapen, inhumanly large cranium was a pinkish-gray in color, spotted here and there with wispy strands of hair. The nose was merely a pair of tiny nares. Its upslanting eyes were dull and fathomless. The limbs were disproportionate, far too long for the torso.

Kane had seen similar hybrid fetuses in Dulce, but the sight still made him feel ill, his belly turning cold flip-flops, his mouth filling with sour saliva. He found a door leading to the glassed-in chamber and went through it, Domi following close behind. He scrutinized the creature within the artificial womb, filled with synthetic amniotic fluid, and knew he was looking at a corpse, as dead as the mutilated human.

He poked the tiny body with the barrel of his Sin Eater and set it to swaying gently. "It's dead."

Domi nodded in satisfaction. "Good."

Kane could not share her glee. Whatever methods had been used to create the hybrids at the Archuleta Mesa complex obviously could not be duplicated here. And he knew the barons would not just give up, resigning themselves to the long night of extinction.

He left the chamber and went back to the door. "Let's move on."

Domi did not respond, but he heard her fumbling with her kit bag.

Impatiently, he said, "Let's go, Domi."

"I heard you the first time," she snapped. "By the way, I think we'd better duck."

He cast a quizzical glance over his shoulder as she stepped away from the long control console. A small metal-shelled oval rested there, as did two others in other parts of the room. Recognition flooded through him like a rush of icy water. Even as he stared at the incend grens, Domi grabbed him by the arm and hauled him down behind a lab table. In a shaved sliver of an instant, Kane saw the console disintegrate in a roaring white flash.

The glassware atop the lab table shattered as if a giant fist had smashed into it. The entire room shuddered brutally. Domi's mouth was open in a shout of elation, but Kane's concussed eardrums could not hear it.

Shards of glass rained on them, and preservative fluids slopped over onto the floor. Despite the barrier of the heavy table, they felt the scorching heat of the thermite charge.

The secondary incendiaries went off in a deadly chain reaction all over the room. Rolling balls of flame overlapped, instantly building to a roaring inferno. The thundering shock waves felt like a storm-driven surf.

Kane made a lunge for the doorway, one hand gripped tightly around the collar of Domi's vest. A hurricane of superheated air struck him from all sides, slapping his breath back into his nostrils. A white nova forced him to squeeze his eyes shut, as it overloaded his image enhancer. Dimly, he heard the squealing rasp of rupturing metal and the splintering of glass.

Kane thrust himself out onto the floor of the office suite, yanking Domi forward in a forced somersault. Groping behind him, his hand closed around the wheel lock of the door. Pulling shut the heavy slab of metal was not difficult. Another explosive charge detonated, and the concussion slammed it closed, though tongues of flame spurted around the edges, melting the rubber seals.

"That ought to start something!" she exclaimed happily, her tone full of glee, her eyes alight.

Infuriated, Kane was just barely able to keep himself from striking the girl. "You stupid, silly little bitch! Why did you—?"

Domi sprang to her feet, her white face twisted into something demonic. "It's war!" she shrilled. "You're the stupid one, all of you—Lakesh, Grant, Brigid—stupid!"

He rose, struggling to regain his composure. "Now they'll know—"

She cut off his words with a savage gesture. "They know already we're here. Now they know that if they try to trap us, it'll cost 'em. Cost 'em big time. They'll end up *praying* we leave!"

Kane stared at her, feeling cold nausea leapfrog in his belly, chill fingers tapping out a ditty of dread up and down the buttons of his spine. What little self-restraint Domi had practiced in the past was now completely discarded. Without Grant as the mitigating influence, the authority figure, she was unleashing all of her bottled-up passions, turning them from love to violence.

Her ruby eyes glared at him, silently daring him to either command her to give up her weapons or take them from her by force. Kane saw no wisdom in attempting either. He turned sharply on his heel, saying, "Come on."

As they strode down the corridor, Kane admitted to himself he was, at that moment, more afraid of Domi than whatever awaited them along or at the end of the passageway. He was just as disturbed by the lack of fire alarms or any commotion at all caused by the explosions. Possibly an automated extinguisher system had kicked in and doused the flames, but that did not explain the lack of personnel.

The corridor ran straight for a hundred yards, doglegged to the right, then ended, but not against a barrier. Kane let out an involuntary grunt of astonishment.

They looked upon a multileveled man-made cavern, so vast Kane could not guess at its true dimensions. The nether end ran away into the dimness. The ceiling was at least three hundred feet above their heads, and dotted with bright stadium lights. It was far larger than the deep-storage chamber beneath Mount Rushmore where they found the Aurora aircraft.

Large containers were arranged in orderly fifty-foot-tall aisles, stretching as far as they could see. Gently sloping ramps led from level to level, linked by passages wide enough for lift trucks and dollies to carry their loads. The ramps appeared to be the only method of getting from level to level. A floor-mounted, electric monorail ran the entire length of the enormous chamber, disappearing between a pair of double doors.

An elevated superstructure was placed between the ground floor and the second level, like an observation post. A short flight of metal stairs led up to its underside. At regularly spaced intervals were wide, square apertures, leading out of the warehouse.

Moving with a silence that would put cats to shame, Domi and Kane eased their way into the monstrous warehouse, using the large containers as cover while they explored the aisles. Once they were between them, the gloom was deep and almost impenetrable.

Most of the containers were of similar size, and all were made of a kind of lightweight, corrugated metal with hinged lids. With his combat knife, Kane pried open the catch of one and pawed through the contents. Nestled within strawlike excelsior and foam padding were broken-down pieces of scientific equipment. He examined the parts of a microscope and other odds and ends he could not identify.

Lowering the lid, he and Domi moved on. They saw and heard no one. Kane felt like an ant trapped in a child's toy box, wending his way around building blocks. Suddenly, a discordant beep emanated from the motion detector.

They slowed their pace at once. Flattened against the crates, they slithered to the floor level and behind the protective shelter of the stacks. On the LCD face of the detector, three, then four, five and six pulsating dots appeared. They moved very swiftly, vectoring in on their position.

Kane and Domi saw them at the same time, creeping from the valley of shadows between two aisles, dark figures, eerie and unnatural, like living shadows themselves. They moved fast and with an unnatural silence.

All of the figures were slim of build, the tallest not much more than five and a half feet in height. Above the narrow shoulders rose smooth, domed craniums, apparently jet-black in color. The hairless skulls tapered to sharp chins, so the impression of the heads was of inverted teardrops.

The bulging eyes were completely round like an insect's. Dark and glassy, they were surrounded by protuberant ridges. Between them, extended in a V, was a pair of insectlike antennae. Kane realized the figures wore night-vision goggles attached to skullcaps, and the antennae were infrared projectors. He had seen a hybrid with a set once before.

All six of them wore tight bodysuits of a dark gray metallic weave, as well as plastic tube-shaped holsters strapped to their thighs. Kane knew that snugged within the tubes were infrasound wands, devices that converted electricity to sonic waves.

They could be deadly weapons, but none of the six figures wielded them. Instead they carried wicked little subguns, Calicos by the looks of them, with 100-round cylindrical magazines and mounted laser sights. Their pale hands were long, slender, with very delicate fingers. The middle ones looked to be the length of Kane's entire hand.

There was no point in trying to hide. Already scarlet threads stretched from the sights and cast red pinpoints on Kane's shoulder epaulets. Kane exploded from his position, bounding to his feet. Domi lunged to the opposite side of the aisle, both people instinctively adhering to the rule of never presenting easy targets in a killzone.

Two of the Calicos stuttered, and bullets peppered the crates behind him. At least three rounds struck Kane's body, stopped by the polycarbonate sheathing. He heard the ear-knocking concussion of Domi's Combat Master cycling through the clip of ammo. Blasterfire thundered in the enclosed space.

Turning, Kane slid between two crates and saw a figure on the other side, trying to cut him off. He raised the Sin Eater, depressing the trigger and unleashing 3-round bursts.

Domi's blistering full-auto fire hammered into the front line of attacking hybrids, lifting them from their feet and bowling them backward.

Kane picked off another man running to assume a flanking position, placing shots through his skullcap. He flailed and went down. Kane continued on through to the other aisle. His body ached from the bruises inflicted by the bullets. The armor stopped the 9 mm rounds, but it did not blunt the kinetic shock much.

As he sprinted down the aisle, his motion detector beeped again. At least ten dots crawled across the

LCD, converging on his position. He reached the mouth of the crate-walled canyon and saw a box-shaped, yellow-painted forklift parked nearby. He raced to it and vaulted into the seat. He keyed the engine to life and put it in gear.

With a whining drone, the little machine leaped forward. He twirled the wheel, steering toward the nearest exit from the warehouse. Over to his left, four hybrids were cutting diagonally across the floor in an attempt to intercept him. He quickly drove between a cross row of packing crates, braked the vehicle and put it into reverse.

With a reverberating bang, the forklift slammed into a series of metal containers forming a tower behind him. The stack teetered ominously for a moment, then toppled heavily onto the four hybrids. They had been running too fast to be able to stop and dodge, though two of them raised their arms and fended off the falling boxes. Kane had no idea what was in the crates or how long they had been stored there, but whatever it was, it was not very heavy.

Kane kept the machine in reverse, and by manipulating the forklift's steering wheel, he spun it on screeching tires in a complete circle, revolving as if on an axis. As it rotated, the flame and noise leaped from the short barrel of his Sin Eater. He played the stream of 9 mm rounds over the two standing hybrids like water from a high-pressure hose.

The first half-dozen bullets sewed bloody little dots

across their chests, smashing them backward into screaming, tangle-footed sprawls.

In the same instant as the Sin Eater began its deadly stutter, Kane saw three more hybrids dashing toward him. One had an infrasound wand in his hand, and its tapered tip blurred as it sent a rippling sonic shock wave surging toward his head.

Chapter 23

All stealth was useless now, Domi knew. She was up against at least a dozen well-armed, swift-footed adversaries. Speed and agility were the tools she brought into play. She had no plan except to evade capture. As a blaster barrel swept toward her, the albino's legs propelled her into a one-handed cartwheel. As her feet spun over her head, the Combat Master spit flame, the recoil only slightly affecting her balance as she landed lithely in a crouch.

She fired a final round and saw a figure drop amid a spray of blood, then she scuttled back into the aisle. Domi holstered her blaster and, bracing her back against a row of crates, she lifted her legs and kicked out at the stack in front of her. They swayed, and when she gave them a second kick, they crashed over. The hybrids managed to get out of their path, but the sharp corner of one container slashed across the top of an oversized head, cutting a large, blood-spurting gash. She was surprised to see that it was red.

The lids on some of the crates popped open, spilling out small machine parts that spread all over the floor and made the footing treacherous.

A clamor of orders and counterorders erupted behind her.

Domi raced across the warehouse, feeling as if her feet scarcely touched the floor. She dashed down a narrow side lane between the aisles, then up another one scarcely wide enough to accommodate her slight frame. The bulky combat vest caught on the corner of a crate, and for a second she was stuck fast. She managed to unzip it and wriggle free, losing the kit bag at the same time.

The hybrids were coming toward her from three sides. That left her only retreat the way she had come—a move that the enemy expected. She chose to disappoint them, climbing up a tower of crates, using the gaps between the individual containers and the wooden skids upon which they rested as hand-and toeholds.

Domi reached the top of the stack and, running at full sprint across the flat surfaces of the crates, she took an alleyway yawning before her in a single leap. She misjudged the distance of the adjacent aisle, came down too low, fumbled her grip on the edge, scraped skin from the palms of her hands and pulled herself atop it. She dashed across the top of the stacks and jumped to another aisle.

Only then did she pause to look back and catch her breath. Her exertions had already drenched her in sweat. Her ragged mass of white hair was soaked through to the scalp, and salty, stinging trickles slid into her eyes.

Domi saw no sign of Kane or any of the hybrids, but she did see the outermost lip of an upslanting, concrete ramp close by, leading up to the second level of the vast structure. Clambering down, she emerged on the far side of the stacks and began running toward the ramp. No one shot at her or tried to block her way.

She loped up it, knowing the ramp was a point of exposure since there was no cover available. When she reached the next level, she did not waste time sighing with relief. It was as dimly lit as the level below and filled with row upon row of the airtight containers. She moved along the sides of them warily, trying to stay close to the shadows, drawing her knife.

The stacks funneled into an open space that had been cleared throughout the center of the floor. On the side opposite her position was a doorframe formed of piled boxes. Domi paused, eyeing it suspiciously. She waited for some sight or sound, staring out with slitted eyes, her thumb resting on the razor-keen edge of her blade.

She did not wait long. Shadows shifted on the far side of the clearing, and she glimpsed two figures stationed seven feet apart against the far wall, aiming their little subguns at the doorway, intending to catch her in a devastating cross fire.

Domi scrutinized the two figures. They were not the slender, small-statured hybrids, but men, human males wearing one-piece coveralls of a drab olive green. She smirked briefly. The hybrids had apparently proved themselves incompetent in a combat situation, so the masters of the art had been summoned, calling in predators to catch predators.

Although Domi despised the breed of so-called new human on general principles, she reserved her most unregenerate hatred for the breed of old human who willingly served them. As far as she was concerned, they were worse than traitors to their own kind; they were groveling, submissive lapdogs.

She assessed the severity of the threat presented by the two men, and in a fraction of a second planned her next move.

As carefully and as stealthily as she could manage, she scaled a stack of containers and crept along the top, intending to reach a point directly above the two men. A gap between the stacks separated her from the position she wanted to reach. She knew if she jumped it, they would hear her. However, she saw a support column only a yard or so away from the gap.

Gathering her legs beneath her, Domi sprang up and outward. Grabbing the post firmly in the crook of her elbow and taking advantage of her momentum, she used it as pivot point. She swung her legs forward and around, sliding down swiftly and landing out of the line of fire next to a box.

When she landed, she bent her legs under her like springs and sprang into a leap. She flew across the clear space toward the man on her left, twisting catlike in midair as she did so. The knife in her right hand slashed out sideways, the edge of it sinking into

his neck. He clapped a hand to his throat, as if trying
to staunch the geyser of scarlet spewing from between
his fingers.

In one continuous, fluid motion, Domi hit the floor,
tucked, rolled, spun herself over and around and
launched herself at the other man.

His reflexes were excellent. He swiveled and
brought up his blaster to fire, but by then Domi was
atop him, feet first in a flying drop kick. The driving
impact of her weight knocked him down, and she
went with him. She stabbed the man with all her
strength, the blade crunching into his chest and
through his heart.

The man jerked, his heels drumming on the floor,
his mouth opening as if to voice a scream. Only a
vermilion torrent spilled out of his lips.

As he went limp, Domi breathed a small sigh of
satisfaction and began withdrawing the knife. A sudden motion at the very limit of her peripheral vision
caused her to turn, but before she could see anything,
a hand closed in her hair in an excruciatingly tight
grip. A neck-wrenching jerk catapulted her off the
corpse. Through the tears of pain that sprang to her
eyes, she caught a fragmented glimpse of a bug-eyed-
antennae head.

Domi kicked herself off the ground, flowing into
the momentum of the heave. She slashed backward
and blindly with her knife, feeling the tip drag
through fabric and flesh.

The hand tangled in her hair opened, she heard a

grunt and Domi flung herself into a headlong somersault. She came out of it on one knee, blade held between thumb and index finger, arm cocked for a throw.

She stared into the shivering tip of an infrasound wand, only inches from her face. She did not hesitate—her leg muscles propelled her in a lunge to the right, her body angled parallel with the ground. Her arm and wrist snapped out and down in perfect coordination of eye and hand. She was not able to see if or where the knife struck because her optic nerves were suddenly overwhelmed by a blinding ripple effect and her head filled with an insect-swarm hum.

Domi hit the floor gracelessly, her entire right side numb. Her heart thudded slowly, seeming to thump irregularly in her chest. Breathing took a deliberate, conscious effort.

Her vision cleared, and she saw the hybrid fondling the knife hilt sprouting from his breast. A red line of blood shone on his left hand where Domi had nicked him. Slowly, the bug-eyed man dropped to his knees, the silver rod clanging dully on the floor. He gazed beseechingly toward Domi, and in an aspirated whisper declared, "I was not going to let you die."

Then he fell forward on his face, expiring very quickly and quietly.

Domi sucked in a rattling gasp and clawed herself forward by the strength of her left arm. Her head pounded as if pickaxes were chopping away at the bone on the inside of her skull.

She fought, wrestled and cursed her way to her knees, then to her feet. The boxes tilted and spun all around her. She staggered, fell to hands and knees, forced herself erect again, her face dripping with sweat. Her right leg shook violently in spasm, and she dragged it behind her like a sack of flour, the toe of her boot scraping against the floor.

The paralysis spread in a wave, numbing her entire body, and she fell, limp-limbed and face forward.

AN INVISIBLE FIST STRUCK the side of the forklift only a few inches from Kane's leg, metal slivers rattling against the armor. He threw himself into a sideways lunge, out of the machine. He felt a pins-and-needles tingle high on his left thigh.

He hit the floor, rolled and got to his feet, keeping the forklift between him and the infrasound wands. He squeezed off another triburst that drilled a hybrid through the middle, slapping him off his feet.

Although Kane could not see her, he heard the boom of Domi's Combat Master. About twenty yards away, he glimpsed an antennae skullcap and the cranium beneath it breaking apart under the impact of the .44-caliber slug. Blood gushed down the hybrid's face as he flailed over backward, arms windmilling.

A silver rod swept toward him, and Kane's steel-spring legs propelled him into a flat dive. His blaster belched flame and thunder again, and a bug-headed figure shrieked, slapping at his right shoulder as the bullet bit a chunk of meat and muscle out of it amid a spray of blood.

Kane kept moving, never still for a microsecond, ducking and weaving, dodging the flashing wands as they hummed and shivered. Survival depended on movement. Having been on the receiving end of the ultrasonic kicks delivered by the wands, he knew how quickly they could disable. The rods flailed at him like whips, buzzing at him like insects, and the helmeted men wielding them panted in exertion and frustration.

Kane was able to sidestep one of the hybrids completely, and he went running past him. He received a spinning crescent kick against his back, which snapped his spine. A hybrid was able to lurch forward and graze Kane's leg with the shivering, humming tip of the silver rod. Pain stabbed through his body, and bringing up his Sin Eater, he shot his assailant once through the night-vision headset and knocked him backward.

Pivoting, Kane ran toward the open doorway. His leg twinged as he sprinted, but he paid it no attention. The hybrids only halfheartedly gave chase, since Kane was far fleeter of foot, and the triburst he fired behind him discouraged pursuit.

He pounded into a murky corridor, turned the first corner he reached and kept running. Like the other hallways he had seen in the installation, the floor was of dust-filmed linoleum. When he reached a pair of swing double doors, he pushed through them and paused to regain his breath and thumb a fresh clip into his Sin Eater.

He looked around and saw he stood in a huge kitchen, with at least eight ranges, twice again that many sinks, refrigerators, food lockers and freezers. He figured as vast an installation as Area 51 appeared to be, this kitchen was probably only one of dozens scattered throughout the place.

He waited for a count of sixty, and when no sounds of pursuit were forthcoming and his motion detector did not register any movement, he tried raising Domi on the comm-link. He received no response, but he tried not to worry about her. The girl was as self-sufficient and resourceful as anyone he knew, including himself.

Kane glided silently through the kitchen, his boots making almost no noise. He walked through a huge dining hall and found himself in a corridor that was dimly lit from overhead bulbs encased in wire cages. The hallway was lined with numbered, electronic-locked doors.

There was a small circle of one-way glass set in each door. Kane peered through one. All he saw was a tiny room, almost a cubicle, with a snoring man, a human male, sprawled naked on a narrow cot.

Kane moved on, senses alert, his finger on the trigger of the Sin Eater. He heard the murmur of voices somewhere ahead of him, so he slowed his pace. The voices were coming from inside one of the rooms, so

Kane very carefully looked through the one-way glass in the door.

Although the lighting was poor, he saw the room was much more spacious than the first he had peeked into. He also saw another naked man, but this one lay spread-eagled on a metal framework. He was bound to it by canvas restraints crisscrossing his chest and chrome shackles around his wrists and ankles. A strap of leather over his forehead pressed the back of his skull into canvas webbing.

A molded plastic object resembling a respirator mask concealed the lower half of his face. Vertical slots perforated it, and Kane realized it was a muzzle. The eyes above the mask were wild and wide with sheer, abject terror. The man's hair-covered chest rose and fell in spasmodic jerks. Veins stood out in stark relief on his neck.

Kane's eye caught a flicker of a motion at the opposite end of the room. Two figures shifted in the gloom with the graceful, studied movements of hybrids. Both were females, a little less than five feet tall. One wore a crisp white coverall over her compact, tiny-breasted form. Her huge, upslanting eyes were of a clear crystal blue, her pale delicate features elfin and beautiful in an unreal way. The silky blond hair topping her domed skull fell in wispy ringlets to her shoulders.

The other female hung back, out of the imprisoned man's field of vision. At first, even second glance,

Kane was not sure she was even a living creature. She seemed more like a mannequin.

She was naked, her body gleaming in the murk. Her thick jet-black hair fell to her shoulders, the ends flipping inward. The color was such a dead black, the texture so unnaturally shiny, Kane knew it was a wig.

Her high-planed face was so thickly made up with rouge, powder and lipstick she resembled a malevolent doll. Her hazel eyes were starkly outlined with mascara.

When the female in the white approached him, the man on the framework trembled violently, and faintly Kane heard him shouting. The hybrid did not speak to him or even appear to hear him. From a pocket of her coverall she produced a small tube, similar in size and shape to that of toothpaste.

Squeezing a generous portion of a semitransparent gel onto his chest, the hybrid used the palms of her hands to spread it over his upper body. Her movements were deft and mechanical. The prisoner shuddered at her touch, his eyes rolling in animalistic panic. When his torso glistened with a thin film of the substance, the female stepped away. Kane saw her gesture toward her nude companion, indicating she should continue the ministrations.

The bewigged hybrid did so, stepping with lithe grace to the man and laying her delicate, inhumanly hands on him. Whereas the woman in white had spread the gel in a desultory fashion, the naked female caressed him slowly and even lovingly.

Her hands made slow, languorous sweeps over and around and down his body. She bent her shiny black-haired head, as if whispering endearments into the man's ear.

Inside of a minute, the prisoner stopped shuddering, but his limbs still shook. With a jolt of nausea, Kane understood it was due to building sexual arousal. Evidently, that was the response the two hybrids were hoping to elicit. The blond one said something to her companion, who instantly transferred her attention to the man's organ. As the nude female climbed up onto the framework, straddling the man's pelvis, Kane turned away from the window, cold sweat collecting between the lining of his helmet and his hair. It seeped out and slid down his cheeks and as he retraced his steps, returning first to the dining hall, then to the kitchen.

He could only hazard a guess at why the hybrid women were using some kind of aphrodisiac to bring about sexual excitement in the trapped human male, but he was fairly certain it had something to do with the dead fetus.

Without access to the cloning, ectogenesis and artificial-gestation techniques the hybrids employed to reproduce, they had become desperate enough to at least experiment with conventional means of conception. Kane did not even want to think about possible success ratios.

Kane tried raising Domi on the trans-comm again, but once more she failed to respond. He crept out into the corridor and back to the warehouse. He stood there, flattened against the wall, scanning the area just beyond the doorway with his eyes and the motion detector. He saw nothing, not even the corpses he and Domi had made.

As he stood there, trying to formulate a plan of action, he heard a woman crying out, faintly, but loud enough so he heard the fear and pain in her voice.

"Kane! Help me! Kane—"

Chapter 24

The gloom between the endless rows of containers made everything a flat gray monochrome to Kane's visored eyes. He moved swiftly about a hundred paces from the doorway, then paused in the deeper shadows next to a double-stacked aisle of the crates. He held his Sin Eater at waist level. Even with his night sight, the light was sullen and gray.

He had no idea where Domi might be. He was not even certain it was the girl who called for help. He tried to bring to mind the exact sounds, recalling the high pitch.

Forcing himself to breathe quietly and smoothly, Kane moved swiftly down between the rows, following one aisle, which seemed to always lead into another. Though he consulted the motion detector frequently, the LCD remained placid. Then, suddenly, it uttered a beep, and a green dot pulsed at the far edge of its face.

He came to a halt, peering ahead. Something moved through the shadows ahead of him, a ghost in the dimness, not clearly visible, then it was gone. He heard no sound of footsteps, and the indicator light no longer registered on the detector. He went on, coming out of an aisle.

The narrow-gauge monorail track led across the vast floor space to disappear in the darkness beyond wide-open double doors. The track was serviced by a small shifter engine whose chromed nose was thrust out between the doors that opened into the cavernous interior of the warehouse. Nobody was in sight.

A half-loaded flatcar stood on the track, and the shadowy figure Kane had glimpsed a few moments before flitted through the open double doors. He paused, refusing to chase after it. He was being deliberately lured somewhere—he had no doubt of it. He also had no doubt it was not Domi who had called out to him earlier. That meant someone in Area 51 recognized him, and the possibility of who it might be sent chills through him.

He stepped out from between the stacks, and walked along the track toward the doors. He saw nothing until he neared the flatcar, then he heard a flat, whipping crack and a bullet winged past his head. It ricocheted from metal somewhere behind him. The echoes of the shot were swallowed up by the high ceiling.

As he dived for the floor beside the track, the blaster snapped again and the slug hit the rail near his feet and screeched off into the gloom, leaving a bright scar on the steel to commemorate its impact.

Kane got up and sprinted toward the flatcar. A third shot followed him, but he received the impression it was an afterthought, as if the shooter fired only for effect. He found shelter behind the half-loaded flatcar, crouching beside it.

The female voice shrilled, ''Kane!''

Straightening, he craned his neck to see over the boxes on the car. Another shot split the still atmosphere of the enormous warehouse, and a round gouged a furrow in a crate lid. Although it had struck nowhere near him, Kane ducked back and swore. At least he had spotted the shooter's position. A twinkle of muzzle-flash showed in a small window on the elevated superstructure.

Still and all, he was trapped in the huge, open warehouse, and though sheltered by the flatcar, he was too far now from the aisles to make a run backward, and too far for a sprint through the open doors. He had nowhere to go. Tentatively, he stretched out his left arm and moved it back and forth.

The motion detector lit up with green dots, beeping each time it registered a signature. The glowing icons slid across the LCD, marching inexorably on his position, from both sides. He counted eight of them. He suspected the sniper had deliberately missed his shots, firing at him to force him to ground while reinforcements advanced.

He cursed and looked around the flatcar he was crouched against. He noticed it had its rear channel chocked to prevent it from rolling backward. He saw how the track extending across the warehouse slanted

toward the open doors, running right past and below
the observation post.

Kane lowered himself to his knees and moved toward the front of the flatcar. The chocks jammed between the channel's bolster and track were little
wedges of hard rubber, like doorstops. Fortunately,
both chocks could be reached from his side, and he
did not have to crawl under the car to loosen them.
Even so, it was difficult to get enough leverage to
release the stops. He had to lie flat on his back, working at them for several long minutes with his knife,
pausing now and then to listen for footsteps. When
he pulled the last chock of rubber free, he was
drenched with sweat, and the flatcar still remained
motionless.

Crouching, he crawled to the rear of the car, put
his shoulder against one corner of it and shoved hard.
For a long moment, nothing happened. Then he heard
the creak of metal, a heavy groan, a screeching rumble of metal grinding against metal. Slowly, it rolled
down the track.

Kane moved with it, staying in a crouch, using the
crates on the car to shield his body. He thought he
heard another cry, calling out his name. The flatcar
gradually gained momentum, and within seconds he
had to trot to keep up with its increasing speed. It was
heading straight for the nose of the shifter that protruded out of the tunnel.

When less than ten yards remained, Kane leaped
upon the flatcar, keeping low on the floor behind the

crates and boxes. He wriggled between and around
them to the other side. The car vibrated and rumbled
beneath him as he lay flat. The chromed nose of the
engine seemed to rush at him, swelling in his vision.
At the last second, he rolled off, turning his roll into
a running leap. He lunged for the shadows beneath
the superstructure.

The crash when the flatcar collided with the nose
of the parked engine was thunderous, echoing within
the high, vault-walled room. Metal impacted against
metal with a prolonged, nerve-racking screech.

The boxes and crates tumbled to the floor, break-
ables within shattering and jangling. Kane reached the
protection of the stairway as the echoes of the crash
died away. An almost continuous series of beeps
sounded from the motion detector, and though he
could not see or hear who was approaching him, they
were close and they outnumbered him by a wide mar-
gin.

Not caring to stand his ground and shoot it out,
Kane crept up the stairs, his body pressed against the
right-hand rail. He held the Sin Eater in a two-fisted
grip. When he reached the top of the stairs, he raised
his head above the edge of the floor and took in the
scene with one quick glance.

The square room was dark except for the feeble
illumination peeping in through the window. There
was no furniture except for a very old desk. A man,
a human male, with broad, down-sloping shoulders
and a face resembling old leather in texture and color,

held a rifle to his shoulder. He was well over six feet tall, weighing perhaps 250 pounds. He was dressed in an olive-green jumpsuit.

A female hybrid stood beside him, standing on tiptoes to peer out the window anxiously. Delicate, lovely and with reddish-gold hair, she whispered, "I don't see him, Hank."

"That's because Hank's looking in the wrong place," Kane said quietly.

The man whirled to face him, moving faster than Kane expected, so he did not waste time with niceties. He squeezed the trigger stud of his blaster. The report was almost deafening in the enclosed space.

The roar that tore from Hank's throat when the 9 mm Parabellum round slammed into the center of his chest was almost as loud. His bellow combined shock, pain and rage. As he fell back against the wall, he shoved the female aside and down behind the desk.

Kane heard the clang of metal behind him and pivoted at the waist. Another human male, dressed in the same kind of coverall, was making a desperate lunge up the steps, wielding a Calico subgun. He was screaming something in a language Kane did not understand.

The Sin Eater roared twice and clipped off the rest of the man's scream. One of the steel-jacketed slugs drove through the crown of his head, and the other punched a red-rimmed hole in the base of his neck. He tumbled head over heels down the stairway.

Kane turned his attention back to Hank, who was

still on his feet. He fired the rifle from the hip, working the trigger. Pulling his head down, Kane heard the bullets ricocheting from the metal risers behind him and smash into the floor above his head. Splinters blew out in sprays.

Kane realized the man was wearing a Kevlar vest beneath his coverall, and when he raised his head and blaster again, he adjusted his aim and squeezed off a single shot.

A spot of crimson bloomed on Hank's broad forehead, and part of his skull and scalp floated away behind him. Throwing his arms out wide, the big man crashed backward against the wall, then toppled forward on his face. The entire superstructure shook from the impact of two-hundred-plus pounds of deadweight hitting the floor. To his amazement, a wail of horror arose from behind the desk, from the lips of the hybrid.

There was a scuff and scutter of rapidly moving feet behind him. Kane turned as another coverall-garbed man, a subgun in his hands, raced up the steps. He glimpsed more figures milling about below.

The expression on the man's face was a bare-toothed grimace of unthinking, murderous fury. "You fuckin' traitor to unity—"

Kane pointed the Sin Eater down the stairway and let loose with a short burst. The staccato hammering of the full-auto gunfire filled the stairway as five holes were stitched across the man's chest.

As he tumbled to the foot of the stairs, Kane called after him contemptuously, "Look who's talking."

Kane heaved himself up into the observation post, intent on taking the female prisoner and using her as a hostage if it came down to it. She was stooped over Hank's body, weeping piteously. The sight so stunned Kane, he did not immediately react when he felt the floor under his feet give slightly.

Not breaking stride, Kane glanced down and saw he walked across a strip of flexible metal mesh, like a tightly woven web. Just as the recollection of the shock field in the desert outside of the Archuleta Mesa registered, he reached the edge of the material. He put one foot on the floor while the other remained on the mesh.

He heard a giant pop, as of a giant balloon bursting, and blue lighting flared before his eyes, dancing in an arcing skein along the barrel of his blaster. Pain erupted through every nerve cell. His heart pounded so violently he thought his ribs would break. The agony went beyond anything he had ever experienced or thought he could endure.

Everything crashed in against him, a marrow-freezing cold and a soul-shredding pain.

KANE COULD FEEL nothing at first. A throbbing pain in his head began, like a drumbeat slowly building to a crescendo. His mouth and tongue felt numb, so he couldn't even groan. He could neither feel nor move his arms and legs.

He tried to orient himself, but he could not tell which end was up—not his personal end or the world's. He shivered, then by increments, he became aware of his body again. He felt something cold and very hard pressing against his backside and shoulders.

A soft lilting voice said, "I won't let you die, Kane."

It was a familiar voice, but despite the words, the tone was not soothing or reassuring. It smacked of a threat.

"You won't die," the voice crooned, pitched so low it was a sibilant whisper. "I won't let you die."

Fear and memory exploded simultaneously in Kane's mind. With a straining, convulsive effort, he opened his eyes. He saw a room so dimly and indirectly lit, everything was blurred. He tried to rub his eyes and discovered he could not move either hand or his feet.

He squeezed his eyes shut, then carefully opened them again, focusing them on his body. He turned his head, first to the left, then to the right and finally down. His wrists and ankles were bolted securely by chrome cuffs to a steel-framed, canvas-covered latticework. His body was in a half-reclining position, and his hands were affixed to the frame at ear level. He also saw he was naked, just like the man bound to a similar framework—or the very same one. He opened his mouth and felt the plastic muzzle against his lips.

A pale hand moved into his field of vision and

patted his cheek. The hand was slender, with exceptionally long, tapering fingers. "Back among the living," the melodic voice said. "If you can call it that."

Panic surged through him as his stumbling thought processes finally matched a face to the voice. Baron Cobalt glided to his side, his gaunt face creased in a smile of mock sympathy. He was dressed in robes of shimmering gold, the long flowing sleeves of which were edged with white fur. The satin draped softly over his slight, spare frame gave him a majestic appearance.

Stroking Kane's sweat-damp hair as if it were the coat of a dog, the baron whispered almost lovingly, "My beautiful, treacherous, murderous Kane. I knew you would return to me one day. I do so admire you, although your passions really should be more restrained." His smile broadened, but it did not reach his eyes. "Oh, we have *so* many things to talk about, so much to catch up on…so many mutual acquaintances to gossip about."

Propping an elbow up on the edge of the frame and leaning on a hand, the baron asked in a conspiratorial whisper, "Do you remember how you once throttled me, insulted me, defiled me? What was it you called me?"

Baron Cobalt pursed his lips, pretending to ponder the matter. "Oh, yes. Now I recall. You told me I was a laboratory monstrosity with an attitude—a vampire living off the genetic material of human beings. You called me disgusting."

Kane croaked, a harsh, incomprehensible gargle of sound.

The baron put his ear close to the slotted muzzle. "Pardon? I didn't catch that."

Kane coughed and with a great deal of effort managed to husk out, "Dickless...I also called you a race of jealous, dickless cowards." His voice was so faint, and muffled by the muzzle, he barely heard himself.

Baron Cobalt heard him. The twinkle of feigned good humor in his eyes blazed to fury, burning hot and molten. His delicate nostrils flared. "At least my kind are not genocidal *monsters!*"

The words burst from the baron's mouth in a high-pitched shriek of rage, amid a spray of spittle. His hands knotted into fists, the knuckles straining against the finely textured skin so tightly, it appeared as if they would split the flesh. "Which is worse, Kane? We use your kind, that is true, but we use only enough of you to survive. Your savage acts have brought *my* kind to the very brink of extinction!"

Kane tried to make himself laugh. In a strained, pained whisper, he demanded, "That's supposed to make me feel guilty?"

A sneer twisted the baron's features, turning his sculpted face into an ugly mask of contempt. There was desperation in his eyes, and the terror of a man driven beyond the bounds of reason. He inhaled a deep breath, as if to calm himself.

"We are a young race," he stated, no longer shrieking but with an unmistakable quaver underscoring his voice. "We are hybrids of human and those you call Archon, but our Homo sapiens genes spring from the very best stock. And for that reason more than any other, you apekin hate us. But as we need your ape's blood to live, we spit on your ape minds."

Baron Cobalt passed a hand over his forehead and sighed wearily. "I told you once before that creation of the new humanity was a matter of natural selection, and to accept our intrinsic superiority as we accepted your kind's innate inferiority. We are better suited to this world, to guide it and reshape it in a new, more productive image.

"But your ape's mind wouldn't permit that, would it? So now our carefully structured, orderly world is in turmoil. Hell creeps upon us, the dark angels of chaos, the very same angels you serve, wait to reap what you have sown. It is only right and just that humankind must provide our salvation."

The baron stepped away, paced nervously, then returned, breathing deeply through his nostrils. "Do you realize how little your kind has advanced in the last five hundred years? The last thousand? All of your achievements were transitory, shiny baubles and toys tinkered together to deceive and placate the masses. None of it was of any true worth, none of it had lasting value. There was no beauty or truth to any of it, or it would have transcended your ape roots and survived to be cherished by the generations that followed.

"Even now, two centuries after the nukecaust, humankind continues to live only by sheer momentum, by force of habit. You have no passion to create, only to destroy. Humankind is spiritually bankrupt and obsolete."

A dry laugh creaked out of Kane's mouth. His voice was growing stronger, no longer as hoarse. "But you still need us...the new humanity can't live without the old apekin."

Baron Cobalt nodded. "I've already admitted that. Aren't you the least bit curious why you're not dead? Don't you wonder why I'm telling you all of this?"

"Because you're a blowhard or crazy or both?"

The baron's mouth quirked in a moue of distaste. "Hardly. I've told you so you'll be prepared for your new life. You're staying with me, to serve me as you vowed to do upon your indoctrination into the Trust. I swear to you, I won't let you die...not until you have repaid your debt, returned what you have stolen."

"What have I stolen from you?" Kane challenged. "I've only reclaimed what the barons, the hybrids robbed from all of humanity."

"You've stolen lives, Kane." Baron Cobalt reached out and fingered away a lock of hair from Kane's forehead. Gazing into his eyes, the baron said sincerely, affectionately, "But I'm not punishing you. I'm doing all of this for you. For the future."

Kane tried to snort but could not pull it off. "How do you figure that?"

"The only characteristic your kind and my kind

share is the biological imperative to procreate.'' The baron made an imperious, beckoning gesture. ''Don't you know that hybrids generally take on all the positive attributes of their parents, becoming the most exceptional specimens?''

A pale face suddenly thrust itself into Kane's range of sight. Framed by glossy black hair and thickly coated with cosmetics, the face was like that of an evil, grinning doll. The smile on her ruby red lips was subtly cruel. A faint whisper slipped between them. ''You won't make up for Hank, but you'll have to do.''

Then Kane felt her hands on him, applying a warm gel that spread a wonderful heat over his body. It did not warm the horror frosting his brain.

Epilogue

Erica van Sloan tottered as she walked, unsteady on her feet even with Sam holding her hand. Many, many years had passed since her legs had possessed any feeling or supported any weight, and the prickling sensation of returning circulation was excruciating.

She bit back groans, too happy to be ambulatory again to permit a preoccupation with transitory pain to dilute her joy. As they walked along the corridor, Sam said, "You're nervous, Erica. Don't be."

After the barons had departed Front Royal, Sam beckoned her to follow him into the jump chamber. He did not mention their destination, nor why Balam stayed behind, and she was not inclined to ask. The love, gratitude and even devotion she felt for the child overwhelmed her, canceling out all conditioned predilections toward suspicion.

They materialized in a gateway unit with rich, golden walls, as if ingots had been melted down and mixed with the armaglass. As they strode along a low-ceilinged, stone-block-walled corridor, Erica wondered if they were in a redoubt, a COG installation, or somewhere else entirely. She did not know why, but she felt they were deep underground. She sensed inestimable tons of rock over their heads. Hesitantly, she asked, "Where are you taking me, Sam?"

"To show you how to reach the man I need. He will be of great use to us...or so Balam has said."

Erica ran her tongue nervously over her lips, once more pleasantly surprised by their restored fullness and pliancy. "Tell me about Balam. Is he your father?"

Sam smiled up at her impishly, his eyes glinting with a buried spark of amusement. "He is not my father. Oh, no...not my father. He is my guardian, my teacher, my mentor. But not my father."

"Then who are your parents? Where do they—and you—come from?"

"I came from here," was the blithe reply. "As did my father. As for who is my mother...I suppose you would hold that position."

They reached a set of double doors. Erica stared down at him, her mind awhirl, her heart churning with conflicting emotions.

"Or," Sam continued in the same breezy manner, "to be more precise, you contributed many of your characteristics to my overall genetic code. If you like, I'll introduce you to my father."

The doors swung open without Sam touching them. Erica followed him into what appeared to be a gulf of deep space. The walls, ceiling and floor of the room were all black, a total black that seemed to absorb all light like a vast, ebony sponge. It was a blackness so deep it wearied the eyes trying to see some color or shadow within it.

But the room was not completely without light. Occupying the center of it from floor to ceiling was a transparent sphere six feet in diameter. Within the suspended globe glittered pinpoints of light, scattered seemingly at random, but all connected by glowing lines.

Erica paused to examine the sphere, but Sam kept on walking. She followed him, squinting into the gloom. The boy stopped before a niche in the wall and announced, "Here is my father. It's way past time you two met."

A light recessed into the ceiling suddenly flashed on, casting a funnel of illumination on a long, deep, transparent-walled tank. Within, floating in a semisolid gel, lay a very tall, almost skeletally thin figure. It was human shaped, but by no means human.

Its cadaverous frame and narrow, elongated skull were completely hairless. Long slender arms terminated in four-fingered hands tipped with razor-sharp spurs of bone. A central ridge dipped down from the top of the domed head to the bridge of the flattened nose. The lipless mouth gaped slightly open, revealing double rows of serrated teeth.

The brownish-gray skin, wrinkled and tough, stretched over protruding brow arches and jutting cheekbones. There was a suggestion of scaliness about it. A short tail extended from the base of the spine, tucked between the thighs.

Erica recoiled in a spasm of primal loathing. Involuntarily, she cringed, stumbling backward a pace or two. Sam steadied her with a hand, and she distantly noted the pebbled pattern on his fingers was identical to that on the hide of the preserved carcass.

"Balam tells me his name is Enlil." Sam's voice was a reverent murmur. "The last of the Annunaki, the last of the Serpent Kings, the source of myths, religions and the root race of Balam's people."

Smiling, Sam tugged at her hand, drawing her closer. Very confidently, very persuasively, he declared, "There's nothing to be afraid of, nothing at all. Don't you know that hybrids generally take on all the positive attributes of their parents, becoming the most exceptional specimens?"

* * * * *

Don't miss the next
exciting episode of
THE IMPERATOR WARS
trilogy, entitled
TIGERS OF HEAVEN
coming in February.

**A journey through the dangerous frontier
known as the future...**

JAMES AXLER

DEATH LANDS®

Zero City

Hungry and exhausted, Ryan and his band emerge from
a redoubt into an untouched predark city, and uncover a
cache of weapons and food. Among other interlopers,
huge winged creatures guard the city. Holed up inside
an old government building, where Ryan's son, Dean,
lies near death, Ryan and Krysty must raid where a local
baron uses human flesh as fertilizer....

Take
2 explosive books
plus a
mystery bonus
FREE

OUTLANDERS®

FROM THE CREATOR OF

AMERICA'S POST-HOLOCAUST HISTORY CONTINUES....